CHILDREN
OF THE
FUROR

TOO rarely do we find a book by a Christian author and presented by a Christian publisher that in one daring sweep speaks impellingly and inoffensively to a broad segment of the religious community as well as to the secular. Roger Elwood in *Children of the Furor*, his most forceful work yet, has joined with Regal Books in a bold venture to prod an unwary public into startling reality.

Reports of organized skinhead infiltration are disquieting. Are the neo-Nazis even now stealthily amassing a militant offensive—preparing to take up their positions? *Children of the Furor* makes it inescapably clear that such likelihood needs to be seriously considered.

Elwood treats a shocking subject with amazing sensitivity as only an author with a deep burden for the world and a surpassing love for Christ can do.

Dwight Hooten
Emeritus: Director Periodicals Div.,
Tyndale House Publishers
Executive Editor, *The Christian Reader*

CHILDREN OF THE FUROR should be compulsory reading, not just for every God-loving American, but every decent, thinking adult in the world.

Mary Dorr
President
Excellence in Media

WITNESS a hard-to-forget series of chilling accounts born of a Satan-inspired, anti-God, anti-Semetic mind-set."

"The many 'furors' of this book will astound you as they reflect realities of man's sin, corruption and attempts of violence against God's people."

"Don't say 'It can't happen here.' It's happening and it's dramatically portrayed in Roger Elwood's, *Children of the Furor.*"

"Victims everywhere! That's what strikes you about this book. And, the Answer, Jesus Christ!"

"This book reads like what could be tomorrow's most disturbing newspaper headlines. Pray that our children won't become more children of the furor."

"It's really lord Lucifer and his aides against the Lord Jesus and His people, dramatically portrayed in an array of characters woven throughout an astounding story."

William E. Sutter
Administrative Director
The Friends of Israel Gospel Ministry, Inc.

IT is not often that a Christian can read a fast-paced, thought-provoking adventure where the main character draws upon the Lord for his strength, wisdom, and problem solving.

Imagine fighting off the fiery darts of the Evil One, "testing" the spirits to determine their source of identity, and using the whole armour of God, all set against a backdrop of international conspiracy, law enforcement and intrigue. *Children of the Furor* does just that.

Roger Elwood has woven into the story line a gripping account of the underground skinhead movement and the horror that can result from following the Evil One.

Mike Lynch
Vice President
Joni & Friends

A NOVEL BY
ROGER ELWOOD
AUTHOR OF THE BEST-SELLING *ANGELWALK*

CHILDREN
OF THE
FUROR

Regal Books
A Division of Gospel Light
Ventura, California, U.S.A.

Published by Regal Books
A Division of GL Publications
Ventura, California 93006
Printed in U.S.A.

Library of Congress Cataloging-in-Publication Data

Elwood, Roger.
      Children of the Furor / Roger Elwood.
             p.   cm.
      ISBN 0-8307-1438-3
      I. Title.
      PS3555.L85C47 1990
      813'.54—dc20
                                            90-43087
                                              CIP

2 3 4 5 6 7 8 9 10 / X3 / KP / 95 94 93 92 91 90

Rights for publishing this book in other languages are contracted by Gospel Literature International (GLINT) foundation. GLINT also provides technical help for the adaptation, translation, and publishing of Bible study resources and books in scores of languages worldwide. For further information, contact GLINT, Post Office Box 488, Rosemead, California, 91770, U.S.A., or the publisher.

Warren Wiersbe
—who encouraged me
to write for the battlefield
and not the bumper sticker.

And Mark Maddox
—for whom it is less difficult
to write my very best.

Weakness has to be knocked out of them. In my [view of the new order] a youth will grow up before which the world will shrink back. A violently active, dominating, intrepid and brutal youth [who is] indifferent to pain. There must be no weakness or tenderness whatever. I want to see the gleam of pride and independence of the bird of prey....In this way I shall eradicate the thousands of years of human domestication....

—Adolf Hitler

ACKNOWLEDGMENTS

WRITING even for Christian publishers can be filled with moments that are frustrating, though in most instances, no one *intends* them to be so. These disillusioning episodes occur principally with publishers who have forgotten the ministry aspect of what they are doing. For some, the bottom line of profits and sales is well-nigh worshiped, with any salvation of souls considered merely a by-product—perhaps.

In any event, that is why I am grateful to the Lord for guiding me to the publishers for whom I now write. For my friends and associates at Gospel Light, the *ministry* is paramount. A book is not simply a book, frivolous in its purpose. Everything fits into a plan, a plan dedicated to the honor and glory of Jesus Christ.

The ministry aspect of publishing fits into that plan, yes, and so does Christian love, frequent expressions of it, by letter or phone or in person. But that shouldn't be surprising, when you think of it. For what is any ministry worth without that very love?

INTRODUCTION

WRITING CHILDREN OF THE FUROR has been the roughest possible experience because it may be the starkest of my recent novels. I have tried to be direct and honest, alerting those who read it to some harsh truths. We do not necessarily honor the Lord when we couch everything in tender words. Such words may actually be misleading and may not help enable readers to endure the realities of life.

I always try to remember that Satan is referred to in Scripture as the Arch Deceiver. Deception can come in a variety of forms. One of these is the notion that we should never grapple in nitty-gritty terms with the sweat and the strain, the blood and tears of life, facing these head-on. Instead, so the thinking goes, we should just maintain a few positive thoughts and we'll somehow manage to get through life.

How deceptive indeed!

When Corrie ten Boom's sister was dying in a concentration camp, Corrie's thoughts were as depressed, as negative, as sorrow-filled as we could imagine. Just look at the story of Job in the Old Testament. And we also have Christ's own words: "My God, my God, why have You forsaken me?"

Where was positive thinking during these instances?

Being a Christian means we are equipped to face *life*. We must not accept some Pollyanna heresy that disarms us instead, making us fair game for the enemy of our souls.

CHILDREN OF THE FUROR may be an emotionally wrenching experience for many. That's what I intended each day as I sat down at my computer and asked for the Lord's guidance—a goal which many brothers and sisters in Christ held up for me in their own prayers.

—Roger Elwood

I believe that it is God's will to send a boy forth...to let him grow to manhood, to raise him to be Führer of the nation....There is a higher Providence, and we are nothing but its tools....

—Adolf Hitler

PROLOGUE

EIGHT-YEAR-OLD Kent Dalham's days were filled with sharp images of bombs falling and collapsed buildings and debris clogging the streets. Perhaps the worst part of the German air offensive against London was the uncertainty, which undoubtedly Hermann Goering had planned as part of his strategy against England—psychological warfare that could be useful indeed in its debilitating impact upon the populace.

Like everyone else in the city, Kent and his parents never knew when the flat in which they lived would be hit and the nightmare regularly engulfing others would involve them more intimately, beyond the role of mere spectators watching the suffering of those around them without experiencing anything tragic themselves.

To be eating a meal, and suddenly find yourself having to leave, to rush out into the street.

To be playing with your children and to hear the sirens.

There was some warning, of course, but not much, and always the haste, the haste to get to a safe haven.

Some never made it to the shelter, entire families dying in the streets or else inside buildings when they didn't flee quickly enough.

Sometimes a husband survived, and the wife perished. Or the wife remained while the husband perished.

Many times children were left without both parents. Or a mother wept over the pathetic little body of a beloved infant.

Young Kent remembered so clearly his mother, Martha Dalham, who looked deceptively frail yet remained as well-organized, as disciplined as ever. He fancied in later years the likelihood that even if a bomb had demolished a building two doors down the street it wouldn't have sent her into hysteria and indecision. She would simply have gotten her young son, and whatever she had put aside for emergencies, and the two would have left the flat, hurried down the stairs and then run outside to the appointed air raid shelter two blocks off Carnaby Street.

She was that way about every crisis, life-threatening or otherwise. When complimented by a friend, when appreciated by Kent's father or Kent himself, she would shrug and say it wasn't her, but the Holy Spirit working through her.

If Kent were scared when the blitz of London was raging, if he started to cry, she would grip his hand tightly and repeat the 23rd Psalm, not so much merely *saying* the words as almost singing them, the sound like the music of a choir of angels guarding their path.

His tall, handsome father, Arthur James Dalham, was involved in the diplomatic service, but Kent discovered later that the elder Dalham had other assignments as well. Even as an adult, Kent was never told everything about his father's work, apart from occasional mentions of subversive groups.

At first all this seemed adventurous to a youngster. But then the dangers involved in his father's occupation became clearer, especially when Kent was a teenager and able to comprehend more of the complexities of international intrigue.

*So his mother and he were together often during the war years, but time with his father was considerably rarer, such moments cherished. Since there were few of these occasions, he tended to remember most of them, tended to compartmentalize them in his mind, like beloved remnants stored in an attic, and taken out and reminisced over when the mood struck...especially one day after the three of them had spent a quiet time in St. James Park, and Kent Dalham saw clearly quite another side of the man he loved very much.*It was toward evening.

They were hurrying back to their flat in anticipation of the intruding German bombers, having been alerted by the telltale sirens and as always, a short while later, that sensation of the ground shaking beneath them.

"They're earlier tonight!" his father exclaimed.

"Anything to confuse us," his mother agreed.

Seconds later, a building collapsed directly in front of them.

The street was blocked.

"We'll have to go another way," the elder Dalham said.

Just as they were turning, Dalham noticed a woman with a small boy hanging onto one hand; the two were covered with blood.

"Take care of Kent," Dalham said, kissing his wife, then hurrying across the street.

Later Kent learned that his father stayed with the woman and her son until he was assured that they both had proper medical attention. But that wasn't all. He also had been instrumental that night, during that time away from them, in the apprehension of the Nazi sympathizer responsible for informing Berlin that two of Britain's most important spies were temporarily being housed in that specific section of London.

Kent was unable to understand the whole matter of spies for a long time. How could they sell out their friends, their country like that? How could they just throw away any concern for other people in their lives—people who had seemed to mean a great deal to them?

For Kent, even after the war, a long while after in fact, it was inconceivable that money alone was the answer. But then what sickness twisted their minds to do what they did?

That evening, though, such thoughts were still unborn, and it wasn't until Kent happened to hear the spy's name that he spoke up.

"Daddy, I have a friend with the same name," he told his father.

"It's a common one, son," Dalham replied.

Kent was silent then, hoping that his father was right and that this was just a coincidence, and that would be the end of the matter.

Not so.

The next day some bobbies were standing out in front of the flat where Kent's friend lived.

"Dad, that's Sean!" he exclaimed.

He groped for another explanation. Perhaps the officers were there for an altogether different reason.

Surely it couldn't be that his father had tried to hide the truth from him? The thought arose, but then he realized that his father, away from home as often as he was, couldn't possibly have been aware of all his son's relationships.

The door to the flat was being opened then, and Kent saw his friend Sean holding his own mother's hand as they walked down the steps to the street. The boy noticed Kent, and in that brief moment of eye contact, Kent saw someone his age who suddenly seemed ever so much older. But then Sean turned away, obviously ashamed.

Later in their own flat, after that latest air attack had subsided, Kent asked his father to tell him what was going on. Art Dalham did his best, but the subject was a complex one for a young boy. Yet one word did help fill in *some* of the blanks.

Nazis.

The entire family had been involved in espionage.

"Even Sean?" Kent asked.

His father nodded sadly.

Kent was devastated.

"Why?" he asked simply.

"They serve no one but an evil leader named Hitler."

Kent remembered hearing about this Hitler in school and elsewhere, but he had never paid much attention.

Now he did—in fact, in the weeks and months to follow, he soaked up all that he could absorb, all that an eight-year-old's mind could comprehend.

But he still could not quite cope with the why part, the motives. What sort of person could get Sean and his parents to engage in such betrayal? Hitler was someone to run from, not to be loyal to, someone to hate, not almost to worship.Ultimately Kent and his mother had to return to the United States, but Art Dalham was asked to remain behind. He was to be involved in the Nuremberg Trials as a member of the American prosecuting team responsible for pleading the case against the war criminals who either had not died or had escaped undercover, in most cases, to be apprehended years later.

All three wept when they said good-bye, the beginning of a separation that would go on for a number of months. Kent would have that memory for the rest of his life—not only because of the separation, but also because of a remark his father had made.

"We've survived this latest war, Martha," he said. "Because of the grace of God, we're among the lucky ones. We all have a country to return to and it won't take a great deal to get our lives back to normal. But not the Germans, not the everyday people who were seduced by their leaders. Their cities are in ashes at their feet. Their institutions are a shambles. Life has been reduced to a primal level. None of this will ever be forgotten. Some will learn to cope but others will carry an overriding sense of bitterness with them for a long time to come."

He paused briefly, then added, "I fear what the hostility being bred will mean for Kent's generation, the price he and others like him will have to pay. How long before a few Germans feel a compulsion for revenge? And what will they do about it?"

...a compulsion for revenge.

Kent wasn't at all sure what that meant, but his father's manner at that precise moment sent shivers up and down his spine.

Part I

We...were like a bit of
sandpaper which, rubbed a
few times, becomes useless
and is thrown away to be
burned with the garbage.

—Benjamin B. Ferencz
From *Less Than Slaves*

1

IN the weeks and months to follow, they would think about their first reactions to that awful sight, experienced soldiers almost unable to continue past the ditch that had been dug around the entire circumference of the camp. Chunks of lime had been poured into it and then water to create a chemical reaction of significant heat and steam, the mixture later cooling to produce a fine, dry, white powder.

Through the thin cloud that remained in the air, they could see portions of bodies, men and women who had been thrown into the ditch while still alive, who with the little strength they had had tried to climb out, dying in the process. Some died with hands frozen in mid-air, fists clinched in utter agony, a few with their heads above the surface, lips pulled back, often showing bare, lacerated gums, the teeth having been pulled out by the maniacal resident dentist.

Several of the soldiers could go no further, overcome with nausea, though most were able to jump over the ditch. One, however, sickened by the stench, the nightmare sights, miscalculated and fell into a mass of bodies; he had to be pulled out, screaming.

Not every prisoner had been disposed of outside the camp.

Impaled on the front gate and at irregular intervals on the barbed wire fence surrounding the camp were other dead Jews, their bodies like hapless puppets, their limbs askew.

The soldiers hurried past, as much from the odor as the sight.

Once inside the camp they surveyed the layout.

"Like boot camp," one remarked.

"Yeah," another agreed. "Like..."

At the opposite end they could see tall brick chimneys, black sooty smoke billowing out from the tops.

The ovens. Four of these. Constructed of red brick, the top of each oven rounded.

Two of the heavy metal doors, caked with rust, were open.

"Oh my g—!" a grizzled old sergeant said, blanching. "Babies, children. Half a dozen all crammed inside."

"Jew babies become adult Jews," another remarked ironically.

They inspected the rest of the camp: the barracks littered with excrement, dried blood on the floors and walls, along with some fresh puddles of it; the single large gas chamber, two trucks parked up close, their exhausts connected to two pipes leading inside, an alternative to hauling in canisters of gas; a concrete block wall, with a line of bodies in front, bullet holes through their temples, their necks, their chests and abdomens.

"Looks like Mauthausen," remarked one of the older men. "Heard about that one! Wasn't supposed to be an extermination camp, but for the six and a half years it existed, more than 36,000 executions were performed."

None of the soldiers could face any of this with professional indifference. Few tried to keep up appearances. Many had to go off to one side, vomiting their disgust.

"I walked through a slaughterhouse once," recalled one of them. "It smelled the same, you know."

And then they approached a one-story, wood-shingled building at the west end of the camp.

The medical laboratory.

If anything could conceivably be worse than the rest of what they discovered, the lab was—a single over-sized room, with windows set high in the walls, a raftered ceiling, several tables littered with formaldehyde jars containing surgically-removed body parts.

And in the rear of the lab, with a folding partition around him, the sole survivor: a pale aged Jew near death, strapped to a thin mattress resting on a bare gray metal frame, blood being drained from his body through plastic tubing in all four limbs.

Later he told them an experiment was being conducted to see how long it would take him to die.

"How could the Nazis have kept this a secret?" a sergeant asked, his voice husky with shock. "How could we not have known?"

"People knew," a private told him. "People *had* to have known."

"But people said nothing."

"Until now."

"Yeah, too late for the dead."

Finally, after airlifting the old man to a nearby hospital, most of the soldiers left, to return to nights torn by the worst dreams of their lives. A few were necessarily stationed behind to safeguard the evidence until a full cleanup battalion could be dispatched. All media coverage was banned for the time being, with only official military photos allowed to be taken of the camp interior, of the ditch around it, of the sign to the left of the front entrance, a sign reading:

DACHAU II
Portland, Oregon

2

*H*E remembered his wife's perfume. It was often the trigger to reliving memories about her, when he could smell it in the air, worn by someone else.

Chantilly.

She adored the scent, and he adored it because of her.

He would buy her assortments for special occasions: perfume, talc, bath oil, soap.

It was a gentle fragrance, gentle like Valerie herself. He would enjoy the scent of it on her skin as he held her close, at night, the soft feel of her making his heart beat always faster, the two of them grateful that they had one another and, later, the two children.

And then it ended.

The reality, with a terrorist's hidden explosive.

The dream, with the jarring sound of a telephone's ring-ring....

The call came well past midnight. Perhaps Special Agent Kent Dalham should have been accustomed to such intrusions, but he had never reached that stage despite more than a decade of service with the FBI. He pulled himself out of sleep, grumbled, reached for the receiver, dropped it, fumbled in the darkness, then found it, his fingers numbly closing around the middle. Finally, he held it against his ear, his throat dry from snoring, his voice cracking.

"Hello...Dalham here," he managed to say.

Headquarters in Washington, D.C.!

He listened carefully, adrenaline pushing past the tattered ends of sleep still clinging to him.

"Good G—!" he started to exclaim, but stopped himself as he listened to the details that were being given quickly, succinctly.

Hundreds dead. Many still not identified. But a list has been started, the names cross-checked with missing persons reports from all over the country.

Teenage girls thought to be killed near their homes but their bodies unaccounted for, instead kidnapped and sent to Dachau II.

Runaways from rich families, poor families, middle class families—scores of them found.

Elderly men and women reported missing, assumed to have wandered off in a daze of senility.

Dead. Their bodies piled on top of one another...in a patch of Oregonian forestland.

The report was overwhelming.

How could it be? he asked himself. *How could anything like this—?*

He said that over and over in his mind, never finishing the sentence because the report up to that point was scarcely believable. He kept slipping into fleeting denial, only to have Bureau conditioning kick in, with the realization that the agent at the other end of that connection was cold-hard serious.

"I can be at the airport in an hour," Dalham finally said, clearing his throat.

As soon as he hung up, he jumped out of bed, packed some clothes, an extra revolver, ammunition—then showered and started to shave. He paused for a moment, looking at himself in the mirror.

Not a bad-looking man in his mid-50s...some grey hair...a few more wrinkles...only moderate bags hanging from his lower lids. The rest of his body was firm, his biceps and pectorals pronounced, with none of the flabbiness that can come with the middle years of any man's life. Working out in a gym was a requirement for FBI agents, but he would have done it anyway.

He chuckled as he thought of those who compared him to a younger, undissipated Spencer Tracy.

For a moment images of his wife and children surfaced. He stood there with razor in one hand, leaning on the other as it rested on the edge of the bathroom sink, vignettes relived from the all-too-brief time they had had together.

How lonely it has been, he thought. *Years later, how much I long for you all...*

He shook himself out of that moment of reflection and finished shaving. Then he got dressed and hurried outside to his car. He stood for a second in the chill night air, enjoying the bracing feel of it against his face and down his lungs.

"You know what's going on, Lord," he whispered as he was getting into the car. "The future is in Your hands. Please guide Your servant! I pray this to You through Your holy Son Jesus Christ in the Holy Spirit."

He waited for a second or two, gripping the steering wheel, his head bowed, and then he turned on the ignition of the dark green four-door sedan.

On the way to Phoenix International, he thought about what he had heard over the phone.

A concentration camp in the midst of the Oregon forests!

After 22 years as a special agent, much of his time undercover, he had gone beyond being shocked even at the worst atrocities. Mass murders, brutal rapes, sadomasochistic torture scenes—there was virtually no depravity he had not witnessed, including the recent upsurge in satanic cult killings.

In Mexico...

The site was littered with buried bodies.

And the artifacts of deluded men chained to worship of the Prince of Darkness.

There had been other ghastly revelations over the years. He remembered being on the scene at Jonestown, examining the grisly aftermath of Jim Jones' madness.

The worst part was seeing the children, crumbled like human dolls in the dirt, most holding the hand of a parent, obeying that parent with trust.

All those children!

There were occasions when the rush of nightmarish images reached such a level of surfeit that some of his fellow agents came close to resigning, not from fear of danger, but from disgust at seeing the corruption to which human beings could sink, the memories surfacing often in the middle of the night, tearing past their lips in cries of shock and nausea.

He remembered the story of one agent who earlier had brought down a man guilty of trapping teenage boys and then torturing and murdering them.

I was happy to waste him. He lunged for me and I fired, the first shot spinning him backward. I made sure the nine others all hit him in the temple, the neck, the stomach. I didn't allow the slightest chance for that monster to survive.

Later I tried convincing myself that it was only self-defense on my part.

The agent came to Dalham's apartment one afternoon and let loose a torrent of emotion, confessing that he was near collapse.

"I got revenge, Kent," he blurted out. "I'm not a Christian like you but I think of myself as reasonably civilized. Yet I couldn't *stop*! I felt *triumph*! I had been the messenger of justice. Surely there was nothing wrong with that."

He fought hard to control himself as he talked.

"It was what he had *done*, Kent. Can you imagine what it's like to put a shovel to dirt and then uncover the bits and pieces of children?"

The agent then had fallen, sobbing, into Dalham's arms. The two of them worked through it together as friends, taking a few days off and driving to a retreat operated by the Navigators ministry outside of Colorado Springs.

And now, Dalham thought, *am I about to face a critical juncture like that?*

A modern Nazi extermination site!

Even the mere anticipation of such a reality tore at his carefully-spun cloak of self-sufficiency, of not letting any perverse circumstance cause him to act or think in anything but a coldly logical manner, keeping his emotions in check and the contents of his stomach in place.

This one's going to be tough, Lord, he prayed, *truly tough this time.*

It was bad enough at that mass murder scene in Texas a few years earlier, where a psychopath was shooting from a county building at everyone in the park below.

Screaming everywhere...people bleeding...paramedics trying to reach them and getting shot themselves.

But that was the work of a single individual, an individual possessed by hatred and a thirst for revenge. He had been abused in his childhood and couldn't sustain any lasting relationships since then, his frustration building up and then erupting, volcano-like, in a burst of violence that lasted for hours.

This latest situation's different, Dalham thought. *If the Bureau is right, this is big-scale, with extensive planning and many participants.*

Planning...

Details so perfectly set in place that no one outside knew.

Yet how *could* it have been kept a secret?

That was one of the questions nagging at him throughout the trip from Phoenix to Portland.

Who was bribed to keep quiet?

How many sold their souls?

It was the same during World War II. Collaborators, desperate for their own survival, did anything necessary to last another day, another week, another month, however long they could, even if this meant pretending they didn't know anything about Auschwitz I, II and III, though their town was just "across the road."

"The most disturbing thing for any of us to recall about those people," a woman who survived confinement there once had told him, "is that they managed to continue their lives with some kind of normalcy, a normalcy bought and paid for by the anguished cries of sick and dying Jews!"

She had become physically ill with the recollection, ashamed of herself for harboring bitterness so very long.

"I want to let go of it, purge all this anger," she told him, "but I can't. All this time, it has been there, at the very center of my being!"

A short while later, he was able to witness to her about Jesus Christ, and she made a profession of faith.

Months passed, and then he got a phone call from her.

She sounded so different! he thought as the memory surfaced, as he remembered what she told him.

"I was freed from Auschwitz nearly forty years ago," she said, emotion clogging her voice. "But ever after, my life had been in another prison, a prison *inside* me. When I accepted Christ, all that changed, all that changed *completely!*"

And now, another camp: DACHAU II.

Several hundred bodies. Mottled in shades of black and blue, from gas, from beatings, from exposure to the elements.

Only one survivor from the group.

Dalham remembered a harrowing tale from 43 years before, told by the Oxfordshire Yeomanry, a British infantry company. They had liberated Belsen, which didn't have gas chambers. Instead, its 37,000 prisoners had been punished by starvation, disease and execution by a firing squad. When British soldiers arrived, some of the Jews, desperately weak and ill, died as they were gathering around their liberators.

A woman begged for milk for her baby. She held it up to one of the soldiers. He saw that the infant had been dead for days but nevertheless he poured some milk on those hard, black lips. The mother was overjoyed, thanking him again and again. Still holding the baby, she walked away a few yards, stumbled and fell. The soldier rushed over to her. She was dead as well.

"From everywhere they came, a long, sad, doomed march," remarked a general later, after tabulating the identities of those at Belsen. "German Jews, Poles, Czechs, Austrians and others, directed through the network set up by Himmler and Eichmann and other madmen."

Forty-odd years ago...

After all that time—more than four decades of looking back on the Holocaust, the wrenching lessons supposedly impressed upon two other generations, constant reminders through the media, endless proclamations from heads of government about never letting it happen again—humanity, having looked through the doorway to hell, seemed determined to keep it shut and locked.

And yet now...

The disappearances of a dozen or so men, women and children would have been puzzling enough, but this number meant something far more.

He asked the stewardess if she could have the heat turned up a bit, and yet he suspected that the thermostat's setting wasn't why he felt so cold.

Dalham was picked up at the Portland, Oregon airport in a grey four-door sedan and driven two hours out of town to the remote, densely forested site.

The fellow agent in this case was a woman. Unlike some others in the Bureau, that didn't bother Dalham at all; he had worked with female agents before.

"A long drive," Maggie Fincher warned him, looking more like a red-haired schoolgirl than an experienced agent.

"Away from everything?" he replied.

"That it is."

A few minutes passed.

"Quite a sight, Kent," Fincher remarked, not taking her eyes off the road that soon began to slice through deep forestland.

"Any clues?" Dalham asked.

"Not many. There's a report on the backseat. Can you reach it?"

After retrieving the manila folder, Dalham leafed through the various sheets of paper inside.

"Only one survivor," he said, repeating what he had been told over the phone.

"So far," Fincher told him.

"Where *would* you find any others?"

"Under those piles of bodies."

"You mean not all of them might be dead?"

"It's possible. The Army guys found a middle-aged woman who was barely alive but died minutes later."

"The report suspects skinheads, not the punk-rock variety but those in the neo-Nazi movement," Dalham noted.

"Who else with this sort of thing?"

Fincher was right. Satanists had a different *modus operandi*, though there were many variations within their approach to murder.

"No sacrificial animals in the vicinity?" Dalham asked.

"Only men, women and children."

Dalham had had contact with the neo-Nazi element over the years—from the riot at Meriden, Connecticut to the Skokie, Illinois incident. Often he found the younger ones to be strangely pathetic, driven into their rebellion by home lives filled with abuse in a variety of forms—incest, beatings, rejection—that had ended any emotional bonds the kids might have ever felt with the families. So they became friendly with some Aryan Underground member and were sucked in by a specious atmosphere of belonging.

Abuse again!

A thread running through virtually all of the mass murderer cases I've ever studied or been assigned to.

From childhood, grievances harbored, festering, waiting for the right channel to retaliate.

And so it had gone with Hitler himself, plagued by the possibility that his grandfather had been Jewish, suffering persistent mistreatment by his father, a constant grind of angry words, beatings, more.

Somewhere along that twisted path, young Adolf groped for some way to strike back, some way to realize the vengeance building up inside him, ready to spew forth in Pompeiian fury.

"It's interesting, Kent," Fincher remarked as though reading his mind. "In a real sense, when they become skinheads, these guys do belong. That's what they're looking for...as well as an obsession to get even, you know, payback time."

"But they're too dumb or deceived or maybe both to realize that, just as Hitler's soldiers were sacrificed by the tens of thousands, they also are expendable. It's a group, yeah, but so are lemmings before they go over a cliff!"

Fincher paused for a moment, then added, "Kent, it must be kind of ironic for *you* to be sent here."

"They told you about my father?"

"*Everyone* knows about that man."

Dalham blushed a bit, not realizing that the whole thing was quite *that* well-known.

"It must have been something for him in those days."

"It was," Dalham agreed, "it was."

He lapsed into silence, thinking back, the memories never less than fresh, always ready to come to the surface with the slightest provocation.

Dad...

Weary after the Second World War, anxious to get home, ready to board a plane, then being called back, asked to forestall his return in order to cooperate with Chief American Prosecutor Robert Houghwout Jackson at the International Military Tribunal in Nuremberg, Germany. From November 1945 through October 1946, a full year of hard, disturbing work.

Sir Hartley Shawcross of the British team called you the most organized and disciplined man he had ever met, Dalham reminisced. You helped organize the trials, yet you were content to let others gain the glory.

You were the one who discovered Goering, dead, in his cell, just two hours before he was to be hanged.

You demanded that Goering's body be put on a stretcher, and taken to the gymnasium where the gallows had been set up for Von Ribbentrop, Keitel, Kaltenbrunner, Rosenberg, Frank, Frick, Streicher, Jodl and, finally, Seyss-Inquart.

Goering had cheated the judicial process of his own hanging. But Dad, you determined that his body would be placed with the others for the world to see.

Even with justice served, there remained the daily reality of life for those who survived the crimes that had earned death sentences for that handful of deranged men.

He remembered his father, who was to serve with the military in its pursuit of the surviving Nazi war criminals, telling him about the sight of living human skeletons peering out through barbed wire fences. Arthur James Dalham had walked up to several, telling them, "You are free. You *are* free!" But they all stared back at him, as though reluctant to believe that wonderful truth for fear that it was nothing more than an hallucination induced by hunger, disease and endless months of seeing their families, their friends put to death.

"What drives people *today* to do the *same* thing apparently?" Dalham said aloud.

"I have lots of theories," Maggie Fincher remarked, "though I can't say how valid any of them are."

"Bounce one off me."

"All right. Communism seems to be waning, Kent. You and I both know that. We'd know it if we weren't in the line of work we are. We'd know it just by reading the papers and listening to the television news programs."

"And with one totalitarian system crumbling, there's always another waiting to take its place, is that what you think?"

"Right on the money, my friend. Crazy idea?"

"Not at all," Dalham offered. "Human nature has never evolved into a better form, with nobler aspirations, since the Romans crucified their criminals."

"We've gotten worse, then?" Fincher asked somewhat naively, her youthful, freckled face quite intent.

"Probably. I think of the latter verses in Romans 1."

"God giving them over to a reprobate mind, that sort of stuff."

Dalham stiffened at the "stuff" categorization, without bothering to ask the other agent how it was that she knew about that portion of Scripture.

Fincher noticed this and apologized.

"Sorry, Kent. That was careless. Sorry..."

"No problem. Tell me more about your theories, Maggie."

"That's the most sensible one, I guess. Down with the Commies, up with the neo-Nazis."

"Why now, though? Today?"

"Whenever there is a great surge in masses of hurting people, confused people, the extremist groups reap a harvest."

Dalham nodded.

His father became quite senile long before he should have because of Alzheimer's, but there were lucid moments, moments when the old sharpness, the facile mind returned, to latch onto something on television or in the newspaper.

One night the elder Dalham heard a report about a series of synagogue desecrations in the Tucson area.

"Watch out, Kent," he said, his voice really not above a whisper. "A few months ago, it was Boston; earlier it was Miami. Something's going on."

The son had smiled at the aging father, not taking much of what he said very seriously in those final days.

"Thanks, Dad, for pointing it out to me," he had replied. "I'll be on the lookout for things like that from now on."

A few months later, that mind would never again flash any light of intellect or reasoning or insight, lost in a maze of disorientation into which Alzheimer's had pushed him repeatedly, until he could no longer find his way out...

"Dad..." he spoke aloud, though not intending to do so.

"What was that, Kent?" Maggie Fincher asked.

"Nothing. Just remembering."

"A different world today, and yet the same," Fincher added.

"It is, Maggie, it is."

Both were silent the rest of the way, each mulling over in their mind the cesspool into which they had been called to step.

3

EVEN the recollections, searing in their etched clarity, that had been passed to him by his father did not entirely prepare Kent Dalham for what he saw as soon as he got out of the car.

Overhead the branches of trees laced together to form a ceiling of sorts.

"That's how they were able to avoid detection for as long as they did," Fincher told him, noting the obvious.

Power saws and bulldozers had been the instruments to scoop out of the thick forest a clearing of a dozen or so acres.

Little could be seen from the air, hints of buildings perhaps but nothing else.

"Runaways, the elderly, schoolgirls, others, all kidnapped presumbably," Dalham said, surprised that he could speak at all.

"That's probably only part of it, Kent," Fincher added. "Think of the skid rows across this country—adults in their 20s, 30s, 40s—people *available* to the devils who did this, just like fruit off the trees in an orchard."

Now lifeless, cold bodies.

All the preparation in the world—all the paternal memories, all the TV mini-series, all the historical *facts*—could never have been adequate to make Dalham ready for what he saw.

And what he smelled.

He was given a gas mask, not for safety but to mitigate the odor.

Just before he slipped the mask on, a vagrant breeze brought the stench to his nostrils, and he nearly gagged.

The scene seemed unreal, men rendered anonymous by the masks they were forced to wear, faceless entities digging down into a mass grave and pulling out body after body after body.

But only their sense of smell was protected, leaving the other senses to wallow in what had to be done. They *saw* the corpses, *touched* them, *heard* the cracking of bones, which happened no matter how careful the soldiers were; and they *tasted* the sickness in their stomachs as, despite how tough, how experienced, how conditioned they might be, each one in his own way reacted to the nightmarish task being performed.

As Dalham and Fincher stood and watched for a few nearly intolerable minutes, the mere role of spectators to such a grisly business making them uncomfortable, forcing them to view it all without getting their hands dirty, Dalham thought he may have heard the faintest of sounds.

He strained his ears, not at *a* sound—there were plenty of these, the *grunts* of the soldiers, the *slithers* and *squishes* and *plops* and the rest. No, he heard something else, someone crying, gasping, faintly at first.

"I don't hear anything," Fincher said when Dalham asked her. "Where is it coming from?"

Dalham walked forward, close to the edge of the ditch. He cocked his head.

Fincher was to his left, doing the same.

"Kent!" she exclaimed. "I think I do now. Someone's—"

Others had heard it by then, muffled, trembling, a cry, then a split second of silence, then another cry.

"Help me!"

In heavily accented English.

Yes. Someone was calling.

"Help me!"

Under the layers of bodies, probably near the bottom.

Alive!

The process could not go measurably faster. The bodies had to be identified; they couldn't be tossed haphazardly to one side or the other, some quite bloated, not from their diet but undoubtedly pumped full of gas, puffing them up, bodies that gave a kind of posthumous *sigh* when picked up, however gently.

Moments later the source of the noise had been found.

A little boy, not more than seven years old.

Not a Jew. Nor black.

Hispanic.

Carved across his forehead in ugly festering cuts was a single word: *Spick*.

"They hate everyone who isn't a WASP," Fincher remarked.

"The Aryan dream," Dalham added, "summarized in a dozen words: 'blood pure and untainted in a race destined to rule the world.' Hitler and virtually everyone else in his inner circle was obsessed by the doctrine. Bastardization of the German race was to be avoided."

The boy was semiconscious by then. Dalham walked up to him.

His speech was garbled at first, spoken in scarcely more than a hoarse whisper.

He was groaning.

"Get a stretcher over here, quick!" yelled one of the soldiers gathered in a small circle around his frail body. Then, realizing that he couldn't be heard through the gas mask, he pulled it off. "Stretcher—now! Hurry!"

"Apar...apar...ap...!" the boy mumbled.

His eyes suddenly shot open, after having been nearly closed, looking at the men around him with their gas masks still on. He tried to pull away but was too weak.

"Somebody get a sedative quick, or this little guy's gonna die of heart failure!" another soldier screamed, his mask off, adrenalin momentarily blocking any awareness of the stench.

"Ap...ap...!" the boy continued to stutter.

Two medics brought the stretcher, lifted him onto it, and started to walk by Dalham.

The boy reached out, grabbed the sleeve of his jacket.

"Ap...ap...apar...a...!"

Dalham took his mask off and bent down beside the stretcher.

"Son, no *habla Español*," he admitted. "I just don't understand what you mean."

The boy's grip had been feather-like but, abruptly, and only for a second, he was able to tug roughly on the sleeve, and Dalham bent down next to his lips.

"*Aparicion! Aparicion!*"

The boy seemed more frightened than ever, saying that word one more time before he fell back against the stretcher and lost consciousness.

Fincher placed her hand on Dalham's shoulder.

"I know what it means, Kent."

Dalham straightened.

"All right, what was he trying to tell us?"

"*Aparicion*, Kent, is Spanish for apparition. That kid was terrified by some sort of phantom!"

4

DALHAM had been aware of the mystical aspects of the Third Reich for a long time. He remembered his father's cautioning him not to dismiss out of hand any remarks about the Nazis being demon-possessed.

"Take Goering," the elder Dalham remarked. "He was one of the more flamboyant of Hitler's henchmen. He did everything to excess: the way he ate and drank, the clothes he wore, the art collection he had built mostly upon a foundation of appropriation from wealthy Jews and institutions he had ordered ransacked.

"But he was also one of the most mystically 'connected' of all the Nazis, and he pursued the supernatural with typical lack of restraint. He consulted clairvoyants. Once he swung a diviner's pendulum across a map in an effort to ascertain the next move of opposing British and French forces. He used rainmakers and hired a scientist to develop a death ray—all presumably under the guidance of occultic influences."

Aparicion!

A word spoken by a frightened Hispanic boy before he collapsed. Any connection with what his father had said?

Dalham and Fincher were sitting on metal folding chairs in the middle of the camp after all the bodies had been cleared from the ditches. Only a small contingent of soldiers remained behind, trying to put some pieces together.

"Is it imagination, Kent, or do I feel a certain atmosphere of evil here?" Fincher was saying.

"I think it's imagination," Dalham told her. "People who go to Auschwitz for the first time have the same reaction. They speak of an odor about the place, a cold, grey deadness, a kind of palpable sadness. It seems so real to them that it becomes a metaphor for evil."

"That might be it," Fincher agreed. "It's all here, my friend. Just as you've described."

Dalham looked about the camp, thinking that it was a striking re-creation of the original Dachau, though on a smaller scale.

Dachau.

One of the earliest camps, built in 1933—a center of medical experiments, in addition to those conducted by Mengele at Auschwitz.

Inmates were injected with malaria, typhus, infectious jaundice. They were forced to drink seawater. They suffered experiments with sulfa drugs, bone grafting, mustard gas.

Mustard gas.

Dalham shivered at the thought. Men, women and children with huge blisters all over their bodies caused by the gas, blisters allowed to become gangrenous just so that the Nazi doctors could see how long it took for them to die.

Arthur James Dalham had told him about a particularly upsetting encounter at Dachau, not worse in itself than seeing piles of corpses or bones clogging the ovens or hundreds of starving inmates too weak to walk after they were liberated by the Allies. Not worse, no, but still something that could never be buried and forgotten in some corner of the mind, agonized over for awhile and then disposed of.

It marked his mind indelibly for the rest of his life.

The sight of mustard gas victims in an advanced state of blistering, their bodies puffed up, every step one of agony, and sometimes they fell, and sometimes they fell, and sometimes...

One of them had stumbled toward Art Dalham, tripping, landing against him.

"The odors, Kent," he had said. "The odors were the worst of it. Like something that had been decaying for a thousand years!"

The elder Dalham rarely showed less than a stoic reaction to harsh circumstances, not wanting to appear weak to his son. But this time, this time was different.

"He died a minute or so later, Kent. I couldn't even pull down his lids. Both were severely diseased."

He shuddered visibly.

"I took a bath as soon as I could, son. A week later, after many baths, I still couldn't feel clean."

"Time to get to get to work," Dalham said finally.

Fincher nodded.

The crematoria were directly ahead. To the right were the gas chambers. Several soldiers were digging out the remains, putting aside any actual pieces of bone among the whitish-greyish powder while dumping the rest into large canisters.

In one of the ovens were the partial remains of several young children.

"It's the hardest to take, sir," one of the soldiers said as they approached. "When this camp was first discovered, a number of the men could stand almost anything, but not *this*!"

The two agents agreed.

One of the children had tried to beat open the heavy door sealing that particular oven, his body frozen like that, his hand still raised.

Fincher turned away. Dalham continued looking, looking inside, trying to visualize what it must have been like, *lying down, feeling the heat instantly, screaming as the door was shut, the only light coming from the heating elements that were glowing bright red...not alone, either, several others with you...the burning, please stop, please stop, and no refuge anywhere, all around you the awful screams, the screams coming from your own throat as well, before your entire body ignited.*

Dalham shut the door quickly.

"I can almost feel the heat," a soldier remarked. "Can you?"

Dalham nodded.

"Look at this, sir," the soldier said.

In his hand was an infant's skull, not much bigger than his palm.

His thoughts went instantly back to an abortion dump site that he had raided years earlier, bags of fetuses piled on top of one another, all killed under the delusion that it wasn't murder.

And now this!

"Couldn't have been more than a year old! What causes people to go crazy like this?"

For the moment, Dalham had no answer.

The laboratory was next.

They saw what the soldiers saw but they also saw more, or at least what the others hadn't been able to verbalize.

"Why weren't we told about *this*?" Dalham asked, shock mixing with anger, the anger threatening to explode. "I can't believe they didn't *discover it*!"

He turned and started back toward the entrance, ready to tear into those involved, then stopped before getting very far.

Remember, Kent. It's only been 24 hours. Nobody's been sloppy. Don't be harsh on the guys. Remember, they were here first; they had to face the shock without any advance preparation.

The lifeless bodies on long tables, yes, those were rough enough to confront; and the vials, containing various fluids. But the cages, the cages in another, smaller room, concealed behind cabinets, it was these that must have caused havoc with even the most disciplined of soldiers.

...in the cages!

People.

All dead.

Dalham and Fincher had seen more bodies outside that building, more bodies by far in the ditch around the circumference of Dachau II.

But *these* were worse, if that could be imagined, worse because of *how* they must surely have died, not "simply" by gas or flames, as monstrous as that was, not by being shot in the head or stabbed in the heart, but with the act of dying, the pain of it, the trauma *purposely* extended in any manner possible.

"This one was abused by electric shock, and who knows what else," Dalham surmised, "to see how long it would be until his heart could no longer stand the strain."

Others.

Stuffed behind bars, packed together like experimental cattle.

"Some may still have been alive when their captors fled, Kent," Fincher guessed.

"Probably," Dalham agreed, "but dead by the time our men got here."

The worst sight was in a cage to one side.

Two young boys.

"Are you thinking what I'm thinking? Could they be...?" Fincher gasped.

"I don't..." Dalham started to say.

He bent down, in front of the cage, looking more closely.

"...think so. I—"

He stood abruptly and lurched from that place, through the lab and then outside. Two soldiers came running over.

"You should have been told, sir," one of them admitted, "but there was just no way to describe it."

"I've heard of...of them at circus freak shows," the other soldier exclaimed, "but I'd never seen anything like that until...until..."

Dalham leaned back against the frame of the building.

"It's the same as 50 years ago," he muttered, wiping his mouth with a handkerchief.

"Oh, yes, sir, that's right," the other soldier added. "I remember something I read from the Bible once, Saint Paul, I think. Well, the old guy was right when he wrote about God giving them over to a reprobate mind. *Some* things change, sir, but not that!"

$$\overline{5}$$

DALHAM and Fincher were sitting in a booth at a roadside diner. Neither had been saying much. They had ordered a couple of sandwiches but these remained untouched.

Fincher lifted a cup of coffee to her lips.

She blushed, smiling weakly as she looked at her hand.

It was shaking.

"Don't worry," Dalham said, noticing.

"You're right, of course, we're not emotionless robots. Maybe Hoover would have liked it that way, but we're not."

"Hoover was strange in some ways, Maggie, but he wasn't quite the monster he was supposed to be, at least not *all* the time."

"Did you ever meet him?" Fincher asked.

Dalham nodded.

"Just a year before he died."

"Tell me about it sometime."

"I will."

They lapsed into silence again.

But not for long.

Two burly men, one probably in his twenties, the other in his forties, entered the diner and sat in the next booth. Both smelled of cigarette smoke, perspiration.

They started gabbing straightaway.

"So you heard about it," the older one asked, "that camp, I mean?"

"Yeah."

"Reminds me of something funny years ago."

"Funny? What about?"

"When they caught that guy Eichmann in Argentina, you know, and flew him back to Israel, well, the kikes were glad to get ahold of him."

Dalham was about to confront the two men for saying *kikes*, but Fincher reached across the table and grabbed his arm.

"We can't change people on the spot, Kent," she said in a low voice. "We can't fight every bigot in the country."

The older man was going on with his story.

"—and so the trial was taped and segments of it played in certain parts of the U.S."

"What's so funny about that?" the younger one asked a bit irritably.

"Well, companies buy commercial time. Everything's got to be sponsored. One company that interrupted the Eichmann trial footage got into a lot of trouble for it."

"All right, I'll bite: What company?"

"Easy Off Oven Cleaner!"

They broke out into uproarious laughter, doubling over in their seats.

Dalham couldn't stand it any longer. He got to his feet and stood in front of their booth, slamming his fist down on the table.

"That's not funny," he said, "not funny at all!"

"What's it to you?" one of the men said. "I don't remember inviting you to our party. You should be minding your own business."

Both men were much larger than Dalham, but he was accustomed to such super-macho types. It wouldn't have mattered anyway—Dalham was fed up with cheap derogatory talk about other human beings simply on the basis of color, race, whatever; and Fincher was ready to join him.

"That's true," Dalham acknowledged. "I *wasn't* invited. But you're going to listen anyway."

Both men started to stand.

"Hold on!" Dalham said, his voice so cold that the other men hesitated.

He took several Polaroid photos out of his pocket and spread these on the table.

"*That's* why it's not funny," he said.

The men glanced at the shots, briefly at first, then with more attention.

"Oh my G—!" they both said after a few seconds.

They sat down, passing the pictures between themselves.

A minute or so later, the younger of the two looked up at Dalham.

"From that camp they discovered?" he asked.

"I took the shots myself," Dalham told him. "Like this one, two boys in a cage and—"

Suddenly the younger man held up his hands. He didn't want to hear the details.

"Mister, I...I don't know what to say," the older one said, deeply embarrassed. "We were just joking around. We had no idea that..."

"It's the same mentality," Dalham said. "From ridicule to contempt and then on to...to that!"

"You've reacted the way you have just from amateur photos," Fincher added. "We were there. We *smelled* the place. We *saw* the lifeless bodies."

"No more Jew jokes," the younger man said. "Man, you can bet on that!"

"You two were there?" the other asked. "How come?"

Dalham took out his badge and laid it on the table.

Both men blanched when they saw it.

Dalham retrieved the badge and started to walk toward the cashier's stand, Fincher beside him. After they paid the bill and had gone outside, they heard someone calling after them.

The older man.

"May have something for you," he said as he approached the two of them.

"What's that?" Dalham asked.

"A town near here. Just a few miles south."

"What about it?"

"A lot of Nazi types seem to hang out there."

"Nazi types?"

"Yeah, you know, skinheads, creeps like that. I'd check it out if I were you."

Dalham thanked him.

"No problem. Least I can do, I mean, you know, what I said back there."

Dalham smiled.

"Thanks," he said.

"Mister?"

"Yes?"

"You forgot the pictures."

The man handed these to him.

"Anybody who does that stuff is crazy or worse."

"Or worse?"

"That's right. This state's been known for some pretty strange goings-on."

"Occult stuff, you mean?"

"You got it."

The man seemed nervous then.

"Gotta go," he said abruptly.

"Thanks again," Dalham said.

As they got into the car, Dalham turned to Fincher.

"Are you a Christian, Maggie?" He asked the question he had intended to put to Fincher earlier.

"I like to think so."

"I am, too."

"I'd never have guessed it, Kent!" Fincher exclaimed in mock surprise, then more seriously: "Why do you ask?"

"Not sure actually, just a feeling."

"A feeling that it helps to have a fellow believer in Christ nearby when you're at the gates of hell?"

"Something like that," Dalham said.

"Let's pray then. Headquarters might think it strange, but who cares?"

And so they did.

$$\overline{6}$$

MAGGIE Fincher liked this new temporary partner. She had seldom worked with anyone as open, as natural about his Christianity or anything else as Kent Dalham was.

So Fincher felt the need to unload something that had been bothering her for awhile.

"It all has been so *businesslike* over the years," Fincher admitted after they had been driving a bit, "like everybody's a cog or a gear or some other part of a well-greased machine."

She had come from farm country in Ohio, where people were still neighbors in every sense of the word.

"I had more of a sense of rapport with some of the *trees* back on our land than I do with most of my colleagues now," she added. "Every one of those trees, it seemed, had been there for a hundred years. The generation before me and the generation before that one knew those trees.

"But with the Bureau, you have efficiency at the expense of warmth, of personality. I find someone I like, someone I can talk to, and all of a sudden he's transferred or he's killed in the line of duty. Or I'm the one who's shipped thousands of miles away."

"But it's a necessary approach, this machine mentality, Maggie," Dalham reminded her. "Any other would mean chaos, unfortunately."

"Unfortunately is right."

Fincher found it interesting to learn how Dalham felt about the machine analogy, but also sensed that the FBI was much more than that to this man, like those who had come to think of the Bureau as a kind of mate by default. She didn't have that perspective, had no need for it since she was married and the mother of a couple of children. But she had been single when she joined, and could understand the passion-by-sublimation baggage carried by agents who had suffered through a divorce or the death of a spouse or who had never been married in the first place.

Fincher sighed as she recalled Thomas Carey, who was in his 80s when he died. Fincher had met the old man at a banquet they both attended three years earlier.

Not enough time, Fincher thought.

Carey was fascinating, with tales from the early days of the FBI, anecdotes involving run-ins with Capone, Netti, other legendary gangsters.

"Most of my life," he had said, "I haven't known anything else."

Many agents had the same view. The Bureau was everything to them. Their dependence on it extended to virtually every aspect of their lives.

"The Bureau's paid my mortgage for most of my adult years," Carey had continued, "and all my doctor bills, all my vacations. They financed my kids' college tuition. They..."

He'd gotten lost then in his thoughts and said nothing further the rest of the evening.

The next Fincher heard of Thomas Carey was the news that the old man, widowed, was found dead and alone on a park bench, pigeons still at his feet, eating the peanuts he had been feeding them.

"I don't think it stops there, Kent," Fincher commented. "You don't expect *feeling* from a machine. Yet the Bureau is so pervasive in our lives that it fosters more than the usual employer-employee relationship. Few of us are into what we do strictly because it's a job. If it were *just* that, I might have quit a long time ago. My family has had to be a part of it also, since we all realize the possibility that I might not come home one day except to be buried. If my desire to be an agent were strictly based on getting a paycheck, then another profession would have rated higher for me because of the safety factor."

"What's the point?" Dalham asked with some impatience.

"I compare it to having a husband who's the kind every woman dreams of, independent, resourceful, a great companion, a wonderful cook—but when it comes to sex, he's as impotent as a block of ice."

Dalham nodded in agreement and admitted, "I've felt that way myself at times. You keep wishing for more humanity."

"But Kent, that's the problem, as I see the matter. It does spring up, something that appears to be a flash of humanity behind the impersonality, but usually only when one of us happens to shed our blood in the middle of some asphalt parking lot or a corridor in a run-down building. Then the tears come, oh they come, and the outrage as well. I don't say it isn't allowed; I don't say it isn't effective at that time.

"And yet, I wonder, how much is *genuine* human pathos or simply well-rehearsed bureaucrats publicly mourning the loss of talent, aware that people are looking, maybe even the media are present...in other words, strictly a theatrical display masking far more pragmatic concerns, like who's going to replace the guy just slaughtered by some terrorist or drug pusher or mass murderer. Don't misunderstand me: I love the Bureau, love what its mission is, and I decided long ago to stay with it no matter what. But Kent, these are some of my concerns. I can't deal with them by ignoring them."

Dalham paused for a moment, considering what Fincher had just said, then replied as perceptively as he was able.

"I don't think anyone *is* taken for granted in this organization. I look at it as more a matter of their assuming in us the kind of competence that simply doesn't have to be coddled or praised all the time. If our emotions were so easily bruised that we had to be treated that way from Day One, Maggie, you know as well as I do that we wouldn't have the kind of resiliency demanded of us in a crisis, especially an extended one.

"As for any sense of loss displayed by the director or anyone else at the top, I really believe what you see is what you get, that it's real grief for humane reasons, not simply selfish bureaucratic ones, when agents die or are otherwise permanently taken out of action. I don't go along with the notion that the Bureau's distress, as it were, is somehow opportunistic, somehow calculating, like pushing a button, and the tears come, along with the eulogizing, and then it's the next guy's time on the conveyor belt."

"But you did agree with the machine description a little while ago," Fincher reminded him.

Neither said anything else for a bit, sensing that they had the makings of an argument—and neither of them wanted to fall into that trap. So they drove on, each leaving the other to private thoughts.

Finally Dalham, in a weary tone, spoke up again.

"If I weren't a Christian, I couldn't stand some of the stuff we have to face," he said honestly.

"That's the way I feel," Fincher replied, glad to get on a different tack. "On Christ the solid rock we stand."

The younger agent thought of her husband and their two children, the family she thought she might never have—but now, years later, she was able to thank God for such a blessing, such a fulfillment.

"You don't have a family, do you, Kent?" she asked.

"I don't," Dalham said. "They died."

"How did that happen?"

"Some weirdos getting revenge."

Fincher saw that Dalham was reluctant to talk, so she didn't pursue that particular matter further.

Brett, Laurie, Susan, she thought, sighing. *Praise God that I have you all to return to after each assignment.*

She looked at Dalham.

How lonely you must be more often than you'll ever admit. How tough to return to an empty apartment after being on the road...

A single tear trickled down her left cheek.

Brett.

I love you so much.

Keep our bed warm until I return...

7

S MOKE.
 They saw it in the distance, coming from the direction of
the town where they were heading.

"That isn't just leaves burning in somebody's backyard,"
Fincher remarked lamely.

She phoned to regional headquarters.

"What's happening?" she asked. "We're approaching
Cedarville."

A pause.

"We'll be there in fifteen minutes or less," Fincher said, and
put the receiver back on its cradle.

"It's the whole town, isn't it?" Dalham remarked.

Fincher nodded slowly.

"We won't find anything left, you know that, don't you?"
Dalham added.

"But I'm sure they've got fire fighting crews there already,
Kent."

"Trust me, Maggie. Trust me on this one."

The past repeated again! The Nazis destroyed more than
one town during World War II, but Dalham was thinking,
then, of Lidice in Czechoslovakia, the community razed in
retaliation for the death of Reinhard Heydrich, who was once
regarded as a possible successor to Hitler himself.

This was done on the direct orders of Hitler himself, thrust
into a particularly bloodthirsty mood by the death of Heydrich, who epitomized everything the *Führer* had in mind
when he spoke of the proud Aryan race: tall, blond, good-looking; a cold, hard intellect; personal bravery.

The assassins were eventually trapped in a church and
decapitated, their heads stuck on poles and displayed tri-
umphantly by the Nazis. But that was only the *final* act of

revenge. As historian Callum MacDonald wrote in *The Killing of SS Obergruppenführer Reinhard Heydrich*, "a blood sacrifice was required to avenge the death of Heydrich. The Jews were the first to be thrown on the funeral pyre...a special train...carrying 1,000 Czech Jews to their deaths in the SS extermination factories. It was followed by two more transports from the ghetto at Terezin. Of 3,000 victims only one survived, a man who managed to jump from the train which carried his companions.... For the Nazis, however, the murder of Jews was almost routine. Something more was required."

Lidice.

As MacDonald continued, "Lidice was to be destroyed. The men were to be shot on the spot and the women sent to a concentration camp. Children worthy of germanization were to be handed over to SS families. The village was to be burned to the ground and its remains leveled so that no trace remained.... Then began the ghastly work of execution...its victims in groups of ten. The bodies were buried in a mass grave by a work detail of Czech Jews from the concentration camp at Terezin. The houses were set on fire and the ruins bulldozed by the German Labour Service....Corn would grow where Lidice once stood as a permanent reminder of the fate awaiting those who defied Nazi rule."

Nothing left, Dalham thought. *Devastated homes were the tombstones...*

That day the "Demon Reich"—Dalham's personal epithet for the Nazi government—had seemed triumphant. Exultant SS officers stood and surveyed the ruins, laughing with self-satisfaction.

"We are invincible," one of them gloated. "Resist us—and be crushed!"

Three years later, their demonic master, the *Führer*, committed suicide in a bunker beneath the devastation that had been dealt not only his beloved Berlin but also all of Germany. His body and that of his once-mistress-now-wife, Eva Braun, were set aflame, the ashes taken to an unknown spot that had remained hidden for half a century.

...*we are invincible.*

How the heathen rage, O Lord!

"Cornfields," Dalham said absentmindedly.

"What's that?" Fincher asked.

Dalham shook himself.

"I was just thinking about why the cornfields grew richly."

"Oh..."

Dalham knew that sounded strange so he explained himself.

"I don't know fully what's going on, Maggie, though I think we both have some strong suspicions."

"Absolutely right."

"How many bodies will become fertilizer for Aryan crops?" Dalham asked.

"Awful thought, Kent! Surely all this won't last long enough for *that* to happen. We would never be that blind, that inept."

"World War II would never have happened if Chamberlain—"

"Theories! The *fact* is that it did happen. You can't blame one man. More than one government was fooled by—"

She turned abruptly and looked at Dalham.

"I hope you're not moving into the prophet business."

Fincher returned her attention to the road directly ahead. Both were soaked in cold perspiration.

Minutes later, wisps of ash were landing on the windshield as they came closer to the town.

The main road was clogged with state troopers and firemen as well as photographers, reporters, others.

"You were right, Kent," Fincher said.

Not one building had been left untouched. Virtually all would be piles of scorched timber and ashes.

People were running in panic. Some of them were aflame. Charred bodies were everywhere.

"Look!" Dalham said, pointing to a piece of canvas hanging from the balcony of a home's second story as the edges caught fire and the whole was consumed in seconds.

A swastika.

After the flames had died down, after virtually every store, every home had been ravaged, with only tottering shells left where there was anything at all, the two FBI agents began the process of trying to find out what had happened, trying to get through the grief, the hysteria, the shock of those who survived.

Scores of people had died. The ones left, who could articulate anything at all, told an astonishing story that was in its own way as inconceivable as an extermination camp in the midst of the nearby forest.

Trailers were brought in to house the survivors temporarily. The seriously injured had been taken to hospitals. Others were treated on the spot.

"They tried to take over the town," said Andy Payne, a construction worker, as he sat sipping some coffee.

"All were skinheads?" Dalham asked.

"Yeah, that's right. At first there were only a few of them, then a lot more. They hung around our bar, our pool hall. They spent some dollars on food, cigarettes, that sort of thing."

"Did you wonder why they picked Cedarville?"

"You mean, what could a place like this offer guys like that?"

Dalham nodded.

"We don't tend to ask a lot of questions out here. The economy's been rocky for awhile. Any money that comes in, well, we don't spook the guys spending it by interrogating them."

"They spent *all* their time in town?" Dalham asked.

"No, they didn't. And they weren't here *every* day. They would come and go at odd hours of the day and night."

"Did they take barbed wire, stuff like that with them?"

"They did, mister, they did. We knew they were up to something but we..."

Payne's hand started to shake.

"...had no suspicion of *what* was going on, I mean, that camp."

"It was hidden away pretty well, Mr. Payne. No one had much of a clue. If it hadn't been for an informant, who knows what would have happened?"

"But where did they get the others to help them? We had only a dozen or so guys here. *They* couldn't have built that entire place."

"It's impossible to tell for sure, but it's not hard to imagine that they spread themselves around, some here, some in other places. *Large* groups create talk, rumors. So they were careful.

"There was evidence of tents. They probably came in from the various communities during the day, did their work, returned every now and then, with some remaining behind to make sure that anybody who may have stumbled on the site was taken care of immediately."

Payne had rested the coffee on a small table at one end of the trailer, and buried his head in his hands.

"I've seen and heard a lot in my life, mister, but nothing like this."

"What caused them to set fire to your town?"

"The mayor and his wife were Jewish. Several of those guys raped her, dumped her in a ditch, thought she was dead. But she wasn't. When the story got out, a bunch of townspeople got a hold of three of the skinheads and made sure they'd never again be able to violate *any* woman."

"*What?*" Dalham said, stunned. "How can you be sure you got the right ones?"

"We weren't sure. We just wanted to send the bunch of them a message. Some places out here still have a sense of frontier justice."

"They *could* have been innocent, Mr. Payne, at least of *that* crime. The wrong ones might have been punished."

"I know! I *know!*" the other said, raising his voice.

Dalham knew the answer to his next question but put it to Payne anyway.

"Were you one of the vigilantes?" he asked coolly.

Payne looked up, his eyes wet.

"I was, Mr. Dalham. I was. And look what it caused!"

"They retaliated by destroying your town."

The man was overcome with grief.

"I don't know where my wife is...I can't find my son, my daughter...My house is gone...*I...I have nothing left!*"

Fincher burst into the trailer.

"Kent!" she said, panting. "I need to see you outside."

"Excuse me, Mr. Payne," Dalham said as he left.

"Kent, there's something else!" Fincher said, still breathless.

"Another town?" Dalham asked.

"Not that. This one's bad, though. Like the camp."

Fincher told him. Dalham's face was ashen.

"We've got to leave now," Fincher added. "Headquarters wants us there as soon as possible."

"What about this place?"

"Later. They want an immediate examination of the new location."

...the new location.

Dalham was glad that he had eaten nothing for most of the day as he prepared himself for what they would face in less than an hour.

$\overline{\underline{8}}$

THE soil had been freshly dug up and then replaced, looking a bit like a farmer's furrowed field but without the furrows.

"Spongy," Derek Hadley, the youth minister, remarked as he stood in the middle of the plot of ground.

Surrounding it were tall evergreens mingled with other trees whose branches were beginning to shed golden leaves.

In the air also was an odor quite vague but unpleasant.

"Notice that smell, Derek," his wife Eileen said. "Like a combination of manure and rotting old wood."

They looked out over the rich-looking bare earth, which came up to the edge of the lake directly in front of them.

"It wasn't like that here before," the woman added. "What could they have been doing?"

"Yeah, Eileen," he agreed, "it's something to wonder about, I mean, why go to the trouble of digging up all this earth and then put it back again?"

The couple were in charge of a group of two dozen teenagers. They had all been in the lake, on rafts, water-skiing behind a rented boat or just having a good swim, enjoying the exercise. One young couple had spent most of the time off by themselves, on a nearby dock, sitting, talking in very serious fashion.

Dusk.

The heat of the afternoon was nearly gone, the light fading slowly, the reddish hues of a vibrant sunset coloring the scene.

Time to gather in front of a large fire and eat and talk and sing.

Most of the teenagers were now coming on shore, prodded by an early evening chill in the air. Three stragglers hurried out of the water when someone shouted to them a special word: food. The couple on the dock finally returned, holding hands, and joined the others.

They all started to sing one of the less raucous songs written by a prominent Christian balladeer.

Several minutes passed before any of them saw what was happening.

The ground.

Derek noticed it first in the waning light.

"Look at that!" he exclaimed.

They saw the ground around them, felt the ground under them...moving.

"What in the...?" someone said.

Not wrenching movement, not like an earthquake, but tiny ripples, with no discernible pattern, sporadic, several in one spot for a few seconds, then nothing, and several more in another spot.

Puffs of dusty earth.

"It's like the ground is bubbling," the youth minister said.

They all got to their feet, backing away from the area immediately around the fire.

"Look!" a teenage girl said. "Behind us!"

Puffs of earth in dusty little clouds arose.

"Where does it end?" Eileen whispered.

"I don't know," he replied. "I—"

Someone screamed.

The puffs of earth were everywhere now, and in their midst human shapes.

Suddenly they all looked at the ground with a growing sense of panic and revulsion.

"Let's get out of here!" one of the boys said.

"Now!" shouted Derek.

They started to pack up. Several of the teenagers were about to put out the fire when directly in front of the flames emerged something else they couldn't see or hear, escaping from below.

Something that ignited when the heat of the flames reached it!

"Gas!" the youth minister shouted. "This entire spot is filled with gas!"

A layer of flame spread quickly.

"Into the lake!" he screamed.

A moment or so later, as they all stood in the cool water, shivering, the ground in front of them became an inferno that soon spread to the surrounding trees.

Forest rangers had spotted the flames, and sounded an alarm; fire crews arrived less than an hour later.

Several acres of forest were consumed but eventually the fire was brought under control.

And then it was time to ponder the cause.

Firemen accustomed to the worst horrors of their profession had no preparation for what they saw.

A mass grave.

Scores of bodies had been buried next to the lake, bodies, it was discovered later, of people who had died after being pumped full of methane gas, gas that began to leak out, troubling the dirt, then causing puffs of dust, the streams of the gas escaping into the night air, instantly ignited by the camp fire.

9

DALHAM and Fincher stood at the edge of the scorched trees, watching the bodies being taken from their common grave and put on trucks. They had questioned the Hadleys and the teenagers. And they had searched the area but found nothing until one of the troopers helping with the bodies walked up to them.

"How about this, sir," he said, handing Dalham a partially burnt sheet of paper. "Found it rolled into a ball, one of the victims gripping it in his closed fist. The edges are singed, but it's quite legible otherwise."

"Thanks," the agent said.

He glanced at the writing on one side of the sheet.

"Just names," he noted. "But look at what these are."

He handed the paper to Fincher.

"Himmler, Goebbels, Heydrich, Mengele," Fincher read, "four of the top Nazis during the Second World War. What could it mean?"

"I don't know right now, but I hate the idea that it's part of a puzzle. I'm not so sure I want to find out what the other pieces are."

The sight before them was as hard to take as anything else that had happened over the previous few hours. Dalham knew that the teenagers especially would be affected perhaps for the rest of their lives.

A pause.

"'Let this mind be in you which is in Christ Jesus,'" he repeated aloud.

"That helps, doesn't it?" Fincher said.

"Sometimes it's the only thing that does," Dalham admitted.

"You've been with the Bureau for a couple of decades. Is this the worst of all?"

"It just might be, Maggie. As bad as other mass murder sites are, make no mistake about that, they're different somehow from this."

"I think I know what you mean. I'm feeling it maybe worse than you. I've not had much of this. I'm kind of new compared to you."

Dalham looked at the younger agent, whom he was beginning to like.

...*I'm kind of new.*

"What sorts of cases *have* you had before now?" Dalham asked.

"Suspected terrorist stuff. Kidnappings. A few bank jobs. But *nothing* compares, Kent, nothing compares to..."

She stopped talking.

Ahead the last of the bodies was being loaded on one of the trucks.

Looking embarrassed and ill at the same time, Fincher turned away, trying to fight yet another wave of nausea.

A moment later she was starting to apologize when Dalham cut her off.

"No need, no need. I did the same thing back at the lab, remember?"

"But it's not the first time, Kent. My stomach's too weak. I wonder if I'll ever be able to take it."

"For a long time, I threw up every other case, it seemed."

"Really? I'm not unusual, then?"

"Oh, no. Talk to some of the other agents. We're trained like automatons, yes, and that's necessary, so I'm not knocking it. But the truth is that our human tendencies *do* interfere. We shouldn't react as you and I have done today, that is, as agents we shouldn't. But as human beings, well, that's another story."

"But you at least don't act very *surprised*," Fincher told him. "It's as though you almost expect stuff like that."

"In a way I do. Not even being a Christian prepares me for it. Yet the Bible is full of revelations about the depths to which people can sink when they are caught up in the depravity of their sins. Christians can't proclaim *complete* ignorance, in any event."

"But some preachers talk about thinking positively, ignoring the filth and the crime and all the rest."

Dalham waved his hand at the now-empty grave.

"Ignore *that*, my friend, and you give encouragement to the vermin who murdered those people. Evil triumphs when those who are appalled by it simply stand around and moan and groan yet do nothing."

"You know, Kent, I worry a lot about comedians who use racial slurs in their routines. That one, you know, the vulgar guy that even jaded critics find offensive. I think he's a menace."

"I agree. I suspect the KKK may be his biggest fans. If it were up to me, he wouldn't be able to get a job anywhere."

Dalham looked up at the fading sun.

"Getting late," he said. "Let's find a motel somewhere near here. I'm dead tired."

"Me, too," Fincher agreed. "Any place's fine with me."

They hopped into the car, not noticing a last ray of sun bouncing off the lens of a pair of binoculars at the opposite side of the lake.

The little community—it didn't seem big enough to be called a town—was south of the one that had been torched. There was an old gas station, a general store, a dozen houses and a small motel that surely must have been a last resort for weary travelers.

The few pedestrians stopped, looked at them curiously, then went on about their business.

"Bet property's cheap here," Fincher said, trying to deal with the strangeness.

"Buy some before the boom starts," Dalham replied in the same manner, for the same reason. "You could make a mint."

"The only time that'll happen here is if somebody starts a candy factory."

Dalham chuckled.

He looked forward to working with Fincher, glad she wasn't a complete rookie, despite that earlier protest. Kent Dalham didn't have his father's legendary patience.

They pulled up in front of the motel, which had been freshly painted.

"Not the best," Fincher said, sniffing the air.

"What do you mean?" Dalham asked.

"The paint. Cheap stuff. I can tell from the odor. It won't last."

Score another one, Dalham thought admiringly. *She's going to be a good partner in this mess.*

As the two of them walked inside, they noted the worn chairs, the pot-bellied clerk, the snowy TV reception.

The clerk nodded, handed Dalham the keys.

The two grabbed their luggage and turned into the corridor adjacent to the front desk, walking slowly first to Dalham's room, where they intended to talk for a bit. Once inside, Fincher sat down on the nearest chair.

"First the camp, then the town and now this," she said, thinking back over that lakeside site.

Both had been trained well, but neither had had such an appalling series of encounters in a single day.

"It's been less than 12 hours, Kent," Fincher was saying.

"And all *here*," Dalham remarked, "in the middle of Oregon, not some Central American country."

"Or Baghdad."

Fincher nodded wearily as she sat down on the edge of one of the chairs, taking off the wrist band where her so-called pancake holster was attached.

"Weird area," she said, thinking of how everyone looked at them as though they were foreigners.

"It is," the other agreed. "The people all seem—"

Despite their training, neither could have been prepared for the motorcycle smashing through the window or the door ripping off its hinges at the same time.

Dalham had already taken off his own pancake holster and placed it beside him on the bed. He reached instinctively for his Smith and Wesson 357, wishing for a split second that the Bureau had already switched to the more powerful 10-millimeter automatic that was supposed to become standard issue at some point.

In an instant he saw six skinhead youths piling into the room. Two were hit in the chest by shots Fincher fired with well-trained accuracy, one in the neck by Dalham. A skinhead plowed into Fincher. Dalham got off a shot that caught him in the shoulder, sending him stumbling back from the other agent.

Fincher's revolver had been knocked to the floor; she was reaching for it when another skinhead dove for her, a large knife in one hand. Dalham felt something hit the back of his head. As unconsciousness swept over him, he heard Maggie Fincher's dying scream.

10

WHEN Dalham regained consciousness, he saw that he was in a mammoth barn with the smell of old wood rotting and horse dung. Moonlight filtered in through windows just below the roof and slots in the large door at each end. Over the entrance was a banner that read:

> Black may be beautiful
> And tan may be grand
> But white's still the color of
> The BIG BOSS MAN.

Dozens of skinheads were gathered inside, on the hayloft and standing on either side of the entrance. An odor of sweat mingled with that of the wood.

Dalham tried to move but couldn't, groaning as pain shot up from both ankles.

"We took care of them," said a tall, muscular skinhead standing directly in front of Dalham, two others to one side. "They're not broke but battered real good. You don't go nowhere."

The others roared with delight.

"We believe in equality here," the tall one added. "We treat all nigger-lovers the same."

More laughter.

"But blacks aren't the only ones you hate," Dalham said, spitting out the words through his pain. "How about the Jews? the Catholics? the Puerto Ricans?"

"That's *right!*" the skinhead exclaimed. "Man, thanks, thanks for reminding me. Ain't he smart?"

The crowd shouted its agreement.

"How could you hold the beliefs that you do?" Dalham asked. "How can you throw everything else aside and turn to such hatred?"

"Believe?" the other repeated the word. "I'll tell you what we *all* believe in."

He raised his hands as though in command.

"Tell him, guys. Go ahead and tell him!"

"White power!" the crowd screamed as though on cue. *"Whiiite power!"*

They kept repeating the words, over and over, louder and louder.

Dalham tried to stand but his ankles were useless. He fell back against the straw-littered ground.

The tall skinhead, a scar across his right cheek, was obviously in command; with a single gesture he silenced the crowd and turned to Dalham.

"They call me Pecarsky," he said, leering as he bent down over Dalham and then proceeded to stomp the heel of one boot onto Dalham's left hand.

Dalham screamed, his face contorted in pain.

Laughter again.

"Only one thing wrong," Pecarsky said as he swung around and faced the other skinheads.

"What's that?" they asked.

"He don't look like no kike," Pecarsky roared in mock disappointment.

"Maybe he's a faggot!" someone from the group yelled.

"Are you queer?" Pecarsky asked Dalham.

Oddly the pain was passing, and though he couldn't stand, Dalham managed to push himself to a sitting position.

"If I were, would you take a knife to me as you've done with other homosexuals?" he demanded. "Is that how you get your—"

Pecarsky lashed out across Dalham's jaw, nearly breaking it.

"None of your business how I get my jollies, *mister*!" he shrieked.

"Did I hit too close to home on that one?" Dalham shot back. "Guys who have to assert their so-called masculinity before a crowd have been known to be closet queens!"

Pecarsky whacked him again. Dalham felt two teeth loosen. As he tried to speak, blood dribbled over his lower lip, a mouthful of it, and he gagged.

"Cat got your tongue?" Pecarsky chuckled.

"Rip it out," somebody shouted.

"Grab him!" Pecarsky ordered the two skinheads standing nearby.

One of them grabbed Dalham's wrists, the other wrapped an arm around his neck.

Pecarsky was on the ground with them. He took out a switchblade, exposed the knife, forced open Dalham's mouth, reached in with his free hand and got hold of the other's tongue.

The crowd was in a frenzy.

"Do it! Do it! *Whiiite* power in *action*!"

"Wait!" one of the two skinheads holding Dalham hollered, though he could hardly be heard.

Pecarsky snapped a look at him.

"Why?" he asked. "I'm gonna—"

"He's FBI! We should've paid attention to Arnie. He suspected as much. He trailed those guys from the lake."

Pecarsky stopped instantly.

"How you know?" he said, his words slurred, his eyes glazed. "I was just getting off on this—"

"There!" the skinhead pointed. "His ID—there—near his foot!"

Pecarsky saw the badge and ID in a leather case that had slipped out of Dalham's pocket.

He reached for it, picked it up, squinted at the photo, the rest.

"He's a Fed!" Pecarsky shouted as he stood up, held the case out, waved it around in the air.

The crowd became immediately silent.

Pecarsky, his face covered with perspiration, knew he could lose control of the other skinheads if he let them feel intimidated, most of them not eager to lock horns with the FBI, at least not just then. He had to do something forceful, even irrational, something that fed upon their hatred, not their fear.

So Pecarsky spun around, glowered at Dalham.

"That don't mean we ain't gonna kill ya," he said. "It means we're just gonna take *longer* doin' it."

He threw the leather case back on the ground.

"I got an idea," he bellowed. "The Feds like everything nice and legal. That's what we'll do."

Pecarsky turned to the crowd.

"*We'll put him on trial!*" he said. "Okay with you?"

As he talked, he waved his hands up and down as though to fan a strong response.

And that was what he got.

"Do it! Do it! Now!" they shouted back, their momentary hesitation forgotten.

"Who's the prosecutor?" Pecarsky asked everyone. "I need a *volunteer!*"

There was only a second of hesitation.

"Fredrickson! Fredrickson!" someone shouted. "He's the type. Get him to do it!"

"That's right," Pecarsky agreed. "The guy's perfect."

They all waited for the chosen one to step out from the crowd.

Dalham grimaced with sudden slashing pain that ripped through his body. He knew he could be dead before long, the way his father would have preferred to die, actually, though "preferred" may not have been quite the word—defying a bunch of maniacs, better than the slow dissipation of senses, of stability, of coherence that had drained away the last few years of his life.

"*Better to go to heaven fighting the Devil with all your senses!*" *Art Dalham would say when he could get the words together, when*

*the loss of those senses momentarily ceased, and he could think with
a measure of clarity, though that clarity itself was so transitory.*

"I can't stand being so helpless, Kent," he would say at other
times. "I can't endure just lying here, knowing I can't go to the bathroom without help, knowing..."

That recollection passed as Dalham saw a moving figure in
the semidarkness, walking down the ladder from the hayloft.

Fredrickson stood in the middle of the floor.

Pecarsky introduced him after a fashion.

"Your prosecutor," he said, smirking.

An odd expression on his face, Fredrickson looked at Dalham, then at Pecarsky.

"Who'll *defend* him?" Fredrickson asked.

"Why, he's going to defend himself!"

At that, the crowd broke out into near-hysterical laughter.

"Is that fair?" Fredrickson surprisingly asked.

Pecarsky exploded.

"Who said that it *had* to be? Now you've been appointed to
do a *job*. Are you going to go ahead with it? Or do you want to
be put on trial along with this nigger-loving Fed?"

Fredrickson winced a bit, then: "I need 10 minutes. You
gotta give me 10 minutes."

"For what?"

"To prepare a case!"

Pecarsky was going to curse at him but stopped short, eyeing the other carefully.

"All right," he relented. "Do what you have to. But not
more than 10 minutes. Understood, *mister* Fredrickson?"

Fredrickson nodded and left the barn briefly.

Dalham was running on a sudden surge of adrenalin,
amazed at how clear his head was. With the pain in his ankles,
his sore jaw, he shouldn't have been coherent, but he was.

Praise You, Jesus, he said to himself. *Give me the wisdom, the
words.*

"Get me something to sit on!" he shouted.

One of the two skinheads with Pecarsky turned to him for approval, and when he nodded, the other left the barn, returning a couple of minutes later with a rickety wooden chair, and helped Dalham to sit on it.

Dalham focused on his location a bit more clearly.

Somewhat less than a hundred skinheads were in the barn, in the hayloft and on the ground, at the opposite end from where he was sitting. In addition to the patches and slivers of moonlight, illumination was provided by gas lanterns placed at various intervals.

Their faces...

Some were only teenagers. Others seemed to be in their mid-20s. None wore the capes, the pointed hoods of the KKK.

They consider the Klan stodgy, too timid. The older generation gotten fat, complacent, wallowing in the status quo.

Many had swastikas tattooed on their arms, some with these on their foreheads.

I bet, Dalham thought, *every one was beaten as a child; some were forced into incest with a father, a mother, perhaps both. All had to get out.*

"How many of you have fathers, mothers who care whether you live or die?" he asked.

Pecarsky screwed up his face and pretended to cry.

"How saaad!" he mocked. "You're tryin' to get us to cry, tryin' to get us to feel sorry for ourselves and maybe *you* at the same time. That way we won't harm you no more."

He raised his hands above his head.

"Am I right, brothers?" he demanded of the crowd.

"Right! Right! Right!" they howled.

"Now keep your mouth shut or I'm gonna break your jaw so you'll never open it *ever* again!"

Dalham fell back against the ground, his mind spinning, trying to concentrate but failing to do so except for a single name, a name that refused to be buried by the nausea and the pain.

Fredrickson.

He repeated that name to himself several times. Why did it sound so familiar?

Before serving in Europe just prior to World War II, Art Dalham had worked with military intelligence headquarters in Washington, D.C. He had been alerted to the increasing popularity of the KKK and what it portended. But there wasn't much he or anyone else could do until they found out about the Nazi connection that the Klan tried to keep absolutely hidden.

Adolf Hitler apparently was funneling money through dummy companies to the KKK, principally with the aim of making sure that the Klansmen were armed.

"It isn't for cultural enrichment," read the memo directly from J. Edgar Hoover. "Please check this through your overseas sources."

The elder Dalham spent a number of weeks trying to put the pieces together. There was little success until one man was sentenced to lifetime imprisonment.

Clarke Fredrickson of Ohio!

"He should have been on the FBI's payroll!" Art Dalham exclaimed. "His behavior discredited the Klan to such an extent that membership quickly went from 6,000,000 to 300,000. The blessing is that we could sit back and watch it all from the sidelines!"

But more than that, out of a desire for revenge after the Klan withdrew its support of him, the former "ruler" of Ohio turned over secret documents to Federal and state authorities, documents that showed Fredrickson himself had Nazi ties, as did other Klan members throughout the country—with further participation in bootlegging, prostitution and other illegal activities, all in an organization that publicly condemned such practices when practiced by others.

Clarke Fredrickson...

Dalham repeated the name.

*I wonder...*he asked himself.

He shrugged, initially discarding the notion which seemed uncomfortably coincidental.

More compelling was the need to plan his "defense" in the few minutes that remained until the hand-picked "prosecutor" was supposed to return, knowing that his attempt was probably doomed since his "jury" was hardly impartial.

Lord, I need the words. I don't have them of my own wisdom. Please tell me what I need to say.

"Good, Fredrickson!" Pecarsky's voice interrupted. "Your victim's been waiting for you."

That voice tore through his thoughts.

Dalham looked up. Just a few feet away was the same young man, who needed to prove that his opponent was worthy of death—or his own standing with his fellow skinheads would be in jeopardy.

Fredrickson pointed directly at Dalham.

"Is he *guilty*? Tell me!" he hollered, giving the impression of one who was trying to stir himself as much as those in the audience.

The crowd yelled, "Hang him! Haaang him!"

Fredrickson tried to smile but failed.

"You bet we will!" he managed to say.

They went wild then, stamping their feet, pieces of straw and dust kicked up. All of them started to stand, ready to lynch Dalham as soon as they could get the rope around his neck.

Pecarsky proceeded to calm them down.

"Who's the leader here?" he shouted.

"*You are!*" they yelled back.

"And what did I say about all this?"

"A trial!"

"Good. Now, shut up and sit down. Let our buddy here do his job."

They obeyed, obviously accustomed to following Pecarsky's orders.

Dalham saw that Fredrickson was uncomfortable.

"Why are you here?" Fredrickson demanded. "State your purpose."

"Because of what you all did a few miles from here. Because of that man-made hell you constructed. Don't tell me that surprises you?"

Fredrickson blinked several times in rapid succession.

It doesn't, mister. I tried to stop it. I told them it was wrong. But they were under orders.

"You let your bigotry—"

"Wait a minute!" Fredrickson broke in. "What's wrong with bigotry? Don't we have the freedom to say what we want, think what we want, do what we want in this country?"

"Of course. But you let your bigotry become violence, aiming that violence at innocent men, women and children who happen to be black or Jewish or Catholic. That camp is the worst example, but there are others. From what I hear, we may have a war going on soon."

"They've taken over this country," Fredrickson repeated some well-worn invective, sounding as though he'd memorized every line from various Aryan pamphlets, "denied millions of Americans the chance to have good jobs or any work at all. They *caused* the Great Depression by manipulating commerce, the banking system, the government itself. And then they formed the Federal Reserve with the excuse that they could better control the economy and make sure nothing like the Depression would ever happen again. And all the while the Jews get rich, the wop millionaires are getting fatter and fatter *while we suffer!*"

Several skinheads yelled expletives.

"Do you honestly believe that *crap*?" Dalham shot back.

"It's the truth!"

"It's propaganda, and you know it. The kind of stuff Goering and others turned out in the Third Reich. It's no more accurate today than it was then. Just an excuse to round up anybody not of pure Aryan blood."

"Are you calling me a liar?" Fredrickson asked icily.

"I think the people you believe in *are* liars, yes."

Fredrickson walked up to him and was about to hit him across the mouth.

"Go ahead," Dalham said. "You can slap me all you want. At least I'm not a woman. Someone like Clarke Fredrickson was the real expert with that sort of thing!"

The other hesitated.

"Go ahead!" the crowd demanded. "Bash him one!"

Fredrickson did just that, and Dalham sprawled on the floor.

"Are you going to rip my shirt off and do to me what Clarke did to Madge Oberholtzer fifty years ago?" Dalham asked, somehow ignoring the pain that made his surroundings spin.

Fredrickson grabbed him under the armpits and lifted him up.

"You don't talk about him like that!" he demanded. "You stop it *now!*"

"Just because he was a once-legendary Klan leader? Or maybe it has something to do with your being the child of his bastard son?"

Dalham was gambling wildly with that one. But he realized he had to do everything he could to unhinge the other.

Fredrickson froze.

"Isn't that why all of you are here tonight?" Dalham said, his voice becoming hoarse. "You have no leaders worth the title anymore. Clarke Fredrickson was an alcoholic who demanded that the *other* Klansmen never *look* at a bottle of liquor. He was an abuser of women at a time when the KKK professed to *defend* their women! After the Klan yanked their support, he let the Federal and state authorities have secret documents that revealed the weak underbelly of the entire movement. He used helpless women, he drank himself into a stupor *and he betrayed six million KKK members clear across this nation!*"

"What else we got, Mr. FBI Agent?" Fredrickson yelled at him. "Tell me that!"

Still holding Dalham with his left hand, he took his right and tore open the white tank top he'd been wearing.

Scars across his chest.

"Just like my grandfather did with that girl, my father did with me! Who do I have but others like me?"

He turned Dalham around to face the other skinheads.

"It's like you say," he shouted. "We don't have a lot of money. Society hates our guts. So we have to..."

"Build a death camp and get rid of everyone you don't like because of their race, their religion."

"We want *purity*," Fredrickson said in a curiously mechanical tone. "We..."

"What about moral purity? What about crimes so awful that they've been condemned for half a century? Is the road to *purity* paved with the carcasses of your helpless victims?"

Dalham saw that this moralizing was having little effect.

"How were you able to build that camp?" he continued, changing tack. "If you're so poor, where did you get the money? What do you know about the money men, their motives? They might be just *using* you for *their* purposes."

Fredrickson was seething but said nothing. Nor did the others.

"*Someone* financed that place for you!" Dalham went on. "Someone bought the ovens, the barbed wire, the building supplies. Who conducted the so-called experiments in that lab? How many of you know *anything* about medicine, surgery?"

Trying to look contemptuous, Fredrickson let go of Dalham, who hit the ground painfully.

Looking up at the skinheads, Dalham managed to stay conscious for a few moments longer.

"You've exchanged one merciless group of your masters for another," Dalham continued. "Whoever it is calls the shots, it's not any of you. You're just their puppets. When will you stop being *anyone's* puppets?"

He heard laughter then, laughter so strong that it seemed to fill the entire barn, from wall to wall, ceiling to ground.

His vision faded, the shapes of a hundred young people wavering in the semidarkness. But more than these, something else quite different appeared abruptly, with panic erupting throughout the group, skinheads running, knocking each other down, some falling off the hayloft to the ground.

Just before a tenebrous wave enveloped him, Kent Dalham could feel intense, sudden heat as the barn burst into flame, and shrieks filled the air.

Part II

I measure every Grief I meet
With narrow, probing Eyes—
I wonder if It weighs like Mine—
Or has an Easier size.

—Emily Dickinson

Give sorrow words; the grief
   that does not speak
Whispers the o'er-fraught heart
   and bids it break.

—William Shakespeare

11

*D*EATH *seemed imminent in the hours after he was rescued by a force of fellow agents who had been tipped off by an anonymous informer. Later a report given to him by FBI doctors confirmed this with some hard medical facts, but at the time, he had only his own battered perceptions to go by—these compelling indeed, bits and pieces of memories like a badly edited film flashing in, then out of his mind...the deaths of his father, his mother...then of his wife and two children.*

Laughter.

He heard it in the midst of the maelstrom that followed that final blazing image in the barn.

A voice so *familiar*!

He strained to hear it more clearly.

Valerie!

And then two other voices from memory, though he couldn't be sure whether it was memory or perhaps this was what dying was like before being translated into the next realm.

Kent Jr. and Sean!

How could it be, Lord? They're gone.

The Bureau had been their substitute, garnering his devotion, displacing everything but his dedication to Christ. All three had died violently, not at the hands of skinheads but of another terrorist group that had long threatened activity against the families of FBI and CIA agents. He had been sent to Florida to investigate a possible espionage case involving Cuban agents near Key West. Valerie and the boys had just gotten ready for church and were piling into the family car. When she turned on the ignition, the bomb that had been rigged under the hood blew up, the explosion killing them instantly.

Seven years ago...

No one had ever questioned his performance as an agent; in fact, he had built a fine reputation for himself within the Bureau. He was considered one of the braver agents, one of the more methodical, indeed an example of how good a product of the FBI could really be. He had been given a number of special commendations over the years, which hung on the wall in his den at home.

Kent Dalham ultimately became an even better agent. But for awhile just after the tragedy that took his loved ones that Sunday morning, he almost had to quit the Bureau altogether, instead of merely taking a leave of absence.

Valerie.

I couldn't even lean over and kiss you one last time, the thought flashed across his mind.

Kent Jr. and Sean.

Just six years old, just four.

The coffins sealed.

To see you all just once more, just one final moment...

He was informed about what had happened just an hour after it happened and boarded the next available plane.

Pieces of the car still remained on the street and pavement in front of their home.

And some blood.

Just a tiny puddle of it.

He stood before that spot on the cement. How upset he had been when either Kent Jr. or Sean cut themselves while playing and came to him or their mother crying.

Being a father was precious, Lord...

And now...

There was nothing left of the three of them, nothing physical.

Warm bodies he once had touched and held, hands that had run their fingers through Valerie's pure blonde hair, lips that he had kissed.

The Bureau gave him a leave of absence, as long as he needed. That decision surprised him later, when he felt well enough to consider it. While his superiors were hardly ogres in such matters, the Bureau did function smoothly primarily because it had specific policies and procedures, and these had served it well for half a century. The way he was treated seemed a sharp break from such cases in the past.

Ironically some brothers and sisters in Christ became like the ill-advised friends of Job, giving him advice that could have impaired his emergence from grief rather than provide any help. They were the ones who urged him not to continue with the Bureau, insisting that any profession that required inflicting violence on other human beings was, by its very nature, a stumbling-block to Christ-centered living, and surely—they rambled on—surely, God was trying to tell him something, trying to get through.

Then one day, as he was visiting his family's graves in a cemetery directly outside Washington, D.C., he saw another funeral a few plots away to his right, and he decided to walk on over to it, standing to one side as the priest spoke.

"Juan was the victim of an unprovoked attack," the elderly man was saying. "He was totally innocent. He died because there is in this world a spirit of evil."

Those last dozen words!

...he died because there is in this world a spirit of evil.

Spoken to his very soul.

Dalham continued listening carefully, taking in every word, tears in his eyes at the answer that was becoming clearer and clearer at a point when he desperately needed it.

"We have no choice but to resist evil," the priest continued, "and to support those who try to shield us from it. Juan was alone when he died, not one of us to help him. Each time we hear someone call a police officer "pig," we should rush up to that individual, and tell him, 'Are you crazy? Where would we be if there were no police to help?'"

"But the police weren't *around* when Juan was shot," commented someone from the group of mourners. "What good did they do for him?"

"You know why that was so?" the priest said in rebuke.

No one answered.

"They weren't around because they had to be some place else raiding yet another rock house," he continued. "It's time we get real, as our teenagers say! How many of us in the Hispanic community have done *anything* to help stop this curse of drugs? How many have looked the other way simply because those at the source, the Columbian drug lords, happen to be Hispanics getting back at the *gringos?*"

The old man wiped his eyes with a tissue.

"Juan was one of us, *amigos*. His death brings devastation to every adult and young person here."

A short while later, the crowd dispersed, the boy's parents lingering a bit and then leaving. Only the elderly priest remained.

Dalham hesitated, then walked slowly up to him, introduced himself.

"I am Father Pablo Rivera," the old man said. "You heard my words?"

"I did, father, and appreciated them."

"It was not such a good eulogy. It was not what I intended."

"But the Holy Spirit must have moved you to say what you did."

"I suppose so, my young friend. Why does all this concern you so much?"

"I have been working for an organization that is concerned with certain matters of internal security."

"Sounds as though you have to be careful about what you say."

"You are correct, sir."

Father Rivera looked at him intently.

"You seem troubled, son."

"I am."

"How can I help?"

Dalham told him the dilemma.

"I can say only this," Father Rivera replied. "Anyone who stands against corruption, who tries to safeguard the innocent from a fate like little Juan's is doing nothing to be ashamed of. I'll go even further: He honors God because he is acting as a warrior against the attacks of those who pledge allegiance by their actions not to the Lord but to the *enemy* of our souls."

The old man reached out and put his hands on Dalham's shoulders.

"I cannot walk the same path you do," he said with a kindness on his face that could never be forgotten. "But if there were not men like you, I would be standing by many, many more graves like this one."

After going home, he sat quietly in the living room, designed by his wife with her usual flair for interior decoration, every curtain in place, the carpeting a perfect match, the furniture arranged just so.

The odors!

He could still detect traces of Valerie's perfume in the air.

Those sounds!

Something like a faint echo of the boys playing seemed to remain.

I'm listening, Lord.

He strained to hear those sounds more clearly, those precious sounds once accepted as normal, now gone for all time, then fell back against the sofa, sighing as the tears came again.

After a few minutes, Dalham stood in the doorway to the bedroom his sons had been sharing. Nothing had been touched, clothes on the floor, a couple of toys, the little pinball machine. A pair of shoes lay in one corner.

He walked down the hall to the master bedroom. After entering, he opened the large walk-in closet, saw her dresses, blouses, coats on one side, his own garments on the other. Lying on the floor was a piece of lingerie. He picked it up, held it to his face, remembering.

On the nightstand beside their bed was a photograph of the two of them with Kent Jr. and Sean.

He went over to it, picked it up.

His emotions were especially strong then as he recalled that photo session and the photographer remarking afterwards about how close and loving the four of them were.

Families across the nation torn apart.

Dreams rendered meaningless by bombs, by bullets, by knives.

Priests and ministers and rabbis delivering graveside speeches trying to weave the events of tragedy into some coherent tapestry.

He sighed as he put the photo back on the nightstand.

"How do I cope, Lord?" he asked aloud. "Tell me how, please?"

What Father Rivera told him began to make more and more sense as that day passed, then another.

But if there were not men like you, I would be standing by many, many more graves like this one.

Dalham recalled a number of cases where the saving of lives had indeed been the outcome, including those protected from gangland-style "execution," primarily because they had revealed details that led to the arrest of key members of the Mafia.

"During the final years of Hoover's reign, well, we just didn't pay that much attention to organized crime," he was told one afternoon by a fellow agent named Doug Buchanan as they manned a stakeout together, the two of them sitting in a car across the street from a suspected Mafia-owned floral business.

"Why do you think that was the case?" Dalham asked, remembering rumors that he'd heard over the years but to which he had paid little heed.

"No one can say for sure," Buchanan remarked. "When he was older, maybe suffering a touch of senility, though that wasn't talked about very much, he equated subversion with the communists and other terrorist groups. The mob somehow seemed less of a threat to the old man."

But for most of Dalham's career at the FBI, which had been taken over by other directors, attention to problem areas became far more balanced, with no predetermined tilt toward one group or the other, though a perceived threat of increased hostile activity from Middle Eastern sources in recent years was changing that balance somewhat.

Dalham remembered when every other report seemed to be based upon emergency action to thwart a move by radical Moslem paramilitary groups against targets on U.S. soil. It was a miracle that virtually none of this leaked out to a panic-prone public.

How many men, how many women, how many children are alive today because of what we have been doing? How many families saved from wrenching tragedy?

When he asked himself questions akin to those, he knew there was not much more to say, that everything he had been digesting all boiled down to that kind of nitty-gritty reality, and there was suddenly no doubt in his mind about remaining with the Bureau until he was legally required to retire or some assailant was a little quicker than he was.

That second prospect never bothered him after Valerie and the boys had died. While they were alive, he was devoted to making sure they had as few burdens as possible should he die on the job. But now he had only himself. Agents would ask him from time to time how he could seem so unconcerned about danger that might prove fatal someday.

"I don't believe that life ends *here*," he would say. "I sense with certainty that Valerie and my sons are alive."

Yet invariably came the next question: "But we can't see for sure what it will be *like* on the other side, so how can you be so confident? How can you *know* that they are experiencing anything better than *this* life?"

Dalham would smile and reach for his Bible, often to the accompaniment of groans from his reluctant partners but then, usually, silence as he read the promises from Scripture.

Days or weeks or months later, the ones who accepted Jesus Christ into their life sometimes had that life ripped from them, not a few dying in his arms as they whispered in awe about music sung by a chorus of angels.

That was when Maggie Fincher re-entered his mind, especially that last, awful image as she was dying, her face a contorted mask of pain and then sudden peace as her lifeless body hit the floor, and Maggie's murderer stood over her, laughing....

12

DALHAM hadn't realized that recovery would be hastened by research that gave him more insight into those who had brutalized him but, to his surprise, the doctors at the hospital where he was confined indeed encouraged him to learn more.

"Confronting the source of your pain," he was told by one of them named Dr. Amory, "is the healthiest approach you can have."

And so he did.

He learned that the skinhead "is immune to reasonable propositions. He is convinced that he *is* reasonable, and that his enemies are not. Having burned his bridges behind him, broken with his family and old friends, he cannot go back. He is committed to his involvement in the group. To renounce it would be to repudiate himself....

"His personality and prejudices have become crystallized around a set of actions and dogmas. They are irreversible. Any external stimulus which threatens to penetrate his armor and make him see the absurdity or injustice of his position is rationalized to further harden his rigidity. He has joined the movement at least partly because it handed him stereotypes in place of his vague notions and saved him from having to think things out for himself....

"With his weakened conscience and consciousness, he can no longer respond spontaneously, however he may appear to be doing so. He has *become* the movement. All thoughts and feelings that are at odds with it are snuffed out. This is what gives [him] the air of a one-dimensional man. He lacks depth. There is a limited range of possibilities open to him. If one wants, therefore, to convert him back [to normalcy], one finds that there is nobody home. His mind is shut tight....

"The ability to exercise his own judgment, having atrophied, is never restored. Even if he should drop out [of that one group], he will quickly seek and find another. Like a drug addict who needs his fix, he cannot live [otherwise]."[1]

...he cannot live otherwise.

For the typical skinhead, all normal and objective processes of thought and reasoning had become distorted. He was a vengeance machine, fanatical about getting back at those he deemed responsible for the pain in his life.

But more than that, Dalham discovered, much more than that.

Skinheads were indoctrinated in a thirst for vengeance that preceded all of them by nearly fifty years.

"And there [at the end of World War II], prostrate among the debris, was Germany's young generation, a youth surrounded by broken symbols....Germany's post-war youth grew up among the ruins, lived in them, queued among them and indeed received its education in them....Together with their mothers they cleared the streets of rubble, they stripped the ruins of their wood for fuel, and whole gangs of boys and girls were posted along points of the railway lines where coal trains had to slow down, to board the wagons and in a matter of seconds throw down enough coal to fill a few bags. They raided vehicles—preferably belonging to Americans—for food and cigarettes and funneled them into the black markets of the cities."[2]

For many German young people, it was bone-deep bitterness that drove them into the neo-Nazi groups that arose out of the rubble of the Hitler Era. For a time, these were confined to Europe, but they spread to the United States.

At the same time came a rise in occultic activity.

Dalham sat back in the hospital bed, considering the two situations: first, an underground network of disadvantaged young people, abused and rejected, their lives being destroyed by parents in particular and society in general. Their hatred toward the Establishment was a continuation of post-war animosity toward the conquering Allies—now directed toward anyone who wasn't "white and pure and non-Catholic," with the Roman Catholic Church seen as an instrument of "nigger-loving leftists and dirty Puerto Ricans and other scum."

Then there was the occultic trend, also continued from the ruins of the Third Reich. For many people, it was a way of obtaining power over the lives of others, usually destructive power, power that culminated in violent death, as in Matamoros, Mexico; as in the case of Richard Ramirez, California's Night Stalker; as in a growing number of other cases.

At some point the neo-Nazis embraced the world of the occult, just as a previous generation had decades earlier. In doing so, skinheads felt that they had the ingredients to become almost unstoppable, with Satan as an ally!

Dalham remembered the barn, that sound he heard toward the end, just before he fell into a cold and awful abyss.

He heard laughter then, laughter so strong that it seemed to fill the entire barn, from wall to wall, ceiling to ground.

He put the books aside and fell asleep, grateful that the Lord gave him the kind of restful peace he needed just then.

13

WHEN Dalham had recovered enough to walk a bit, he overdid it, and collapsed halfway down the corridor outside his room. But by fits and spurts his strength returned, and he was able to go outside.

Days later, he stood on the rolling expanse of lawn that surrounded the hospital, breathing in air that had a touch of mountain snow in it. He felt as though he had taken a bath and was now clean for the first time in a long while.

He walked slowly, his ankles throbbing a bit.

Ahead, in a wheelchair, he saw a frail-looking figure alone except for a nurse who hovered several yards away.

Dalham approached him.

The old man heard him, turned his head slightly.

Dalham recognized him instantly.

"Sir?" he said somewhat tentatively.

"Yes?" the old man replied.

"You're Solomon Hillel Schechter, aren't you?" Dalham asked.

The old man squinted, then smiled.

"I am!" he said, pleased by the attention. "For a moment I thought I recognized *you* as well."

Schechter called for the nurse. When she came over to him, he asked her, "Would you find a chair for my friend to sit on?"

She nodded agreeably and left for several minutes.

"You were the only one to survive, sir," Dalham recalled.

"The only one, yes," the old man agreed, savoring the words. "What is your name, my friend?"

"Kent, sir, Kent Dalham."

"I'm Solomon Hillel Schechter," he said, forgetting that Dalham already knew that. "Most people consider that a mouthful—but I ask, what can be done now?"

He chuckled a bit at that, then coughed painfully. The nurse was returning with a folding chair, and she expressed worry about him.

"I'm fine," he told her. "Bless you for your concern—and don't tell me about this sort of thing being your job. For you, it's something more, my dear."

She blushed, opened the chair for Dalham, and then returned to her nearby "station."

"They've got to treat me right," Schechter added mischievously, glancing out of the corner of his eye at the nurse, obvious affection mirrored on his face.

Dalham's admiration for the old man was growing steadily.

"I can identify the whole crowd," Schechter continued. "Maybe those punks thought I would be too scared if I ever did get out."

He shook his head vigorously.

"That didn't work the first time," he smiled proudly, "and I haven't suddenly turned coward after 45 years!"

"Who were they?" Dalham asked.

"Kids mostly. To me, anybody under 30 is a kid, but these were *really* kids, some in their late teens, others not older than mid-20s."

"You said you can identify them? *All* of them, Mr. Schechter?"

"The leaders in any event—probably not the grunts. But the leaders, ah, yes, down to the last little punk."

The old man noticed Dalham's questioning expression.

"You can't quite believe that, can you?"

"It would be quite remarkable," Dalham replied, trying to be sensitive to the other's feelings.

"I listened to their voices," Schechter continued. "I saw their faces. I had a long time for the sound of their orders to sink into my mind, voices filled with the same loathing as before. And those eyes—the old coldness back again!"

My young friend, if you only realized why such things could never be forgotten, even by someone of my years.

We heard the voices from hell, saw the demons themselves for days after being liberated, yea, for weeks, for months, for years.

That is why we continue to hunt down the war criminals. When we know the last one is gone, only then can we hope to exorcise their awful legacy from deep within us.

For a moment Schechter's mind seemed to be wandering.

"What did you say your name was, young man?" he asked then.

"Kent Dalham, sir."

Schechter lapsed into silence briefly, and then his countenance brightened.

"Praise God!" he said suddenly. "No wonder you looked familiar."

"I don't understand, sir," Dalham told him.

"Arthur James Dalham! Are you—?"

Kent Dalham was nodding even before the old man had finished the sentence.

Tears streamed down Solomon Hillel Schechter's face.

"Mr. Schechter, are you all right?" Dalham asked.

Schechter wiped his eyes with the back of his left hand.

"God can bring joy out of any despair," he said. "Kent Dalham, your father liberated nearly a thousand prisoners from Treblinka. He personally gave me a cup of water. Think of it, *clean* water!"

Sobs forced him to stop briefly.

Arthur James Dalham.

There was a point in Kent Dalham's life when his father's shadow seemed to smother him, when everyone was saying, "Oh, you're Art Dalham's son," and he had to struggle to achieve any sense of self-identity. But he had ultimately come to regard the image the elder Dalham projected as a profound blessing and not a curse. This metamorphosis had culminated only a week after he joined the FBI.

He was at headquarters, getting acquainted with Bureau routine when a fellow rookie, sitting at another desk across from his own, picked up the phone to answer a call that had just come in from "upstairs." Dalham couldn't control a fleeting smirk as he saw the other man's expression and noticed instant beads of perspiration on his forehead.

After he hung up the receiver, he looked across at Dalham.

"Kent, I...I..." he tried to speak without stuttering but failed miserably.

"Calm down. After all, you didn't get a call from God Himself, did you?"

The rookie blushed.

"Depends upon how you look at it, Kent. That was from Hoover."

"You mean his secretary or Tilson's, for that matter."

"No, Kent, that's not what I said. I *meant* Hoover!"

It was Dalham's turn to act queasy.

Lord, he prayed silently. *Are they canning me already?*

He swallowed, then added, *Lord, I'll need you by my side when I enter that man's office.*

"Thanks," he told the other rookie.

"Good luck, partner—buckets of it."

Dalham headed first for the men's room.

Anyone who met with the director had to be perfectly groomed, not a hair out of place, clothes fitting just right, shoes shined.

Do I need a shave? he asked himself. *Maybe he'll overlook it.*

Five minutes later, he was shown into J. Edgar Hoover's inner sanctum.

That was in 1971, a year before Hoover's death. The man had aged rapidly in the two years since Bobby Kennedy had been assassinated.

Dalham stood at strict military-style attention.

Hoover grinned and asked him to sit down.

A smile. He doesn't seem upset. I might be overreacting.

"I personally approved your acceptance into our little group," Hoover said slowly, chuckling a bit. "'Little group' *used* to be an accurate description, I suppose, but no longer. Still, out of just under 20,000 employees, special agents represent only about 40 percent."

"Thank you, sir, for letting me come on board," Dalham said earnestly.

"You *earned* the privilege, Agent Dalham. Anyone who can pass training at Quantico as well as you did *deserves* to be here."

Dalham found the popular image of the man conflicting with the flesh-and-blood reality across from whom he now sat.

"How can I be of service, sir?" Dalham asked, hoping to find out a bit more quickly why indeed the Director had wanted to see him.

"I can imagine how tough it has been living life as Art Dalham's son," Hoover spoke sympathetically.

"Thank you, sir. My father served his country for many years. He was admired by many people."

Hoover leaned forward on the old desk that had been his for decades.

"And I, Special Agent Dalham, continue to be one of them."

Dalham was uncomfortable. This was not the J. Edgar Hoover he had imagined, not at all.

"I have been accused of keeping files on thousands of people," Hoover continued. "It is said that I have information on rock stars, movie stars, senators, diplomats, company presidents, many others. I won't respond directly to any of that, of course."

He tapped the intercom and asked his secretary, "Bring me the Arthur James Dalham file."

Less than a minute passed before that file was handed to the Director.

He let it rest momentarily on top of the desk.

"Some people *demand* surveillance," he said. "That actress, for one."

Anger spread across his face.

"Going to Hanoi, laughing and joking *with the enemy!*"

Dalham nodded in agreement; he happened to be in total sync with Hoover on that one.

Hoover snorted with contempt.

"Many Americans lost sons and husbands to the very enemy she found so charming. Can you imagine such a woman, Special Agent Dalham?"

"I suppose I can *imagine* anything, sir," Dalham said, stepping out on potentially dangerous ground, "if I consider what the Bible has to say about the nature of man."

"The Bible?" Hoover repeated.

"Yes, sir, I am a Christian and I believe totally in what the Word of God has to say."

Hoover fell silent for a moment.

"You seem quite sincere, Agent Dalham," he then observed. "I have not always heard such things from people who meant what they were saying."

"I could not live each day properly without starting it in prayer."

Kent Dalham, know when to speak up, when to keep your mouth shut! J. Edgar Hoover is hardly a candidate for conversion at this stage in his life. And yet look at his eyes...

"We must talk further someday, Agent Dalham," Hoover said.

Dalham swallowed hard.

Hoover then waved his hand through the air in an impatient gesture.

"Enough of these digressions!" he said sternly.

He tapped the file folder.

"As I was about to say a moment ago, even your father didn't escape my scrutiny."

Dalham, confused, said, "But I thought you said you admired my father."

Hoover's expression turned cold.

I questioned him!

And then Dalham, rushing over his words in his mind, realized his mistake: He hadn't addressed the Director as 'sir.'"

"Sir, forgive me, I meant no disrespect," he said, hoping that no damage had been done.

Hoover seemed to be placated by that.

"Your father once reacted in the same way about some matter, and *he* wasn't shot at dawn, was he?"

A grin curled up the sides of Hoover's mouth.

"Thank you, sir," Dalham replied, his heart rate immediately calming down.

"I want you to have your father's file," Hoover said abruptly.

Dalham didn't know what to say.

"It is only the second time in nearly 40 years that I have turned a file over to the subject or a member of that subject's family."

"I am honored, sir."

Hoover picked up the folder and held it briefly.

"I have only one regret, Special Agent Dalham."

Dalham dared not probe the Director but his very manner asked the question anyway.

"That I never gave it to Arthur James Dalham—while he was alive," Hoover said, that pause uncharacteristic.

Dalham wasn't sure whether to wait for Hoover to hand the folder to him or cautiously ask for it.

"I will not have your knuckles beaten bloody if you reach across my desk to take this folder from my arthritic old hand!" Hoover remarked, enjoying the embarrassment caused the young rookie by his remark.

Dalham took the folder, noting silently how thin it was.

"Go now, Special Agent Dalham," Hoover said then. "My duties do not allow the luxury of wasting any more time."

"Thank you, sir," Dalham said with genuine relief and gratitude.

But Hoover had already turned to other considerations, barking an order over the intercom.

As Dalham was leaving the inner sanctum, he turned for a moment. J. Edgar Hoover was leaning back in his chair, his eyes closed, his head starting to droop a bit.

Dalham shrugged mentally and left, anxious to read the contents of the file.

He glanced at his watch.

It was near enough to the end of his shift that he could check out and head straight for his apartment. Once he had arrived and sat down on the sofa, he placed the folder on his lap, not knowing what he would read when he opened it.

A single sheet of paper.

He half-thought of looking around the apartment, wondering if anything had fallen out of the folder.

Then he picked up that lone sheet and struggled with a scrawled note signed by J. Edgar Hoover:

> I am thought to be a very hard man. I have convinced myself over the years that being stern and authoritarian is the only way I can get people to follow my every order.
>
> But you, Arthur James Dalham, are successful in an area where I am a complete failure. I have respect from fear; you have it from love.
>
> This is the only sheet of paper that will ever be in your file.
>
> JEH

That was the beginning of Kent Dalham's realization what his father cast was not a shadow, but something much brighter.

14

WE take so much for granted," Solomon Hillel Schechter was saying, his voice bringing Dalham out of that flashback. "Think of it: Clean water was more welcome then than any strongbox filled with gold or diamonds!"

"What was it like back there, Mr. Schechter?" Dalham asked.

"At Dachau II?"

"Yes, sir."

"Amateur night, amateur night! But even rank beginners can cause death, can bring pain, can act insanely. They were like young men possessed with some kind of evil spirit."

"Just like their predecessors?"

"Just like the original Nazis, yes. All of them had some mystical connection, though it was only Goering who seemed *obsessed* by the occult."

"The others were possessed but may not have realized it."

"Indeed!" Schechter said, pleased that the younger man had made the connection.

"What else could explain the sheer intensity of their barbaric conduct? It couldn't have been mere madness."

"I agree totally! The ferocity, yes, and the scale upon which they spewed forth the Nazi plague. Whatever I experienced was repeated in the lives of millions of others."

Schechter went on to relate one incident in particular.

"I was shoved into an excavation in the ground with a dozen other men."

"All of them Jewish like yourself?"

"*That* was a major difference from the war years. True, there were Gypsies being annihilated in those days, other non-Jews; but I saw only a handful, frankly. This time, though, I was confined in that excavation with several blacks, two Puerto Ricans and half a dozen Jews."

"Was there iron grating over you, sir?"

"Yes. At least we weren't suffocating for lack of air, as many did when they were buried alive at the death camps in Germany and Poland. But when it rained, the skinheads would leave us for many hours in the muddy water. One Latino died of pneumonia later; most of us got sick in one way or another."

The old man shivered, drawing a blanket tightly around himself.

"The worst moment came when they took a black teenager and tied him to a stake in the middle of the camp. They beat him. They cursed at him. They called him 'Nigger! Nigger! Nigger!' over and over again. And then they poured gasoline over him and set him ablaze. His screams could be heard throughout the camp."

Schechter's eyes were bloodshot as he looked directly at Dalham.

"Two other Jews and I were given the job of burying him. As we untied him and laid his body on a stretcher, something fell from his hand, a tiny New Testament, its pages untouched somehow by the flames.

"As a Jew I was tempted to leave it there on the ground. But I didn't, Kent Dalham. I picked it up, stuffed it into my pocket, and proceeded with the burial. Later, I took it out, and read through those little pages, and passed it to others in the camp. It didn't last long, no matter how careful we all were. But we had memorized much of it. They couldn't wipe the words *from our minds*!"

He reached out and took Dalham's hand into his own.

"We wouldn't have been able to go on without that New Testament," he said, his voice trembling. "They all died, yes, but they did so with courage. I can't explain why they're gone, and I only am left. God knows that, though I don't. As long as it is in *His* hands, nothing else matters."

They both fell into silence for several minutes. Then Dalham asked the other man again about identifying the skinheads.

"Bring me whatever photos, mug books or whatever else you have, my friend," Schechter told him. "As long as these eyes hold out, I will do whatever I can."

Dalham had two more questions, among the most crucial of all.

"Do you feel like telling me a bit more, sir?" he asked.

Schechter nodded.

"I have lived through hell to spend another day, week, month, whatever I have left in the bright sunlight. I have the best care. And I can help you get the monsters who did these unholy things. How much *better* could I feel, young man?"

"Do you have any idea how they could have gotten away with what they did?"

"I heard them talking from time to time, something about bribing officials and—and there was a comment about closet Nazis."

"Then someone got cold feet and tipped us off?"

"That or a case of conscience, though it is difficult to imagine anyone from that group being afflicted by ethics or morality or anything of the sort."

"And so they left everything as it was, not even bothering to conceal any of the evidence."

Schechter chuckled.

"There was little time! The Federal and state governments acted more quickly than usual. Those at the camp and their collaborators were caught off guard."

A short while later, Dalham was getting ready to leave.

"Can you stay just a bit longer?" Schechter asked. "There's something else, something as terrible as anything I've told you thus far."

"What could that be, sir?" Dalham asked, his interest piqued.

"There is more involved here, I suspect, than simply a few officials accepting bribes, more even than some Nazis in high places."

Dalham was hardly unaware of what the old man was saying. There had been some revelations about the influence of the Aryans Underground in a region outside of Tucson, Arizona. He had had some peripheral involvement which, while slight, was enough to give him some insight into what was going on. And one of the national news magazines did an investigative piece about the head of the organization who had resided in that area and ran a so-called "respectable" business which was nothing more than a cover for the activities that were of far greater interest to him. He came across as a nice guy on the surface, while engaging in a campaign of corruption at the local government level.

But Schechter acted as though he was hinting at something else.

"I'm not at all sure if I know what you mean," Dalham admitted.

"Companies, Kent Dalham. Companies willing to provide monies to *finance* what is happening."

He lowered his voice.

"Do the names of Fendorf, Holzhauer, Lotman mean anything to you?"

"Yes, sir, they do. Fendorf, Holzhauer and Lotman were three of the principal firms cooperating with Hitler during World War II, among others, that is."

How well Dalham knew! His father had taken it upon himself as a personal cause to go after certain men in those firms, while acknowledging the decency and integrity of the overwhelming majority of executives and workers in each case.

Fendorf.

Dalham winced at the recollection.

Deiter Fendorf wanted a factory owned by a wealthy German family, but they refused to sell. Fendorf then contacted Hermann Goering to make "arrangements." As a result, men who worked a lifetime to build up a company had to get rid of it at near-bankruptcy prices or face internment in a Nazi concentration camp.

"Fendorf maintained labor offices in France and other nations," wrote a friend of Art Dalham's who had compiled a book about Nazi corruption and crime. Fendorf "drafted workers for employment in their plants, *even going so far as to enter into direct negotiations with concentration camps for the services of the inmates."*

And doing absolutely nothing in the process to alleviate the awful conditions in the camps!

"These companies still exist, to a greater or lesser extent," Schechter said ominously.

"Yes, I know, but what?"

Dalham considered himself reasonably unflappable. But the implications of what Solomon Hillel Schechter was suggesting shook him just then.

"Be very careful, my friend," Schechter added. "The FBI certainly can survive virtually anything. But individual agents, I'm not so sure."

He leaned over close to Dalham.

"Especially you, Kent Dalham, especially since your father did so much, shall we say, to *embarrass* certain powerful people at those companies directly after the war. Consider what already has happened to you!"

Dalham thanked him and, feeling a little tired, was about to go back to his room.

"I should tell you this before you leave," Schechter added.

"What is it, sir?" Dalham asked, a certain weariness grabbing hold of him.

"The names of the leaders..."

"What about them?"

"Himmler, Goering—the rest."

"I am familiar with them, sir."

"That was what they called themselves."

At first Dalham couldn't figure out why the old man put special emphasis on names that he had heard *ad nauseum* over the years.

Schechter looked straight into his eyes.

"I don't see what—," Dalham started to say.

"Not fifty years ago, dear friend. Not that at all!"

The words came to Dalham's lips in an oddly mechanical manner.

"Today, Mr. Schechter, is that what you're saying? In that camp? Himmler, Heydrich, others—the leaders used *those* names?"

"And Goebbels. Mengele, too. But it wasn't *just* the names."

It must be my weakened condition, Dalham told himself. *I don't know where he's heading with this.*

Schechter seemed to be almost enjoying the puzzlement on the other's face, the manner of one who had special knowledge denied others.

"What I am about to tell you I've not as yet mentioned to *anyone* else," he said, his voice barely above a whisper. "They might chalk it up to an old Jew's encroaching senility, they might indeed!"

Dalham was waiting, only slightly annoyed with Schechter's somewhat toying manner.

The old man leaned forward conspiratorially.

"They seemed quite convinced that they had been taken over by the original monsters, that they *are* Goebbels, Mengele, the rest," Schechter told him.

"And in the background, financing it all..." Dalham started to add, catching the different threads as he was finally able to weave these together in his own mind.

Schechter's eyes widened in the triumph of revelation but also with an edge of fear.

"German money provided by one or more unrepentant industrialists planning another Holocaust from their safe offices in Frankfurt and Hamburg!"

15

DALHAM was exhausted. He had returned to his room in a funk because of what the old man had told him.

After all the intervening years, the layer after layer of insights and unimpeachable historical perspective, after all that, they still...

He slammed his fist against the wall of his room, yelping in pain. He remembered an incident five years before when he'd been riding in another agent's personal Mercedes, one a couple of years old that had been a dream-come-true for the man, bought from a special fund into which he had put money for a long time.

They were approaching the Lincoln Tunnel just outside New York City. Suddenly the driver of another car swung his vehicle in front of the Mercedes, cutting them off. The other agent had to slam on the brakes to avoid hitting the intruder. This caused a chain reaction behind them as the next car hit the rear of the Mercedes and others piled up, until half a dozen were involved.

Dalham scrawled down the license number of the car that had caused the multiple accident. They phoned ahead to Lincoln Tunnel authorities. The driver was stopped as he came out the New York side and held until Dalham and the other agent arrived.

They faced him in a small room at the Port Authority Building. The man was in his mid-50s and had a thick Israeli accent.

"Why?" Dalham asked simply.

"German car," the man replied, and then lapsed into an expletive-riddled diatribe, ending it as he jumped out of his seat and lunged for Dalham, screaming, "They're devils. They've never changed! Never!"

Both agents assumed the man was just another disturbed individual. They turned in a report about the incident, and that was that.

How much did he know? Dalham asked himself. *Was it simple bitterness or something else?*

But later Dalham received a brief note faxed to him on a confidential line by the other agent.

> Something to think about, Kent. That guy a few
> months ago? The one who sideswiped us?
> He's dead. Supposedly a suicide...

Aaron

Dalham puzzled over it at the time but got involved in other cases, and the matter slipped his mind.

Until now.

The whole issue of the complicity of major German industrialists in the operation of Nazi concentration camps was hardly new. Yet even noted Jewish activist Benjamin B. Ferencz had never seriously hinted at anything sinister *after* the war— things arrogant and insensitive, yes, but nothing more than that.

Dalham had plopped on the bed after entering his room but couldn't sleep, and ended up staring at the ceiling as he went over Schechter's words again.

German money provided by one or more unrepentant industrialists planning another Holocaust from their safe offices in Frankfurt and Hamburg!

He knew he would have to contact headquarters; the old man had told him but no one else.

But first he needed to learn more, because he had to be prepared to build a case. There was a devil's advocate system that worked well in such instances, and he wanted to have all the facts possible.

The next morning Dalham requested a long list of books, hard copy files, microfiche and the necessary equipment. All of it arrived by special courier that afternoon. In the meantime he had commandeered another room in which to put everything.

What he uncovered brought back fragments of conversation he had had with his father over the years.

"When we went after the German industrialists, we found an attitude among some of them that was nearly as appalling as what we found at the trials of Goering and the others," the elder Dalham said while relaxing after a tennis game with his son.

"Even a few of the Nazis repented," Kent Dalham pointed out.

"Precisely, son. But I don't know of a single instance when *any* of that particular group of so-called businessmen showed what could be called *genuine* remorse."

"The love of money, Dad?"

"I don't mean to be rewriting Scripture, Kent, but it might be more accurate to say an *obsession* with money, a *worship* of it, money on a pedestal before which they bowed. But then I suspect that's what God had in mind anyway."

"I'd like to hear more someday, Dad."

"In this kind of world, Kent, you may *need* to hear more someday."

There were other times when Art Dalham shared similar comments, similar recollections with his son.

I didn't realize the real purpose, Dad, in those days.

He placed the book he'd been holding on his lap.

How I miss it all. People expect me to be like you in all that I do. They expect me to be as intelligent, as strong, as Christ-centered.

Shaking his head as though to clear it of such thoughts, he returned to the book, written by activist Ferencz, a former concentration camp inmate who had formed a group with the purpose of obtaining reparation payments from the German industrialists.

"Even the severe hardship cases of those who had survived work for I.G. Farben at Auschwitz got no more than $1,700 each," wrote the author. "The Jewish slaves who toiled for Siemens had to settle for $825. The AEG/Telefunken slaves received no more than $500, and the Jews who worked for Rheinmetall received even less."[3]

The whole story was appalling. At first Dalham thought he had misread something, but the more he got into the facts, the more ill he felt, especially with regard to one case.

Erich Stier.

Stier was a regular supporter of the Third Reich, depositing not less than 100,000 German marks in the SS coffers. His various companies benefitted materially from the use of cheap labor gleaned from Auschwitz, particularly I.G. Farben, a synthetic oil and rubber factory which was literally right across the street from the Monowitz labor camp, otherwise known as Auschwitz III. Just a few miles west was Auschwitz I, the central or so-called main camp, though it was Birkenau/Auschwitz II, to the northwest, where the five crematoria and four gas chambers were located.

Like Fendorf, Stier aided in the conscription of labor for his companies but unlike Fendorf, Stier's involvement with the Nazis went beyond "mere corporate expediency." He seemed to relish his access to the power centers that controlled Germany during World War II.

Whereas Fendorf took over only one industrial plant by devious means, Stier went about the same approach on numerous occasions with other businesses. According to an expert report compiled during his postwar trial, "Stier, through his intimate contact with the high officials in the Nazi regime, had himself placed in the position where he was the only one permitted to negotiate for a large plant in an occupied nation. The owners thereof were unwilling to sell [in more than one instance but] were compelled to sell at a drastic sacrifice, and Stier thereby became the owner of such added industry without competition from other industrialists. His efforts to procure [many] industrialist plants in different territories were traced in detail."

Yet Fendorf was convicted, while Stier was not!

After the war, negotiations began between a group of Jews and Stier. But little came of these after more than 20 years because "Stier had convinced himself that he had done nothing wrong," and placed no urgency on the matter.

B'nai B'rith and other Jewish organizations labelled Stier a "slave master." They pointed out that the man earned $360,000 a day yet refused even the smallest claims of a few hundred dollars each.

At the time of his death, Erich Stier was the fifth richest individual in the world, having amassed assets worth over one billion dollars, with countless millions handed to him directly from the labors of men, women and children forced to work for him by their Nazi masters.

Dalham closed that little book and sighed, grateful for its insights into the post-war German mentality but sickened by the lack of contrition these men showed—men made by profits and accumulating wealth into soul mates of the maniacs who provided cheap labor for them.

After finding a file of special reports as he was leafing through the pages, he was jolted by something else, another astonishing fact.

The role of certain wealthy Swiss citizens, according to a memo that was many years old.

A country pledged to neutrality was infested with profit-minded men and women who maintained links through Farben with the Nazis.

The Swiss projected an image of neutrality but it was an image some of them discarded whenever there was money to be made," stated one confidential memo. "There is some suspicion that it came to be the perfect cover for clandestine involvement in the German economy from before 1939 up to the last days of the war. These businesspeople were like jackals as they sniffed out every conceivable opportunity to land lucrative deals. If the government knew about any of this, they never admitted it.

Dalham had been nearly dozing off, but that paragraph sent adrenalin rushing through him.

Dachau was a focal point and, to a lesser degree, Natzweiler, which was northwest of Dachau, both close to the eastern end of Switzerland. Swiss millionaires had considerable knowledge of what their francs were buying but went ahead anyway. Electrical equipment, machine tools, precision instruments, even Swiss watches became tainted with the blood of the Jewish labor drawn from Dachau and Natzweiler. And yet some of these same businesspeople were professing public outrage over the plight of concentration camp inmates!

Lord, what a dirty world! Dalham thought. *What a dirty world has been built on Eden's foundation.*
He put that memo aside and leafed through scores of more, as well as letters and other items.

Another proved as startling as the first one: Rudolf Stier has bought substantial acreage in Oregon, claiming that he intends to build a retirement community that will be a model for all others to follow. Zoning and environment studies thus far conducted apparently favor approval.

No code indicating priority status was attached to the brief report, which meant that it was a routine observation, nothing more.
Though the hour was late back East, Dalham phoned Doug Buchanan, another agent, at home.
"Doug, this is Kent," he said.

"Maybe 10 o'clock is a decent hour for a valued friend to phone, Kent, but at 1:00 A.M., anybody who wakes me up is just an intruder who had better justify his call!"

Dalham laughed, then read the memo.

"Ring any bells?"

"Nothing. Now, can I go to—"

Buchanan stopped short, cleared his throat.

"Wait a minute!" he said. "You're there in Oregon now, aren't you? That concentration camp mystery?"

"You got it."

A pause.

"What's the problem?" Dalham asked.

He could hear his friend groan at the other end.

"If somebody had only smelled a rat before now."

"Cut it out, Doug. We're FBI agents, not mystic diviners."

Buchanan paused, then:

"Thanks for that, Kent. I'll hunt up anything else I can find, and fax it as soon as I can. Wouldn't it be interesting if that camp were located in the midst of the land where Stier claimed his 'retirement community' was going to be built."

Dalham was impressed.

"How come you made the connection so quickly?" he said appreciatively.

"I could tell you some nonsense, make you think I was some sort of genius, but that would be a lie."

"Well, what then, Doug?"

"You never knew it but I'm a bit of a history buff, Kent. I find the World War II years particularly interesting. Fascinating! When that report crossed my desk, I dug into the elder Stier's background a bit, all the awful stuff about his use of sick and hungry and even dying Jews to do the labor at his various companies. I found out that Rudolf was his son, and that there was some suspicion about certain 'connections' he had been maintaining over the years."

"And then you went on to other matters, right?"

"Right. Even evil characters—and I'm not saying that Rudolf Stier is as rotten as his father was—even *they* can do perfectly innocuous things. So I figured it wasn't worth any more time."

"Change your mind now?" Dalham asked.

"You bet I have, Kent. There just might be something colossal here."

"Thanks, Doug. Call me when you can."

"I will. Wait, Kent?"

"Yeah?"

"Stier inherited *all* of his father's money. With wise investments, a reasonable rate of return, the guy might have *billions* at his disposal."

"Enough to finance an army."

"And a revolution."

16

*E*LSEWHERE....

The U-shaped desk surrounded him. On top were six computers, two on each side.

He looked at the information on these and grinned. Then he stood and walked from behind the desk to a large window in the suite he leased on the top floor of that tall building.

Hundreds of thousands of them in just this city alone, he thought, his face contorted in a momentary sneer, *scurrying around like loathsome rats, bringing with them the awful disease of their Semitism.*

He thought back to the plague centuries before.

The spring of 1348.

Lake Geneva.

Jews were accused of poisoning the wells.

They admitted it all! After they were tortured, the truth came out. Copies of their confessions were sent to every town within a day's journey.

He licked his lips, his thin, red lips.

In Basel, every Jew in the community was herded into several buildings, and the wood structures set ablaze, and they all died!

Perspiration appeared on his forehead.

In Strasbourg, sixteen thousand were murdered!

Elsewhere hundreds were starved to death...

He had to fight hard to keep a rising sense of exultation from overwhelming him, knowing as well as he did that past history was meaningless.

They're back now, stronger than ever.

He felt almost physically ill as images of Jews filled his mind, their predatory countenances ready to take over every respectable Gentile business, and bleed it dry, cutting quality, boosting profits, burdening the workers.

He turned and looked at the yellowed semitransparent lampshades throughout his office.

Those were the days, he told himself.
The scent of triumph made his nostrils flare.
And so it shall be...again!

17

TIRED from reading, Dalham lay back in bed, rubbing his eyes.

It would be so much easier if you were here, Valerie, and the kids. We supported one another. God never meant for any man to go through life alone, especially the sort of life I've had to lead. Without you here, I feel almost too weak, too...

He snapped out of that train of thought. He wasn't weak, he knew; it was just that Valerie and he had been so interdependent, one lost without the other. That meant their marriage was tremendously invigorating, satisfying, but it also heightened the sense of loss after his loved ones were wiped out.

Wanting some fresh air, Dalham left the room and was at the front entrance when he heard someone shouting at him.

"Agent Dalham, would you please wait a moment?"

He turned and saw one of the doctors rushing toward him, then looked through the glass in the center of the door.

A morose-looking figure walking across the lawn.

A young man in his early 20s, *all the hair shaven from his head!*

Dalham recognized him instantly.

Fredrickson!

"What the—?" he started to say.

"May I have a moment with you, Kent?" the other man interrupted, panting.

Dr. Amory. The chief physician at the hospital.

"What's going on? That happens to be one of the skinheads in the barn."

"Yes, he is. His name is Michael Fredrickson."

"And his grandfather was Clarke Fredrickson. I know all that. What's he doing here in a Bureau hospital?"

Amory hesitated a moment.

"Check my file again," Dalham said angrily. "I think I have the clearance you need before you answer."

Amory looked uncomfortable.

"Forgive me but, you see, that's a special young man."

"Him? I don't see what makes that guy so—"

"He's the informant," the doctor interrupted again, "the one who tipped us off about Dachau II."

Dalham looked outside again. Fredrickson was leaning against a tree, as though suddenly faint.

"Why wasn't I told earlier?" he asked.

"You were in pretty serious shape. We didn't want your emotions to get in the way of your recovery."

"My emotions?" Dalham repeated, then realized Amory was right.

"You're a top agent, Kent," Amory said sincerely. "But it's also because of—"

"—my father," Dalham finished the sentence for him. "All right. You've proved your point. What next?"

"I was supposed to give this letter to you when you had sufficiently recovered."

Dalham took the sheet of paper Amory handed to him. The familiar Bureau letterhead was at the top. It was signed by the Director himself.

> Fredrickson is an important key. He *must* tell us what he knows. But he's been reluctant to talk to anyone, Agent Dalham, anyone, that is, except you.

Dalham looked up from the letter.

"Isn't that overstating the kid's importance?" he said.

"Sessions doesn't think so. That's all any of us needs to know, isn't it?"

Dalham nodded, returned his attention to that single sheet.

> You have the Bureau's full support. And you may contact me directly anytime you wish.

An open line to the director!

Dalham hated to admit it, but he was suddenly nervous.

"You're sweating," Amory observed.

Dalham wiped the back of his left hand across his forehead.

"So I am," he said.

"Not many agents get that kind of letter," Amory added.

"You don't have to tell me that, doctor."

He looked out at Fredrickson again.

"I wonder if he saw an *aparicion*, too?" Dalham mused aloud.

"*Aparicion*? Isn't that Spanish for—?"

"Phantom...*apparition*."

"What's the connection?" Amory asked.

"I'll let you know," Dalham told him. "I'm going outside now."

"Good luck, Kent."

"Yeah. Thanks."

Fredrickson was sitting on the grass now. He jumped a bit when Dalham sat down beside him.

"You know?" he asked. "They told you?"

"I do. They did. Can't figure out why I'm so special, though."

"Aryans Underground hates you."

"I'm one of thousands of agents. They hate *all* of us."

"More than that."

"What makes me different?"

"God's picked you."

Dalham was momentarily startled to hear the youth talk like that.

"Picked me? For what?"

"To be His instrument of righteousness against the worst kind of evil."

Dalham couldn't keep himself from laughing.

"No, it's true," Fredrickson continued, his expression intent. "Please don't laugh."

"Sorry, sorry. Go on."

"That's why I couldn't tell anyone else. *You* were there in the barn, nobody here was. They *couldn't* understand as well as you."

"Nobody has to remind me. I remember every minute of it."

"Do you?" Fredrickson asked.

"Do I what?"

"Remember *every* minute?"

"I was trained to observe everything."

"And that training is infallible?"

"Of course not."

"But the barn was in flames, right?"

Dalham nodded.

"What caused the fire?" Fredrickson asked.

"At least one of those lanterns being knocked over."

"That came later, a minute or so later."

Dalham was annoyed.

"Cut the crap!" he barked. "Get to the point."

"The point is that you're forgetting something. You've got to put in that missing piece yourself. You've got to."

Dalham feigned increased irritation, and got to his feet.

"When there are no more games, we'll talk," he said as he started to walk back to the hospital.

"*Please!*" Fredrickson said. "It's important."

Dalham never knew, during the course of his later life, why he stopped suddenly and turned around, a cold chill grabbing his spine tightly.

"You know any Spanish?" he asked.

"I do, sir. I learned a few words from a—."

"—little Latino boy, isn't that it?"

He reached down and grabbed the youth, yanking him to his feet.

"A little boy buried under *a pile of decaying bodies!*"

"Yes, yes!" Fredrickson said, sobbing. "He was in the camp."

"He almost *died* there," Dalham said. "All he could say was just one word."

The boy reached out, grabbed the sleeve of his jacket. "Ap...ap...apar...a!"

Dalham took his mask off and bent down beside the stretcher.

"Son, no habla Español," *he admitted.* "I just don't understand what you..."

The boy's grip had been feather-like, but abruptly, and only for a second, he was able to tug roughly on the sleeve, and Dalham bent down next to his lips.

"Aparicion! Aparicion!"

The boy seemed more frightened than ever, saying that word one more time before he fell back against the stretcher and lost consciousness.

"I know, I know, I know!" Fredrickson was babbling. "That's what you *have* to remember about that night, sir. You have to believe that it was real...because it was. The *aparicion!* It was there in the barn. That's what you saw. *It was there to destroy you!*"

18

A short while later Dalham was in the room given over to the reference materials he had ordered. Fredrickson had gone back to his quarters.

Dalham sat down in a chair and closed his eyes.

...it was there to destroy you!

He had encountered other so-called supernatural "connections" since he had become an FBI agent, but none as terrifying as that cult of Satanists that could trace its lineage back to the 10th century! When he and several other agents burst in upon them, they were engaged in a ceremony that, during the years since then, he had tried to block out of his mind as much as possible.

Valerie knew that he was more than usually upset after he returned home from that particular encounter.

He gave her only a hint of what had been going on.

She was stunned.

"It's the sort of thing you hear about but don't really believe," she said after the children had been put to bed, and the two of them were sitting on the back porch, breathing in the cool autumn air.

"The problem is that when we don't believe the truth of something like that, we're just not prepared for the reality when it's thrown right in our faces," he had commented.

"Christians seem more guilty of the head-in-the-sand routine than some of my non-Christian friends, Kent."

"You wonder why that's the case. It's puzzling for sure!"

Valerie sighed and looked at the clear sky.

"We're supposed to set our minds on things above and not those below," she said softly, that aroma of Chantilly wafting past his nostrils. "And yet we mustn't ignore what goes on down here. I think God meant that we were to have our goals in heaven but our feet on the earth at the same time. If we aren't prepared for the tribulations in this life, we aren't able to cope with them very well."

He smiled.

"Did I say something funny?" she asked.

"No, you didn't," he replied. "I was just thinking how much of a blessing it is that the Lord introduced you into my life."

He leaned forward, kissed her lightly, then put his arms around her and kissed her again, this time with considerable passion.

Such memories fading as he returned to the reality of that room with those books, and the work directly ahead of him, Dalham wasn't surprised to find that both cheeks were wet.

...it was there to destroy you!

He didn't give much credence to a statement born apparently of Michael Fredrickson's paranoia. But somehow he couldn't dismiss it altogether in view of his own impressions just before he lapsed into unconsciousness in that barn.

Interestingly, one of the books sent to him was entitled *History of the Third Reich*. He picked it out from a pile near the chair and turned to a section devoted to the Nazi extermination camps.

"'Many of the guards slipped into an Aryan form of voodoo, not much different from the Latin Santaria. They would take dolls, give them the names of certain inmates, and stick pins in the arms, the legs, other areas. Later, tired of remote-control sadism, they used human beings instead of dolls.'"

He slammed the book shut and threw it on the floor.

Feeling oppressed, he left the room and entered the corridor outside. Dr. Amory was talking to a nurse a few feet away.

"Kent!" he said. "Glad to bump into you. Could you come to my office for a few minutes?"

"No problem," Dalham told him.

Amory's office was more luxurious than Dalham would have expected, knowing the Bureau's penchant for as few frills as possible: cherrywood paneling; leather chairs; suspended tile ceiling; wall-to-wall carpet; and a large executive-type desk with two computers, a laser printer and a multi-line phone.

The doctor saw him eyeing the setup.

"Special, isn't it?" he commented.

Dalham nodded.

"Not everyone has something like this," Amory said. "I'm a bit pampered, I suppose."

"Which isn't usual Bureau policy."

"How true, Kent, how true indeed. The question is why; I mean, that's what you're thinking, isn't it?"

"Yes, sir, that's about it."

"It's a long story, but let's just say that I have proven myself invaluable to the Bureau over the years. You see, at this hospital, and this one only, we treat only the most special cases."

"And I qualify?"

"You still don't understand how important you are, Kent! And it's not just because of your father."

"The kid, that skinhead?" Dalham asked skeptically.

"That's part of it, yes. You see, I am a holdover from the long Hoover era. You are, too, of course. But I started a good bit before you did. You met the Man only once. But he and I had become friends well before he died."

"He seemed to like my father."

"That he did. I'm going to show you a letter that has been seen by only a limited number of individuals over the past 20 years."

He sat down at the desk, opened the center drawer and took out an envelope, looking at it briefly, then handed it across to Dalham.

"Please," he said, indicating a chair in front of the desk. "Read this."

It was from the Director's office. As Dalham took the letter out he noticed the date: *August 3, 1971.*

"Just three days after I met him," Dalham said.
"And only a short while, really, before he died."
Dalham sat back and read the contents:

> As the years pass, I can feel myself fading more and more rapidly, my friend. There are aches and pains, yes, but it's so much more than that now. My mind! I forget incessantly, it seems; I sit and think about the past for long stretches at a time; I get up in the morning, and I dread the hours ahead, for fear that people will notice that I am no longer what I was.
>
> You know what the worst aspect of all this is? There is no one to succeed me. I don't mean in the Bureau; our laws provide for that so well. I mean another kind of succession, the kind that fathers have when they leave behind their own flesh and blood to continue in their stead. I have friends, and you are one. But there are more enemies than friends for me these days, I am afraid, more vultures circling as though knowing it won't be long before they can swoop, and I can no longer defend myself. There is, however, one young man I wish you would "adopt" for me. Without his ever knowing it, please help him as discreetly as possible. He is the son I never had, the legacy I cannot leave behind.

Dalham glanced up at the doctor for a moment.
"Anyone who believes those who are savaging his memory," Amory said, "would expect a heartless monster, some would even say a pervert. After awhile, rumor constantly repeated becomes a kind of falsely legitimized fact. But the friend I knew, Kent, while riddled with shortcomings, was far, far different from the man depicted by the media."
Amory smiled.
"Read on, and you will realize how special you are," he said gently.

And Dalham did just that.

> Nothing I am asking you to set up must ever be made public. You will have to use every device at your command to keep all this private. If anything ever leaks, there will be every kind of twist and turn put to my motivations, all of which will be suspect. Was he an illegitimate son? Did we have something going on between us, as they claim I did with Clyde? You know what I mean, and you know the truth about me.
>
> Arthur James Dalham is the only other individual who must know the truth.

"My father!" Dalham exclaimed. "He said nothing."

"We had to have the cooperation of a family member," Amory said. "No one else, not even your mother, could be included. All lawyers, all accountants, *everyone* else has been kept in the dark all this time."

Dalham returned his attention to the letter.

> I don't want Kent Dalham given promotions he does not deserve. But I don't want him denied these, either, for reasons of personality clashes, temperament or anything else unwarranted that ordinarily might stand in the way.
>
> I don't want him accorded pay raises he does not earn. And there must be thorough objectivity in this matter. But I am putting up a portion of my estate to benefit him financially when he retires. As you know, I have substantial sums available to me.

When Dalham had finished reading those last few words, he looked up.

"Your eyes are especially wet, Agent Dalham," Amory said.

"I'm sorry, sir, but—"

"Relax. You react as I did."

"It seems more like a will."

"I thought that, too. He left quite a lot of money to Clyde Tilson, of course, and to a handful of others. Yet none of them, not even Tilson, knew about the arrangement regarding you."

"I'm not worthy, Dr. Amory."

"Cut it out. You are. Hoover wasn't naive when it came to judging *people*. Whatever else might be said about him, he couldn't be easily deceived."

Dalham nodded reluctantly.

"I'll need time to absorb all this."

"Fine."

"In the meantime, there *is* something else."

"What's that?"

"Fredrickson," Dalham said. "I want to reach him, Dr. Amory. He's salvageable, I think."

"I agree."

Dalham was about to excuse himself when Amory asked him to remain seated.

"Another matter, Kent."

Dalham was struck by the expression on Amory's face, a combination of anger and fear.

"I have a report here that I received a few days ago. As soon as I read it, my mind was made up. When I saw you with Fredrickson, I knew I was right. You would have gotten a copy by normal channels if you hadn't been here, recuperating."

Amory handed him a sealed manila envelope.

"Take this to your room," the doctor said. "We'll talk tomorrow. You can tell me if you come to the same conclusion I did."

"Fredrickson's a factor, isn't he?"

"That's right, if my hunch isn't misplaced."

Dalham thanked him and left the office. The walk to his room seemed uncommonly long.

19

DALHAM was shaking by the time he had finished reading the bulk of the contents of the manila envelope.

They're trying to do it all over again, he summarized. *They want to reconstruct the Third Reich.*

A small cadre of agents had been gathering facts for months. They worked under special orders from FBI Director William Sessions throughout the United States and, in conjunction with the CIA, abroad as well.

It began in Zurich, led to Geneva and on to Frankfurt and Rome.

No company like Fendorf, Holzhauer or Lotman was itself implicated, at least not officially. But the name of at least one board member from each appeared again and again along the trail that was traced by U.S. government operatives.

Finally the link between them all was uncovered: Rudolf Stier held stock in each company.

Dalham ground his teeth together, the very name sending his adrenalin level shooting upward.

The man who had bought Oregonian acreage for a retirement village!

Dalham was trying to control his anger.

Permanent retirement for Jews, blacks, Catholics, he thought scornfully.

He sat down and reread the portions directly about Stier.

"'Rudolf Stier is a devotee of astrology, tarot cards and other popularized occultic entertainments,'" he read aloud. "'But his tastes run deeper than just these diversions. He spent considerable time in Haiti, studying an offshoot of *Santeria,* the Haitian form of voodoo, which claims the ability to kill by curse as well as raise the dead. If they like you, they promise immortality; if you rub them the wrong way, you die, and often quite horribly.

"'It should be remembered that there is some evidence supporting the view that the AIDS epidemic began, in part anyway, when wealthy homosexuals traveled regularly to Port au Prince for liaisons with special partners there and then returned to the United States carrying the HIV virus.

"'No one should forget that Josef Mengele and others were deeply into germ warfare investigation and related research nearly 50 years ago. How much of all this is interconnected remains to be seen, but we should not overlook the possibilities. Sometimes the most profound developments in history are made up of bits and pieces, with the whole being greater than the sum of its parts.'"

Dalham laid the file across his lap, repeating from memory fragments of the rest of that particular report.

Stier was traced to San Francisco at one point, with some sightings of him in the Tenderloin area. From there he apparently went on up to Oregon. After staying for several weeks, he returned to the East Coast for an extended visit in Washington, D.C.

And then he was gone.

That was a year ago.

What would he be doing in D.C.? Dalham asked himself.

There was a sealed smaller envelope in the larger one. He opened it and found the answer.

"Rudolf Stier was spotted entering the Panamanian Embassy in the second half of November 1989."

Just before Noriega was deposed!

"We suspect he is the source of the leak that tipped the dictator off, enabling Noriega to elude capture as long as he did and leading to an unnecessary loss of lives, American as well as Panamian."

The last lines were the most shocking of all:

"We had Rudolf Stier in custody until a Federal judge ordered his release. An inquiry dealing with that judge is now in progress. We have turned up only one detail thus far. Judge Kramer Buchholtz, of German extraction, has money invested in an American medical

research company owned by a subsidiary of Lotman Industries. Naturally the majority stockholder is one Rudolf Stier."

And Stier was now out of the country apparently, last seen having dinner with an official of the Swiss government!

Coincident with all Stier's activity was the surge in the number of perceived skinheads across the country, perceived being exactly the right word, because it was not a statistic available to any census taker. There were few records of any kind, but the ones that did exist, and the impressions of law enforcement officials in virtually every state, were convincing.

A single individual behind it all?

Dalham couldn't swallow that. Which only made matters worse. If Stier indeed were not alone, who else?

20

"MICHAEL Fredrickson knows a great deal, doesn't he?" Dalham asked Amory.

They were back in the doctor's office.

"I told you yesterday about a hunch of mine," Amory replied. "Remember?"

"About Michael?"

Amory nodded.

"That's exactly what it was," he said. "I think he can tell us a great deal indeed. Are you in agreement with that, Kent?"

"He wasn't an Aryan commander apparently, but he was nevertheless present with them at critical moments," Dalham commented. "I think you may be right on!"

"I gather that some within the Aryans Underground think that his grandfather was given a bum rap, as the expression goes," Amory said. "They are convinced that the KKK hierarchy thought Clarke Fredrickson was becoming too powerful and would force those aging monoliths to swing toward a—."

"—more oppressive stand against the blacks, the Jews, the others they were supposed to hate."

"Absolutely correct, Kent. It seemed to them that the KKK leaders had become too soft, more interested in broader public acceptance than the Klan's original vision."

"The ballot box instead of the battlefield!"

"Again a bull's-eye," Amory said. "When Michael Fredrickson could no longer stand the abuse at home and joined the Aryans Underground, he had ready acceptance. His by-then fellow skinheads relished the irony that his father, a Klansman, created an atmosphere that Michael found intolerable, symptomatic of the KKK's decadence in their eyes, and came to believe that it was only as a skinhead that his life would have any meaning. The little that Michael was inclined to reveal was enough for us to be able to piece together what I've just told you."

"Were they grooming him to be a leader?"

"That seems a reasonable assumption, Kent. And as such he would be privy to a great deal."

"Since everything was being set up so perfectly for him, a group that adopted him as one of their own, a future that seemed unlimited, why would he throw all that away by becoming a snitch?" Dalham asked.

"That is one of the many answers I pray you will find out," Amory acknowledged.

"By the way, I've been thinking: This is not the place for me to try."

"Too 'institutional'?" Amory guessed.

"Not so much that, but it *is* enemy territory, after all—assuming we're still the enemy in his mind."

"Anywhere you want to go is fine," the doctor assured him.

"I haven't thought about where the best place might be."

"I have a suggestion," Amory said.

"I'm open."

"There's a retreat not far from here. It's beautiful, peaceful, with some good people running it. The director and his wife can be as helpful as you want or stay entirely out of the way."

Dalham concurred.

"Sounds good," he said.

"I'll have someone drive the two of you there tomorrow."

Dalham and Amory both stood.

"Thanks," Dalham said. "Thanks for trusting me with that letter from Hoover."

"I really had no choice."

"There's one thing, though, Dr. Amory..."

"What's that?"

"He did insist that my father was the only other person to be told. How come you broke with that?"

"You had a rough time back there, in that barn and afterwards. Your nerves were shattered. You had lost a great deal of self-confidence, Kent. You're much better now. But I thought knowing Hoover's feelings would encourage you in the future."

"Emotional insurance, then? Something to sustain me, is that it?"

"More or less."

"But I have my faith."

"Yes, but remember, God often works through human instruments, Kent. You know that as well as I do."

They shook hands.

"It's amazing," Dalham said.

"What's amazing?"

"How people can enter someone's life so suddenly and change it."

"Hoover was *in* your life a long time ago," Amory reminded him. "You just never knew it."

"I wasn't talking about him so much as about you, sir," Dalham told him.

"I brought you the news, Kent. I didn't *create* that news. I'm here if you ever need me."

"My father said that more than once. I had to get used to the fact that one day he wasn't."

Dalham was about to leave the office when Amory added one other comment.

"Michael Fredrickson is an only child, as you are. You just might become an older brother image to him, Kent."

"Or a father?"

"Yes, that's a possibility, too."

Dalham thanked him and left.

What an extraordinary two weeks—from near-death at the hands of crazed skinheads, to recovery in an FBI hospital, to learning that he'd had, in a sense, a second father. Who could have predicted any of it?

And now, what of *tomorrow*?

The implications of that word!

We steal if we touch tomorrow. It is God's.
As that quotation occurred to him, he stopped in the doorway to his room, his head bowed momentarily.

21

DO you know what it was like?"
"I can't honestly say yes."

"To find your bed violated night after night by your own father. You've never had to face that!"

"That's true."

"Is it any wonder that I had to run away?"

"What about a pastor?"

"We had one."

"You didn't talk to him?"

"I tried."

"What was his response?"

"Some stuff about prosperity and success being just around the corner if I would only have faith."

"But the lack of *things* wasn't the source of your pain."

"Right! The guy never seemed to understand that. He was always after numbers—more members, more donations, new buildings."

"That's an approach that's been infecting more and more churches in recent years."

"Infecting? Yeah, that's right."

"Like a disease."

A pause.

"What happened after you ran away?"

On Hollywood street corners, thumbing customers. Dressed in jeans. Tank tops. Eyes searching each car. Hopping in. The price. Then the place. Sometimes tied up. Sniffing poppers. Getting higher and higher.

And always the shame afterwards.

Tears.

Then on the street again, thumbing the next trick.

"I was in Hollywood. It was an afternoon. Really hot! This guy picked me up. We talked for awhile. He wasn't interested in the usual stuff."

"Another skinhead?"

"No, different. Dressed in a suit. A full head of hair."

"What about the car?"

"Expensive. A Caddy, I think."

"What did he say?"

"All the right things."

"And you were hooked?"

"Yeah, I was hooked. I wanted to take what he offered."

Michael Fredrickson hoped that Dalham would not give up on him. People had been doing that most of his life. He'd had no one for a long time who seemed interested in helping him hang on, except Aryans Underground, and he knew in the end that they would have ultimately ended up destroying what little there was left of him.

Before that, only his mother cared what happened to him.

She had been afraid, afraid of the maniac who was her husband, his father, afraid of what would happen if she defied him.

"But it can't go on like this," she told her son one evening. "I must stop that monster!"

He knew that she would choose a moment when she could either shoot his father or stab him. He also knew that he couldn't let her do that. It was better for *him* to have to deal with his conscience than for his mother to have to wrestle with her own.

So he intended to fix the brakes on his father's car, but never got a chance to do it. His father was drunk one night and lost control of the car. It plunged over a cliff, but the elder Fredrickson did not die. He was totally paralyzed and had been institutionalized ever since.

His mother disappeared after that. He was left with no one.

That was when he found out about Aryans Underground.

That was when another nightmare blended seamlessly with the previous one.

22

THE retreat encompassed 10 acres of ground on the plateau atop a small hill.

Below were two- and three-story office buildings, shopping centers, hamburger joints, the noise of traffic. But the retreat nevertheless seemed totally isolated, an Eden apart from the commerciality outside its boundaries.

Kent Dalham and Michael Fredrickson were sitting in a white gazebo near the western edge of the property.

"So peaceful," the youth was saying. "You know, this is the first time I've ever been to any place like this."

"I thought Aryans Underground gave you a sense of belonging," Dalham remarked.

"Oh, they did, but we were nothing more than a glorified street gang."

"And how many gang members are actually happy? How many can claim *real* peace?" Dalham speculated.

"They'd get high when they're fighting back, when they defend their turf—it's even a sexual thing with a lot of them—but that passes, and it's the same old story."

...the same old story.

Until one night.

"What happened then?" Dalham asked.

"I don't know actually. The leaders went away for awhile, leaving the grunts behind."

"But you were more than a grunt, Michael."

Dalham waited for a response but there was none.

"Do you have any clues?" he then asked.

Fredrickson seemed increasingly uncomfortable.

"Their names had changed—completely different."

"From Smith and Jones and Williams, I bet, to Goebbels, Heydrich and so on."

"How did you know?" Fredrickson asked, surprised.

"An old man told me."

"Mr. Schechter?"

Now it was Dalham's turn.

"You remember him?"

"Yeah, I do. A nice old guy."

"A nice old *Jew*."

"I was never hung up on them like the others. Not all of us were."

"You *pretended* to be anti-Semitic?"

Fredrickson stood and walked from the small gazebo, stopping at the edge of the property, looking out over the commercialism below.

"A lot of us talked the language because that was expected of us," he said.

Dalham was now standing next to him.

"That was the key to belonging, then?" he asked.

"It was. But there *were* guys who *did* hate the Jews and the Catholics. At first I was real scared. They seemed..."

"...possessed?" Dalham offered.

"Yeah, that's about it. They acted like they were possessed."

"Does the *aparicion* have anything to do with it?"

...something else, quite different, appeared abruptly, with panic erupting throughout the group, skinheads running, knocking each other down, some falling off the hayloft to the ground.

Dalham shivered as he remembered that fleeting sensation.

"You said back at the hospital that the *aparicion* was there in the barn, that it was intent on destroying me," he reminded the other.

Fredrickson dug his hands deep into the pockets of his jeans.

"Can you tell me what you meant?" Dalham probed.

"I don't know for sure."

He turned and faced Dalham.

"You're scared, aren't you?" Dalham remarked.

Fredrickson nodded, his face drained of color.

"It's no secret that the entire skinhead movement is evil," Dalham reminded him. "But that's been little more than a convenient label to describe what they have been doing, with no supernatural implications as such. Are you hinting at something more?"

"*Yes!*" Fredrickson yelled suddenly. "We stood at the gates of hell, don't you realize that? We stood there and—and *he* came through. Others, too. They came through and took over."

He raised his hands in front of his face.

They were shaking uncontrollably.

"It's more than hatred," he cried. "It's more than abuse. It's..."

Looking quite helpless and deeply frightened, as though the trauma of speaking in such a sudden rush was too much for him, he collapsed on the soft grass, sobbing hysterically.

Dalham bent down and took the boy in his arms.

"We'll get through it," he said. "With God's help, we will. Please, please believe that, Michael."

Fredrickson looked up at Dalham.

"You don't know what you're saying," he said, his voice cracking. "It's not that easy. They're powerful. They don't give up, they just don't!"

23

SOLOMON Hillel Schechter remembered the young man at the camp, the one who seemed to want to help. Sometimes this skinhead, so different from the others, would show kind little gestures, such as leaving some extra rations. More than once, behind the building where the old man and so many others were confined, they would grab moments to talk in a low voice.

"Why are you here, my friend?" Schechter asked him early on.

Fredrickson hesitated, not accustomed to lifting up the lid of his inner self before a stranger.

"Because—because you look a little like someone I saw in a Bible once," the youth replied with some embarrassment.

"I do?" Schechter replied, genuinely surprised. "I wonder which Bible character that was?"

Looking from side to side, alert to the possibility of being seen, Fredrickson responded, "God."

Schechter's mouth dropped open.

"Some artist's personal vision of God looked like *me*?"

Fredrickson nodded nervously.

"Son, son," the old man added, "I don't know what to say. I don't know how I can repay the kind things you've been doing."

"Just pray for me...please!"

It was then that they both heard voices, footsteps.

"Hit me, son," Schechter said in a whisper.

Fredrickson shook his head frantically.

"Yes—you must! So they don't suspect," Schechter persisted.

Other skinheads were coming around the corner.

Fredrickson hit Schechter across the cheek, and the old man collapsed on the ground.

The intruding skinheads laughed as they saw this happening.

"Good!" one of them said. "Clobber the filthy old kike!"

The two of them, the young skinhead and the aging Jew, found other occasions when they could grab moments of conversation.

Weeks later, Schechter sat back in his room at the hospital, realizing that the youth had been God's instrument in giving him some relief from the awful cruelties at the camp, some relief from the familiar oppressiveness.

I didn't have anyone like young Fredrickson nearly 50 years ago, he thought. *None of those devils showed us anything but contempt.*

He was holding a New Testament like the one he had found in Dachau II.

*I wonder...*he asked himself, regretting that he had not, for some reason, asked his skinhead friend the question that was in his mind now.

He opened it, hesitated only a second, and leafed through its pages, reading verses that caught his attention.

Forgiveness is everywhere. Jesus asked His Father to forgive even those who crucified Him. The sins of the harlot were forgiven.

He paused, dark memories surfacing.

My loved ones gone! Can I ever forgive the beasts who spilled their blood?

24

MICHAEL Fredrickson was shivering as he lay on the bed in his quarters at the two-story motel-like building on the grounds of the retreat.

How can I be so cold? he asked himself. *How can I be so cold?*

Memories.

His father entering his room...ripping the sheets off his bed...that awful, evil smile...the lust on his face.

So long ago, and yet not very long at all.

He tried to get back to sleep but couldn't, and climbed out of bed, walking to the window directly opposite.

Fredrickson looked out over the neon lights below.

My father was a product of that kind of world, he thought.

Flashy and bright, and heady at times.

And empty.

Fredrickson's grandfather had managed to hide a great deal of KKK money, money that his father got hold of.

We never went hungry. I got all the food I wanted but more that I didn't.

At first he submitted to his father's advances, too young to realize that this wasn't normal.

The more I cried, he recalled, *the more you...*

Suddenly he was dizzy and had to sit down in a chair near the window.

When Aryans Underground entered his life, he felt redeemed. He felt pride in wearing their uniforms, felt that at last he had become part of a group that would never reject him.

And then that night, he remembered.

He lied to the FBI agent. He *had* gone with the others, had started to participate with them, had placed his hands on the table, and felt it move abruptly, shaking.

And had run from that room, out into the night!

I couldn't stay. How could I stay? How could I?

It all changed for him after that.

He was allowed to remain but they treated him differently.

I saw only a little of what was happening that one evening, saw their bodies moving like puppets whose strings had been jerked one way, then another.

And then...

As he ran, he heard behind him just two words, just two chilling, terrible words, words he would not be able to forget, nor the harsh voice that spoke them.

25

THE rather strange-looking man stood and walked around the U-shaped desk and out of that office, past a secretary who asked, "Are you going to the sanctuary now?" He merely nodded to her and then continued down a long corridor toward a door at the end. As he came up to it, he took a key out of his right trouser pocket, unlocked the door, went inside and locked it again.

No one else could go in except at his invitation, which he never gave.

He looked around at familiar things.

The photos. The old flags. The medals.

Memories are made of this, he thought to himself as he perversely hummed a certain melody. *Ah, what memories!*

And then he got down on his knees, raising his palms upward before the inverted cross.

26

DALHAM was awakened by someone banging on the door of his room.

He stumbled and fell over a chair after he got out of bed, his knees throbbing by the time he made it to the door.

It was Martin Nancarrow, the retreat's founder, a robust-looking sixtyish man with bushy eyebrows and a commanding manner about him.

"You'd better come quick!" he said.

"What's happening?"

"Michael's threatening to commit suicide. He claims demons are after him!"

Dalham grabbed a shirt, slipped on a pair of slacks and shoes, then followed the doctor.

Fredrickson was standing near the gazebo, at the edge of the plateau.

"Don't!" Dalham begged as he approached the boy. "You mustn't. We're getting so close, Michael."

"Close to *what*?" Fredrickson demanded. "Close to more pain, close to more..."

He leaned forward, his feet inches from the edge.

"I have nothing to live for," he cried. "I don't have the Aryans—they'd never take me back. I don't have *normal* society, as you call it. I have no parents. I am a freak."

"Why do you say such a thing?" Dalham asked. "What is it about yourself that—?"

"My father's abuse, that's what. Because of him I can never be a father myself."

"But you can adopt kids, Michael, if you get your life together," Dalham told him. "You can give youngsters the kind of home *you* wanted."

Fredrickson started coughing, then stopped.

"The only reason you *pretend* to care is that you want me to tell you everything I know, lead you to headquarters. You want *information*—you don't want *me!*"

Fredrickson seemed very weak then, in danger of falling over the edge as much from that weakness as from any desire to commit suicide.

"Can you really *imagine* what it's like to be violated again and again by *any* man? And when that man's the one who's your..."

He let out a single cry—"*Heil Hitler!*"—and jumped.

27

NANCARROW was one of the more prominent Christian counselors, working with ministers, missionaries, businesspeople, young and old, all of whom came to his retreat for help.

"I've had a former president here," Nancarrow had said. "There have been gospel singers, a well-known televangelist, many, many more. I sometimes think that being a Christian guarantees not peace and happiness but rather constant attacks by the enemy of our souls. Those who try to push this prosperity doctrine make the fatal mistake of equating blessings and joy with material rewards from God. How deluded they are!"

They sat in the waiting room of the hospital where Michael Fredrickson had been rushed. His fall from the plateau had been broken by trees and bushes midway down, leaving him with a broken rib and a slight concussion. Nancarrow gave Dalham his impressions of the youth.

"He *thinks* he's seen some awful demonic event," he said.

"Does that surprise you?" Dalham asked.

"Not these days! I used to run into such cases when I counseled with missionary kids as their parents were on furlough, but it was comparatively rare. Now, however, encounters with demonic presences are much more frequent."

"And no longer confined to the mission field," Dalham offered.

"Precisely. In fact, the majority happen right here in the United States. But that shouldn't be so surprising actually. There are many assaults upon young people these days, inside *and* outside the home."

Dalham agreed and told of a case he had been assigned to just a year before.

"There was this family of eight, the parents and six kids," he said slowly. "All of them were abused by either the father or the mother, sometimes both. Finally the kids couldn't take it any longer. They killed both parents."

"I remember some of the details through the media. But why were you called in?"

"The kids concocted a story about their parents being brutally beaten and then kidnapped by unknown intruders," Dalham recalled.

"So the possibility of kidnapping triggered action at the Federal level?"

"That's right," Dalham agreed. "We found the two bodies later."

"You stumbled into quite a mess then, didn't you?" Nancarrow observed.

"I did. Unfortunately, by the time we could piece everything together, the kids had run away. To date we've found four of the six but not the remaining two."

"But wouldn't they all have been together?" Nancarrow asked.

"Two were out at a local store, getting groceries. They fled when they saw what was going on."

"Two more missing kids," Nancarrow said sadly, "two more among hundreds of thousands."

"All of them prey for chicken hawks, pornographers—."

"And neo-Nazi groups!"

"Sadly, yes."

"I see so much pain," Nancarrow said. "I see it even among missionary families. They're held up as examples on the field and when they're home on furlough. But they're just ordinary, fallible human beings. Often the pressure of being *observed* every minute of every day is too much. Kids figure they can't measure up, so they go crazy—literally."

"But with Michael, it *has* been worse, Dr. Nancarrow. He never had any kind of foundation to begin with. There was nothing but the perverted sexual legacy left by his grandfather, which then was inflicted on him through his father. The question is, does this go beyond perversion into the occult?"

Nancarrow rubbed his chin as he carefully considered what he would say next.

"I am not at all sure about Michael. His may be a case of genuine demonic encounter or it may be delusion fostered in an admittedly evil atmosphere."

"When I was in that barn, I thought I sensed something quite oppressive."

"The *aparicion*, perhaps?"

"Michael says that it was there, and it wanted to destroy me."

Nancarrow stood.

"When you're older, you can't sit as long before you become stiff," he said apologetically.

He started to pace as he talked.

"I shy away from demonic explanations for Michael's problems."

"Why is that?"

"A simple truth, my brother. Michael's had so much pain in his life, and he's so messed up inside, that Satan doesn't need to go overboard by calling in his troops. Michael has all the potential necessary for self-destruction without any demonic help. It was only when he met you and one other individual that things changed a bit."

"Me?" Dalham responded, surprised.

"You didn't allow prejudice to affect the way you treated him."

"You mean, I refused to apply his own standards to *my* conduct?"

"That's exactly what I mean. There you are, an FBI agent, well-scrubbed, with normal length hair, on the Establishment's payroll—indeed, someone who should have found Michael, with his shaved head, ragged clothes and sullen manner a real loser not worthy of an instant of your time."

"I saw him as a kid who needed help."

"And that's how you came across."

"You mentioned one other individual," Dalham reminded him. "Who was that?"

"Solomon Hillel Schechter."

"The old guy really had some impact on Michael!"

"A great deal," Nancarrow agreed. "But with that came a problem."

"He saw that Jews weren't the monsters he thought they were?"

"Exactly, my friend! He realized that Schechter was, like himself, a human being caught in a disastrous situation."

Dalham fell silent, briefly, then: "I wonder if Schechter is well enough to travel."

"Here?"

"Yes, right to the hospital."

"And both could stay at my retreat, is that what you're saying?"

"It is."

Nancarrow literally jumped up and down.

"That's a wonderful idea!" he exclaimed. "I would be happy to work with them both."

28

SOLOMON Hillel Schechter was able to discard the wheelchair and walk with a cane, his nurse staying with him at first until he became more confident.

"I am fine," he told her with much appreciation in the tone of his voice and the look on his face, knowing that while her job was to be by his side helping him, this nurse brought something more to the relationship between them. "I need the exercise. I don't want to be an aging invalid. I can't do anything about aging but the rest of it, ah, there I *can* do something!"

She smiled and was about to leave him there in the corridor outside his room when he touched her gently on the shoulder.

"It's funny," he said, "but I've never called you by your full name, Janet Young."

"That's fine," she replied. "Sometimes names aren't all that important."

"I...I..." he started to say but, feeling awkward, stumbled over the words.

She chuckled a bit.

"Mr. Solomon Hillel Schechter tongue-tied!" she exclaimed. "I never thought I'd see such a thing."

"What I'm *trying* to do is ask you a question," he told her. "Are you a...a...Christian?"

"Is *that* it now?" she said, smiling broadly. "Well, that's not so bad. The answer is yes, I am a Christian. Why do you ask?"

"You've not tried once to convert me," he observed.

"I wait on the Lord's timing," she said.

He grunted a couple of times and then waved her away in his usual grumpy way. But this time he was playful, and she left, as far as he knew. Yet he suspected, as on other occasions, that she was hovering just out of sight, ready to help if he fell or had some other difficulty.

Schechter thought he would go outside and get some fresh air, walking the grounds for as long as he could.

It was mid-afternoon.

The grass was well kept, a healthy green. He could smell the odor of fertilizer. Then he stopped short.

The grass was as healthy as this near Auschwitz, he recalled, realizing that the Nazis had used a different kind of fertilizer.

He shook himself and continued walking.

Before he had gotten far, he could hear the nurse calling to him.

"Mr. Schechter! Mr. Schechter! A phone call. You have a phone call!"

There was none of his family left. Who could possibly care about him?

When he got to the phone at the nurses' station, he heard Dalham at the other end.

"It's a strange thing you ask me to do," the old man said after listening to what the other had suggested. "His God is Adolf Hitler. Mine is the God of Abraham. How could we ever be reconciled?"

"I agree that the notion is bizarre," Dalham told him, "but, sir, how many Nazis have ever shown you the kindness he did?"

"I must admit that, in this world, kindness from *anyone* is increasingly rare."

"Will you consider it then, Mr. Schechter?"

"No, my friend, I won't."

"I'm sorry to hear that."

"I don't *need* to consider it," Schechter said teasingly. "What you say about this young man has much impact. I will go, Mr. FBI Agent, I will go."

"May I tell Michael?"

"Yes."

"Wonderful!"

They said good-bye. Schechter, the phone receiver still in his hand, questioned his good sense only for a few seconds, then realized how separate an existence he had lived since World War II: suspicious of people, never marrying, tending to his furniture business and blocking out so many opportunities for relationships with other human beings.

He handed the receiver back to the attendant and returned to his room, sitting down on the edge of the bed.

So lonely...

He recalled a quotation he'd read years before and repeated it aloud.

"Only in a house where one has learnt to be lonely does one have this solicitude for *things*. One's relation to them, the daily seeing or touching, begins to become love, and to lay one open to pain."

Things.

True indeed. He accumulated things that he would cling to in the midst of his loneliness because after all, once bought with *his* money, no thing he owned could be taken from him, as people could be. Increasingly his happiness depended upon accumulating more paintings, more expensive Oriental rugs, more classical albums and new cars. He got them at a dizzying rate, a new one every six months, more watches, more clothes, more...

...to lay one open to pain.

The pain came when the *things* could not give him the fulfillment he needed, any pleasure gained by acquiring them only transitory. And then he had to buy something else. But the "high" never seemed as good as before, no matter how much money he spent.

So he would sit in his spacious house, alone, the maid gone home, and he would look around at the luxuries. Nothing had changed; the loneliness was still there. He could reach out and touch, not another human being, but only a painting two hundred years old, admiring the brush strokes and remembering the thrill of the auction when he outbid everyone else. But there any remnant of joy would end, the old canvas quite cold to the tip of his finger.

...open to pain.

Those words described his life.

Perhaps I've lost the ability to have any kind of genuine communication with people. I've put on a good front all these years, fooling people who think of me as a nice old Jew, warm and friendly.

A lie.

Warm feelings died in the two extermination camps that were his homes for four long years, wrung out of him and countless other Jews, Gypsies and others by their maniacal captors.

The Germans became wild beasts. But so did the Japanese, the Russians, the Italians, the Turks, the Chinese in their treatment of rebellious students, even the British in India! And don't forget the Americans at My Lai—hardly heroes in comparison.

But they weren't beasts at all. They were human beings, supposedly capable of much finer behavior.

And yet...

Why?

That unanswered question drove him into the self-imposed isolation of 50 years, where no one could get his total trust, his complete faith.

If evil could entrap the inscrutable Orientals as well as the civilized Brits and the others, no part of humankind was immune.

Ted Bundy was somebody's boy next door.

Charles Manson hadn't always been crazy.

Ed Gacy—the mass murderer who abused and killed teenage boys and buried their bodies on his property...

His surroundings, that by-now familiar room, the furniture, the pictures on the walls, the window overlooking the expanse of grass he had admired minutes before, all that was once so reassuring now seemed threatening, ugly, as he had a momentary flashback to a crueler time. Like a drug flashback from absorbed chemicals in the body, the memories absorbed by his subconscious gripped him, memories that were recalled without warning—usually the most traumatic of the lot, sending any sense of normalcy into an emotional tailspin.

I've got to get away from here!

He struggled to his feet, suddenly quite terrified, blindly, unreasoningly terrified.

I've nowhere to turn. If everyone is evil, then no one will be able to help me, will want to help me, will do anything but chuckle at my fear, perhaps secretly, thinking that I do not sense that my pain is their exaltation.

Perspiration drenched him. The room became unsteady. He began to fall.

He *began* to, but he did *not*.

He sensed a steadying hand.

"Who's there?" he asked, more confused than frightened.

No answer.

"But I felt your hand," he said, "raising me up. Where are you?"

At his feet was that tattered New Testament.

He hadn't put it there. What was it *doing* there?

He bent down, a bit painfully, and picked it up. Then, holding it in his hands, he walked slowly to the window, looked up at a clear patch of sky.

He heard no voices, saw no sudden sweeping visions, felt no submerging wave of ecstasy. But he *knew* with utter certainty what Almighty God wanted to tell him in that moment.

There is One not tainted by the sins of humankind, is that what You're saying? One who could never betray me? One who, in His very goodness, offers the alternative to everything that has poisoned my existence nearly all my adult life?

The words that generated such a perception had been read in the midst of hell itself, not the hell of Scripture perhaps but the hell generated by those whose very souls had been taken over by...

He left the window, sat down on the bed again and went through the New Testament one more time, feeling as awkward, as disloyal to his own tradition as he had when he read it before. But he did not let this bother him quite as deeply, and he absorbed the verses with greater ease.

...behaving as brute beasts.

The words couldn't have been more sharply etched on the thin paper. Alongside acts of almost inexpressible kindness.

And then, in the book of Revelation, the most astonishing culmination, with images so spectacular that Schechter felt overwhelmed.

And God shall wipe away all tears from their eyes; and there shall be no more death, neither sorrow, nor crying, neither shall there be any more pain, for the former things are passed away.

He closed the Bible and put it aside, savoring those words.

...no more death.

He saw so much of it at the camps, death *inflicted*, not the death of ordinary life, organs giving out from age or sickness, but death handed out as punishment for being what they were: Jews.

The New Testament promised an end to death, an end to crying, an end to pain!

Oh, the sobs that came at night, every night, people beaten, people sick, people fearful of the gas chambers, the ovens, the ditches piled high, people with no hope.

And now a book with the greatest hope of all: a life eternal, free of death!

He started sobbing, unable to hold back his emotions any longer. How bitter he had been over the years, especially bitter toward Christians. He once worked as a cook for the SS commandant at one of the camps. He saw guests arrive for dinner and the commandant say grace or ask one of the guests to do it before each meal, petitioning God's blessings on the Third Reich.

After the war, that image dimmed because he saw how other Christians tried to help Jews rebuild their lives. But such a scene could never be completely forgotten, so grotesque was it.

Now he realized that God planned to eradicate *all* suffering.

Schechter fell back against the bed, the tears drying, as he sighed with anticipation of that day.

But in the meantime we must face what we face.

He found himself considering the plight of Michael Fredrickson. They seemed so disparate as individuals, and yet perhaps not. Both had endured a past that forced upon them a pervasive sense of gloom about their future.

Both of us are victims of the Nazis!

Despite his age, despite the pain in his joints, he shot up straight as *that* occurred to him, the impact of it staggering.

Two generations apart, but the same awful philosophy at the heart of their pain!

Fredrickson had tried to break away from the shackles imposed by first his father and then the other skinheads. In utter desperation he had attempted suicide as a final solution.

For Schechter, suicide also had seemed an option while he was a camp inmate and later, even decades later, during those times when the old melancholy assaulted him, reopening wounds of the past.

Now I must shed those clinging remnants and be free of any desire but helping this young man build a new life for himself. Mine is nearly ended, but Michael has so much ahead of him—if he can exorcise those demons.

"Michael..."

Schechter was surprised at how warmly he repeated that name.

29

*I*F *he can exorcise those demons...*
For Michael Fredrickson, that wasn't something accomplished easily or without pain. It meant going back to his childhood, to terrible memories.

He tried to kill his father, thinking he would enjoy getting back at the man who had tormented him for so long.

He didn't.

And then only Aryans Underground seemed to offer relief from the pain.

"Afterwards, I wanted to die myself," he admitted as he, Nancarrow and Dalham sat in the little gazebo near where he had attempted suicide the second time. "I tried some sleeping pills but didn't take enough of them to do the job. Then I kept on running. The police never found me because that's when I got into Aryans Underground—they're good at hiding guys like me. They swallow you up, and *nobody* from the outside world can easily find you."

His voice was trembling.

"Do you *know* what I did while I was with them?" he asked plaintively. "Can you imagine some of the—"

Fredrickson had to choke back some tears.

"I'm not sure I can continue doing this," he said. "I'm not sure I have what it takes. How can I confront it all?"

He shuddered at the images in his mind.

A group of them got hold of an elderly black woman and they...

"No!" he cried. "It's so many awful things. I can't face it all. I can't."

"You don't *run* from the pain, the guilt," Nancarrow told him. "That only reinforces it, makes it stronger, makes it rise up and accuse you when you least expect this to happen. The pain is there, I know, but you take that pain and examine it, take every single filthy act you've done or witnessed and never

again allow these to dominate you. Otherwise you will be giving to Satan what he wants most: victory."

Fredrickson chuckled sardonically.

"Satan?" he repeated the name. "I know all about him, you
know. I realize that he's been behind so much of my pain. He
uses guilt as a weapon."

Dalham and Nancarrow were beginning to appreciate
Michael Fredrickson more than they had ever imagined they
would.

"You're coming through loud and clear, Michael," Nancarrow told him. "You tried to hide from your pain by joining a
group of others feeling the same way. You reinforced one
another's misery. You said, 'I'm one of you because I've been
hurt like you all have. Now let's strike back at the generation
that's made us so miserable, at the society that would *allow* it
to happen without protecting us.' You never *had* anyone to
protect you before then, Michael. You never even had a childhood. It was ripped from you."

"But what was I to do?" Fredrickson pleaded. "Nobody ever
told me. I couldn't go to my father. My mother was a hooker.
Any minister I ever approached turned away in disgust because
they just couldn't believe what I was telling them about the
old man. If you break somebody's legs, you can't blame him if
he doesn't walk properly. That's what it was like with me.
Aryans Underground seemed to offer me everything I wanted."

Nor was it entirely negative. There had been wonderful
moments when he would sit with half a dozen or so of the
other skinheads, and they would talk about the experiences
that had driven them into the movement in the first place.
The perspective was wrong, but the therapy was correct.

"That part was what I needed," Fredrickson admitted, "on
one level at least. But later I began to see that it was actually
making me worse because—"

"—it associated relief with the need to strike back," Nancarrow gently interrupted, "to terrorize as a purgative for the poison that had built up inside you."

Some of it, Fredrickson thought, *like robbing little convenience stores, smashing synagogue windows and scrawling swastikas on the entrances, yeah, some of it was exciting. But the rest...*

"If they offered you companionship, the rest, then why did you betray them?" Nancarrow asked candidly.

Fredrickson winced at that word.

"They betrayed me actually," he replied.

"There was all this talk about hating the Jews and the blacks and the rest and, later, when it went beyond window-breaking and such, you began to see the real dark side, is that it?"

"Right! Especially when that camp was built and...and those people...those people brought in..."

"You saw clearly how evil the whole thing was?" Nancarrow asked.

Fredrickson nodded slowly.

"How did they go about getting the prisoners?" Dalham probed.

"That was what required the most planning, coordination," Fredrickson replied. "Everything was handled from a central office."

Dalham was taken by surprise with that one.

"I thought the movement was essentially quite loosely-knit, with units in various regions but no real overall master planner unless you count that guy in Tucson."

"He's involved but not the real power."

From the ghettos, Fredrickson remembered.

A prime source. Old men, wrecked shells of human beings. Mostly blacks and some hispanics. The Jews didn't come as much from the ghettos, the skid rows, because not all Jews looked like Jews, not all of them had hooked noses and beady eyes.

"We got them from parks, from homes we broke into, from hospitals and from nursing homes," Fredrickson told them. "The nursing homes were the best. The staff and police assumed they just got confused and wandered off."

"What happened when you guessed wrong?" Dalham asked. "When you thought you had a Jew but it turned out you didn't?"

"They were put in the camp anyway."

"But even from the viewpoint of Aryans Underground, they weren't your enemies!"

"They would have *become* enemies because they would have been able to tell the local cops and the Feds about us. We couldn't just turn them loose."

Dalham had trouble sleeping that night, which was to be expected. He dreamed of a United States plunged into a satanic maelstrom, with the senile elderly herded like cattle into makeshift gas chambers, then shoveled into crematoria put together from parts of ovens, radar, and other junk.

And nothing could be done in this nightmare. The enemy showed demonic cleverness, striking at unexpected places at unexpected times. Aided by provocateurs. Financed by dirty millions paid from the coffers of a few National Socialist fanatics for whom the passage of years since the Third Reich had only heightened their determination to do it right the next time.

Ultimately there was national panic...

During the days to follow, Fredrickson told Dalham and Nancarrow a great deal else. What he could not yet face was what had happened at a seance one night.

"Their attitude toward me started to change after that," he said.

"Why?" Dalham asked.

The three of them were walking slowly as they talked, the retreat a beautiful, isolated place, serene and undisturbed by the surrounding world of neon and cars and frenetic activity.

"Because I didn't *participate*," Fredrickson observed. "They wanted me to become one of them in a deeper way than I had been until that point."

"But what could be deeper than all that you had shared with them so far?" Nancarrow asked.

"It was a baptism, no, it was more than that, really. It was a..."

He stopped walking.

"Please, I'll tell you everything else but I...I can't face that...that..."

"Evil, Michael?" Dalham asked. "Something terribly evil went on that night, didn't it?"

Fredrickson looked at the older man.

"More evil than what you saw at Dachau II!" he said.

"How could that be?" Nancarrow asked.

"Because that camp and all the other things they planned sprang from what went on that one night."

...all the other things they planned.

Fredrickson laid out for them all the details of which he was aware.

Especially the role of Rudolf Stier—a continually lingering presence *in absentia*.

"He visited the camp just once, in the early stages," Fredrickson had said earlier. "I caught only a glimpse of him."

A restless man, he remembered, *short, with eyes that pierced.*

Telling them about grand visions of a recreated world order, raised from the ashes of American democracy...

A new Reich.

"Stier was supposed to be the architect."

"In his own image?" Dalham asked.

Fredrickson hesitated at that.

"I'm not sure. I think he might not have been the one."

"Who else then?"

"I never knew."

There were growing munitions stocks in various regions across the country.

"The weapons are being bought by Stier along with financing from wealthy Nazi sympathizers."

"In the United States or back in Europe?" the FBI agent asked.

"Here! You have no idea how *many* there are. They outnumber closet Communists by a huge margin. Some of them used to be Communists. When they found that movement faltering, they switched over."

"Any philosophy, so long as it is dedicated to the overthrow of this country, is that it?"

The other nodded.

"But not just the United States," Michael Fredrickson said. "They want it all—they want the whole world under their control sooner or later. Europe will fall, according to their plan. Asia. Australia. Everywhere!"

"But it starts here."

"Yes."

"Don't the others know that they'll be thrown aside eventually, and that the big boys will take over, guys who aren't interested in having their empire continue on the uncertain backs of a bunch of kids, no matter how effective those kids might have been proven to be by then?"

"I don't think so. They're so hungry for vengeance that it's blinding them."

The three were quiet for a bit, emotions calming down. And then there was much more that Michael Fredrickson had to tell them, including where the skinhead leaders could be found.

Part III

Power, like a desolating pestilence,
Pollutes whate'er it touches;
   and obedience,
Bane of all genius, virtue,
   freedom, truth,
Makes slaves of men, and of
   the human frame
A monstrous automaton.
—Anonymous

30

THE strange man was ready to give the word. Everyone was in place. It all had been planned for a long time.

He looked at the map given to him by his number two man. On it were round stickers at the points that would be hit.

"Are you pleased, sir?" the other asked.

He nodded as he said, "Indeed I am. Does T.M. have everything ready there?"

"He does, and our field man in Georgia."

He grimaced.

"I wish he'd upgrade that newspaper a bit. It creates a bad image."

"You are correct, sir, it does."

"Later, I suppose. Now..."

There would be outbursts in half a dozen states, spreading to others in a matter of days.

"In the streets of poisoned America!" he exclaimed. "The gutters will flow with the blood of all the niggers, the kikes, those pope-loving wops," he said.

"And the spicks, too," the number two man added.

"Yes! We go after them all, every impure one of them. Himmler, Goebbels, the others all set?"

"To the last one!"

"And you?"

"All the way, sir."

"You're the one planning this. Be sure it goes smoothly."

"I will. My neck is on the line."

"That it is, that it is."

31

DURING the 24 hours just before the FBI was able to get together a group of agents to go after the skinhead leaders, part of the plan Michael Fredrickson had told them about was activated, leading many within the Bureau to agonize for years afterward about their failure to act sooner.

Another town went up in flames—west of the Mississippi, near the Mexican border. The old frame buildings, unchanged for many decades, ignited easily.

It wasn't clear after that where Aryans Underground would strike next.

Until a certain university in New England was torched.

Dalham, at his temporary headquarters in Oregon, saw the report come over the fax. A short while later he received a top secret video made after the fire was put out.

Total devastation at the university. Scores of students died in their dorms.

A narrator intoned: "In retrospect we can see that this particular institution was, shall we say, a logical choice for the skinheads. A significant percentage of its student population was Jewish or black. A racially bigoted student group was kicked out last month."

Then evidence was presented for the rise of bigotry in the ivory towers of the nation's colleges and universities.

"A black student named Charlene Washington returned to her dorm one evening to find her clothes soaked in bleach and the word NIGGER painted on one wall.

"Later, under a rug, she discovered WE WANT YOU DEAD, NIGGER scribbled on the floor. She collapsed and had to be rushed to a nearby hospital to be treated for 'emotional traumatization.'"

The incident was typical, and only the tip of the iceberg. Yet blacks were not the only target.

"Members of the Hillel Foundation at the University of Kansas found a sheet of paper taped to the door of their dorm room. On it were the words: 'Jew-Boys, get out. We're going to burn your Torahs.'

"At Bryn Mawr, freshman Christine Rivera found an anonymous note slipped under her door: 'Hey, Spic, if you and your kind can't handle the work here, don't blame it on the racial thing. Why don't you just get out? We'd all be a lot happier.'"

Dalham discovered that more than 250 colleges and universities, including top schools such as Brown, Smith and Stanford, reported racist incidents ranging—according to one national publication—"from swastikas painted on the walls to violent attacks and death threats."

More recruits for Aryans Underground! Dalham thought.

And it was getting worse. At many institutions, reforms were given lip service but no real support, aided by what was called "institutionalized bigotry"—especially apparent in the lack of minority faculty members at a number of colleges and universities.

Fertile ground for a growing number of skinheads!

Minutes later, Dalham received a call.

It was time.

They found the isolated site easily. Michael Fredrickson's directions had been accurate down to the last turn in a winding road.

They're so confident of their secrecy that they have no guards, Dalham thought, *no elaborate alarm system.*

When Fredrickson had told him what to expect, Dalham could scarcely believe it.

"You mean they're so arrogant they think they're unstoppable?" he asked.

"That's about it," Fredrickson remarked. "Give a group of delinquents tens of millions of dollars, and they'll think anything."

And that kind of money was only part of the bankroll available. The skinheads were but one batallion in the overall war.

"Faulty weapons parts," Fredrickson had added. "Why do you think there's been such a rash of them?"

"Agents inside the defense contractor firms?"

"That's right. So much attention on Communists and Middle Eastern agents and—"

"—next to nothing on neo-Nazis?" Dalham finished the sentence.

Fredrickson agreed.

"For decades we all thought it was over except for a few splinter groups," Dalham mused aloud.

"And some wild kids who would *never* be able to get their act together on a national scale," Fredrickson added.

Enter Rudolf Stier.

The cabin itself was empty.

"They're gone," said Adam Gerber, another FBI agent, speaking the obvious.

"Question is," said Dalham, "have they moved to another location? If they found out Fredrickson is in custody, they might begin to worry that he would snitch."

There were now six agents in the cabin, half a dozen outside on the grounds, several more waiting in a van.

Dalham surveyed the interior.

A fireplace. Several bare wood chairs. A table. An old wood-burning stove.

"*Listen!*"

Gerber had frozen at a sound he thought he heard.

Chanting...

Dalham noticed it then.

"Where?" he said, then realized exactly where.

Below. Under their feet.

Dalham kicked a small area rug aside.

A trap door.

He opened it. Steps.

The six agents went down as quietly as possible.

A tunnel.

The chanting was coming from further down.

None of them was prepared for what they saw as they entered the cavern at the end of the tunnel.

Four skinheads.

Each was holding a knife in one hand.

In the background was a large photo of Adolf Hitler.

To one side were three children, terrified, tied to one another. They saw the men storming in and began to scream for help.

"Look at their *eyes*!" Gerber said.

Dalham saw the expression immediately, like four subjects of a master hypnotist, with eyes looking up at the intruders yet not comprehending that the agents were there.

The agents walked a step closer. The skinheads were gathered in a circle, surrounding a now still and frail little body.

"They've already killed one!" Gerber exclaimed. "They've already..."

Emotion choked off his words.

Despite the screaming, despite the intruders, still the skinheads acted as though they were alone, and continued their awful ceremony.

"No!" Gerber screamed, years of FBI conditioning gone in an instant.

He lunged forward, knocking the skinheads to one side and the other. None resisted. They all fell backward, still clutching the knives, still zombie-like in their stupor.

The other agents managed to subdue Gerber, and he soon regained control of himself.

"Maggie Fincher was a friend of mine!" he said as he stood, half-sobbing. "So is her husband. I love the whole family. She had a couple of beautiful children. When I see this being done to innocent, helpless..."

Dalham and the others understood how he felt. The incident wouldn't go on anyone's report. For a long time Gerber had been a top-notch agent; his career shouldn't be endangered for the sake of that one moment.

They all stood looking at the four skinheads each acting as though slowly emerging from a hypnotic state. Their knives were confiscated.

The remaining children were led out of the cavern by several of the agents. One of them, a little girl, pigtailed and freckled, inexplicably broke away from the others and put her arms around Dalham's leg.

He bent down, picked her up and hugged her.

"You look like my daddy!" she exclaimed.

Dalham blushed, realizing that he hadn't held a child for many years.

The little girl smiled and kissed him on the cheek.

He handed her over gently to one of the other agents. She seemed reluctant to go at first.

"Your daddy will be waiting for you," he told her.

"Promise?" she asked.

"I promise."

He maintained eye contact with her until she was gone from the cavern.

You have a father to return to, little one, he thought. *I have been a father like him, but I have no one like you to return to me.*

One of the agents had broken away from the group and was investigating a smaller, narrower corridor that jutted off from the cavern where they were standing.

He came stumbling back less than five minutes later.

"Barker, you look lousy!" Dalham said. "What's wrong?"

The skinheads were led outside, left in the custody of the agents who had been keeping the grounds under surveillance. Then Dalham, Gerber and Barker went back inside after being assured by Barker that no other men were needed.

"It's not a life-threatening situation," he told them.

He cleared his throat.

"You'll see for yourselves."

After the skinheads were taken to a suitable place for incarceration, Dalham remained behind with Gerber and a couple of other agents to go over the property, especially the extensive underground tunnel system.

Gerber noticed an old clipping in one corner:

WAS HITLER'S BODY
ACTUALLY BURNED
OUTSIDE HIS BUNKER?

"Old story," Dalham remarked.

"I know that, Kent," Gerber replied, somewhat irritably. "But what's it doing here?"

"I have no idea. It's just a tattered old clipping, as far as I'm concerned."

He realized he had spoken sharply, and apologized.

"Accepted," Gerber said. "This spot's enough to fray anybody's nerves."

Eventually they came upon the place Barker wanted to show them: a large cavern piled to the ceiling with armaments.

"Amazing!" Gerber said.

"Look at this label," Dalham said as he pointed to one on the side of a nearby carton.

Gerber bent down to examine it.

"Hamburg. It never ends with these guys, does it?"

Dalham shook his head. "Apparently not, my friend. Apparently not."

Further exploration of the underground nerve center revealed files that contained the location of other skinhead "cells" around the country, into which had been poured substantial reserves of weapons, ammunition, sophisticated monitoring devices and other materials.

A concerted effort by several governmental agencies, spearheaded by the FBI, resulted in nearly simultaneous attacks against the various locations.

The resistance was savage. Fatalities were heavy on both sides.

But ultimately all the cells were nullified, with thousands of skinheads taken into custody.

32

IT wasn't as difficult to meet as either of them thought it would be. Their hatred and bitterness already had been dealt with in moments when each was alone, when each could turn to the Lord and find relief from the emotions that had been poisoning them.

For Michael Fredrickson, it was a great deal more awkward to get on his knees and talk to God. As he told Dalham during a walk the two of them had taken a couple of weeks after he returned to the retreat, "God seemed to have deserted me a long time ago."

But that changed. Martin Nancarrow was an expert at getting people to work through harmful and encumbering defenses and to embrace some needed truths. And despite all the pain Fredrickson had undergone, the fact that he had joined Aryans Underground in the first place showed his desperate search for self-identity and self-acceptance.

Now the direction of that search had been realigned, and Fredrickson's outlook started to alter with surprising quickness, at least enough to enable him to face that moment when he would meet Solomon Hillel Schechter again.

They came face-to-face at the gazebo that had become such a central place for Michael Fredrickson: out in the open, a quiet place where he had tried to take his life and where the pieces of that life were now being put back together.

"I'm nervous," he told Dalham. "I'm ashamed."

"So is Sollie," Dalham remarked.

"Sollie?"

"That's his nickname."

"Oh."

Fredrickson found it difficult to realize the old Jew would be ashamed.

"Why would he? He did nothing wrong."

"That's not quite the case, Michael. He's spent more than 40 years lost in a tangled forest of hatred. You provided the way out. He knows now that hatred is seldom justified, that it becomes a cancer, a cancer that rotted away his personality, his emotions, reducing life to a bleak level of existence."

A frail-looking figure could be seen at the far end of the pathway leading to the gazebo.

"I don't know if I can do this," Fredrickson said, his face pale.

"According to Dr. Nancarrow, Sollie said the same thing yesterday when they talked by phone. Put your fear under the blood of Jesus Christ."

...put your fear under the blood of Jesus Christ.

A strange thought for Michael Fredrickson.

He had thought of blood before only in the context of spilling his father's, of going through with the Aryan dream of killing hordes of Jews, blacks, others.

But now blood was to be a symbol of cleansing!

The old Jew was only a short distance away now.

Schechter saw Fredrickson and smiled as he waved at the young man.

"He seems so friendly," Fredrickson whispered. "Why is he so friendly?"

"Because you were kind to him at the camp, Michael," Dalham said. "And he thinks he hasn't known much of that in his life. Now..."

Dalham hesitated.

"What's wrong?" Fredrickson asked.

"Nothing's wrong. It's something beautiful, Michael, something that reminds me what Christianity should be all about. You see, he told Nancarrow that he's learning to love you."

"But he doesn't know me at all. He has no idea what I'm really like."

"He knows, Michael, what *he's* like, and love is the key to changing him at the same time"—he looked directly at Fredrickson—"it changes you."

Schechter, with Nancarrow by his side, was only a few feet away.

Fredrickson walked forward, stood in front of the old Jew, then burst into tears.

"Forgive me," he said, "please forgive me."

"For being kind—is that what I should forgive you for?" Schechter asked.

"For *ever* hating what you are."

"I forgive you, as God forgives us both."

He reached out his arms slowly and put them around Fredrickson.

"I don't know how much longer I will have in this world, Michael, but I want you to spend that time with me...as my son."

Suddenly the tears were not Michael Fredrickson's alone.

33

MEETING Schechter was not all the former skinhead decided he would have to do.

"I've got to," he told Dalham. "I don't think I'll ever be completely free until I do."

"But what about your mother?" Dalham replied. "Shouldn't you be trying to find her?"

"Yes, I will. But I need to face my father first. I need to get rid of that baggage."

The two of them told Nancarrow what Fredrickson wanted to do.

"I think it's precisely the right thing!" Nancarrow responded. "I think it's one of the two missing pieces in this puzzle."

Next they told Schechter.

"Do you want me to go with you, Michael?" he asked.

"No, Sollie. It's something I have to face myself."

Schechter smiled.

"The Lord will be with you every step of the way."

"I know."

Dalham had been able easily to track down Albert Fredrickson through headquarters in Washington, D.C.

An asylum that was less than a day's trip from the retreat!

Dalham thought about that coincidence, but decided it wasn't so bizarre. Michael Fredrickson had never really strayed very far from where he had been born. There was a strong Aryans Underground faction in the Pacific Northwest, full of restless, disaffected young people ranging from their teens to their mid-20s, proverbial time bombs ready to explode. They haunted the region in search of victims as well as members.

Neither had his father gone far. Quite mentally ill, he was never very logical in his actions. Despite a long record of arrests for an assortment of crimes ranging from petty theft to assault, he decided to stay in that area and not try to get a fresh start elsewhere.

The asylum to which he was ultimately confined was only a few miles from his son's childhood home in a small town in rural Oregon.

Albert Fredrickson.

He had been confined to the institution ever since the accident.

Michael Fredrickson stood in the doorway to his father's room.

Empty just then.

The elder Fredrickson had been taken outside for some fresh air, and when the nurse was momentarily distracted, he had gotten up from his wheelchair and started to wander off.

"Sometimes he's alert, coherent, can navigate pretty well; other times he's a virtual catatonic," the asylum's director, Wayne Bowder, had told him. "We'll bring him back in a bit. Why don't you wait here?"

The room was painted a light gray. There was a metal bed, a nightstand next to it, plus a dresser and a couple of chairs.

Michael walked over to the dresser and saw two photographs in plastic frames resting on top.

One was of Natalie and Albert Fredrickson, looking quite happy.

What a charade, Michael thought. *What a lousy charade!*

The other photo was of his father holding him on his knee. His father was smiling; Michael was not.

Just an hour or so before, you'd... he started to recall, then shut off the memory, wincing a bit.

He opened the top drawer of the cabinet.

Inside was a diary.

His father's.

He lifted it out and began to leaf through the pages.

> I washed my hands real good today, first with soap,
> then with some special stuff for difficult stains.
> My hands look clean now.
> But they aren't.

Several pages later, he read:

> Michael's face is always before me in my dreams. He
> is crying. I want to reach out and beg his forgiveness
> but my sickness won't let me.

Michael sat down on the nearest chair, reading page after page of his father's diary. There was so much more that startled him, that showed a man torn between guilt and a compulsive perversion.

Sickness grabbed Michael's stomach as he read through more of the diary.

It hasn't been just me, he thought. *Dad paid others to be with him.*

His eyes focused on the next page:

> God knows I want to stop. But I don't know the
> cure.

Michael repeated those first six words.

God knows I want to stop...

Michael closed the diary and put it back in the drawer. He noticed something else inside just as he was closing it.

A pair of baby shoes.

He looked at the soles.

On the left shoe were the words: Michael Fredrickson, my beloved son. On the right: A gift from God.

He put them back in the drawer and closed it abruptly.

How could he profess love, and yet give me only torment? What happened to my—?

His thoughts were interrupted by Bowder's voice.

He turned, saw the director standing behind a wheelchair, which he then rolled into the room.

"Spend as much time as you want," Bowder told him. "If you need anything..."

He pointed to the buzzer.

Then the director left, and Michael was alone with the man he had hated most of his life.

Albert was sitting in the wheelchair, apparently unaware of his surroundings.

"Do you know I'm here?" Michael said, standing directly in front of him.

There was no reaction.

Michael threw his head back, hot tears streaming down his cheeks.

"Do you *realize* what I went through?" he shouted. "Do you *understand* what I suffered?"

He had intended to vent all the feelings that had been bottled up inside him over the months, releasing the poison once and for all.

Beautiful Savior...

"What?" he said aloud.

Those words! In his mind, like a distant echo that was coming closer, closer, closer.

Others also.

I'd rather have Jesus...

Where could he have heard such words? Not from his father.

He sank to his knees.

What's happening, Lord? I've done nothing to honor You.

And then he had a mental image of Sollie there in that camp, shivering, afraid, looking so hopeless.

I gave you extra food, water. And now you've come back into my life.

He looked up at his father. For an instant he thought he saw the man's gaze shift away from him, as though his father had been studying him.

Be ye therefore merciful, as your Father also is merciful.

From the New Testament they'd confiscated at the camp, the same New Testament they'd taken from Sollie!

"But how *can* I be merciful to a man who wrecked my life?" he asked aloud. "How can I do what I know I came here to do? Look at him, Lord. How can I forgive *him?*"

The residue of feelings from long years of disgust and hatred had entered that room with him. He now confronted the man who had sexually abused him throughout his child-hood.

But there was suddenly something else.

His father was crying, his whole body shaking.

"*Good!*" Michael screamed. "That's what I do everytime I..."

More words came into his mind.

When peace like a river attendeth my way...

Peace? How could he feel peace now? How?

He closed his eyes.

Take my mind, my heart, my soul, Lord, mold them with Your loving hands. Open my eyes to what You want me to see.

He felt a feather-light touch on his shoulder. Then it was gone.

He glanced up at his father and saw a man looking much older than his physical years, his hair almost entirely grey, his skin quite pale, his head tilted to one side and slightly forward. There were heavy dark circles under his eyes. The backs of his hands were covered with the splotches of kidney disease.

"You look so old," he said.

Yes, Albert Fredrickson looked very old then, helpless. The crying had stopped, and he sank back against the wheelchair, his lips moving but with words spoken so softly that they couldn't be heard immediately.

Michael stood, walked over to his father, bent down, trying to understand.

He couldn't.

Then he saw something in the palm of the man's left hand.

A photograph.

Of Albert Fredrickson's son.

Michael gently opened the fingers of that hand, and took the photo and examined it.

At the bottom were three words:

I love you...

"But, Dad, how could that be?" he said. "How could you do the things to me that you did?"

Another voice then.

Michael turned around, saw Bowder again, standing in the doorway.

"That's where the sickness came in," he said. "That's where the nightmare he'd experienced during his childhood had messed him up inside. We may never know the full extent of his psychosis."

"So you're saying he couldn't help himself?"

"I hate to offer that simply as an excuse, Michael. Nothing he did should *ever* be excused. It is, however, perhaps an explanation...about the only one we may ever find."

"Can I stay for a little longer?" Michael asked.

"Absolutely. There's no time limit."

"Thanks."

After the director left, Michael turned back to his father, smiled.

Several hours passed.

Dalham wasn't becoming impatient. He had been spending the time on several calls to headquarters, though what he was planning had begun before the two of them had ever arrived at the asylum. He was again grateful for what his status as a Special Agent could enable him to accomplish. Considering what he was attempting, the length of time proved to be a blessing.

He pushed back from the desk he had been allowed to use and walked down the corridor to Albert Fredrickson's room, peering around the edge of the doorway.

Michael was sitting at his father's feet, holding the man's hand. There was still no response.

Michael sensed that Dalham was there.

He turned. His cheeks were wet.

"Could you arrange for me to stay here a few days?" he asked.

Dalham smiled.

"Of course," he replied.

Michael nodded.

"That's good," he said, "that's good."

He hesitated, then: "Tell Sollie I'll be back soon. I hope he understands."

"I don't think you need worry about that."

Michael gently tapped his father's hand.

"Maybe I can find Mom someday. Maybe we all can make it."

Dalham heard someone speaking.

It was Bowder.

"She's here," the man said simply.

Michael overheard him.

"What's he saying, sir?" the young man asked.

There was the sound of footsteps, the hint of perfume. Dalham stepped aside.

Michael's eyes widened.

And his father's.

Part IV

Our fathers and ourselves
sowed dragon's teeth.
Our children know and
suffer the armed men.
—Stephen Vincent Benét

34

KENT Dalham knew enough about the crisis to realize the extent of what had been averted. But not everyone did, of course; the media got the essential facts straight, but not much more than that.

> "These skinheads used to be quite small groups. The recent necessity to attack them en masse showed that Federal authorities were greatly concerned about reports that they were in the process of banding together to start a war. But now it has been stopped in its tracks."

That quote stuck in Dalham's mind because, though it was close to the truth, it reflected the conventional wisdom that the threat had passed and a societal sigh of relief could be breathed.

...stopped in its tracks.

He looked at the reports on his desk at headquarters.

We've only delayed things, he thought.

He tapped the report on top of the pile, the one with HEINRICH FLICK on the title page. Inside was a recitation of facts he already knew, but there were others. When one of Stier's residences was raided, this one in upstate New York, agents found a vast library of historical books, many dealing with the Nazi Youth Corps during World War II, tracing its origins back as far as the sixteenth century!

> "At the very core, whether centuries or decades ago, was an emphasis upon paramilitary training, *which they could always rely upon when necessary.* This began after the French Revolution as a defense against the mistreatment of German youth by Napoleon, reemerged in the

midst of World War I and exploded in full force during World War II against the perceived enemy—not a single individual, as with Napoleon, but a single people, the Jews."

Other books dealt with mob psychology, one called *The Business of Revolution.*

In the basement was a cache of explosives, plus certain parts that if assembled correctly could create a nuclear device.

But Stier himself was gone.

As always...

Dalham put the reports aside, glanced at his calendar.

Two more days.

He understood why he was picked to do the next job. Such things were in his family background! And he had been a key figure in the apprehension of the leaders.

Now the next step.

Interviewing the four of them.

I'm supposed to peel them apart and see exactly what started them on the road to their revolution.

He shivered at the possible disclosures that would be thrown at him, not at all sure how he would deal with what he might hear.

35

KENT Dalham was tired as he drove up to the prison. His ankles still hurt, and though he was otherwise well-recovered, his level of adrenalin seemed to be lagging a bit.

He knew somehow that it went deeper than his body's metabolism. He was to do a psychological surgery on those so committed to bigotry and hatred, so committed to revolution and violence that they were obsessed by a mission that consumed virtually every thought, every word and deed, every moment of their lives.

To look into their very souls, he thought. *That's my job, to step into a pit of vipers.*

After half a century nothing was different. His father had been assigned to interrogating the original group of monsters, to try to find out what was going on inside their heads.

I suppose, Kent, many people envy me. A certain mythology has grown up around the Nazis. I met Hermann Goering! Some folks seem to feel that I missed the boat by not getting his autograph!

It was an assignment not without its price for Arthur James Dalham. For weeks afterward, he could not sleep well.

"The delusion!" he would say. "The demonic delusion that eradicated any sense of decency, any shred of compassion. More than one spoke with little or no emotion; they were killing machines, son—cold, efficient, indeed monstrously efficient.

"And yet the brilliance most of them possessed! If earlier in their lives they had turned a different way, gotten in with a crowd other than the National Socialists, the whole world would have been different today."

Now in the 1990s, not the 1940s, once again Jews had been blamed for everything that was unfortunate in the lives of their tormentors.

The young man's face was covered with perspiration as he ranted, his nostrils flaring:

"They're scum, human garbage. They have grabbed control of the banking system. They dominate the media. We are here to terminate them, to get America back to its roots."

Now the situation was reversed. The leaders commanding those who had imprisoned him, however briefly or primitively, were now incarcerated, and *he* was going to interrogate them.

He had to admit that he was gloating somewhat, wanting to rub their noses in what had happened, the presumed collapse of their revolution. But he couldn't allow pure emotion to affect his conduct over the next few days. He had to be objective, analytical, had to put outrage in some inaccessible part of himself.

Before, I had to face their hatred, he told himself. *Now I have to put it under a microscope, understand it and see whether it can be stopped from spreading.*

That last thought was the most unnerving of all.

All terrorist acts had stopped. But the silence alone didn't totally reassure Dalham.

What if I fail in getting to the nucleus of all this, finding the hows and the whys and the rest? What if others smarter than I am also fail? What next? Cancer undetected can be fatal.

A couple of minutes after he parked the car, he was taken to meet warden Elliott Lewisohn.

As he walked down one long corridor after another, he noticed the guards, several of the prisoners.

Tense.

He had been to prisons before, many times in fact, and while none were scenes of unbridled joviality, he had never encountered one with such an atmosphere of tension, not even San Quentin just before a riot had broken out.

Finally he approached the warden's office and stepped inside.

The man sitting at the desk directly ahead was large, his weight probably approaching 300 pounds. But he was quite tall and the bulk was well distributed, just the sort of individual to intimidate almost anyone in a prison.

Lewisohn got up from behind the desk and greeted Dalham heartily.

"I admired your father," the warden said. "Remarkable individual."

"That he was, sir," Dalham replied.

"Cut the sir, please. Call me Elliott."

Dalham relaxed.

"Thanks, Elliott."

They engaged in pleasantries for a couple of minutes, and then Dalham asked, "How is it working out with the new prisoners?"

Lewisohn's manner changed.

"Too early to tell," he replied, barely opening his mouth, as though the words were being forced out. "They're safe for the time being."

"You said 'for the time being'?" Dalham probed. "How did you mean that, Elliott? Have you some reason to expect trouble?"

Lewisohn's temper flared.

"Considering the *type* of prisoner we are referring to, yes!" he said, this time spitting the words out.

Instantly regretting his manner, Lewisohn apologized. As the two continued talking, Dalham realized the unique position the other man was in, unique and uncomfortable.

"I am a Jew," Lewisohn remarked. "At a very young age I endured what has come to be called 'the Holocaust.' I lost my parents at Chelmno, one of the lesser-known camps as history treats it, but actually a main extermination center in Poland."

Dalham indeed was surprised, admitting that he hadn't heard of it.

"This isn't unusual," Lewisohn told him. "It was reserved *exclusively* for Jews, mostly the sick ones. It was so ghastly there that the guards received a bonus of 15 *reichsmarks* for each day that they remained."

"Due to the exterminations?"

"Not entirely. Other camps were larger and gassed many, many more victims, yet no extra *reichsmarks* were paid, as far as I know. At Chelmno, however, the guards were constantly exposed to infections as a result of all the diseases carried by the inmates."

"I suppose the Nazis didn't want to contaminate the healthy work forces at other camps."

"Precisely. Once inmates died of natural causes or being gassed, their bodies were put into an efficient *Knochenmuhle*. That's a fancy word for a machine with a simple purpose."

"I know what it was," Dalham hastily interpolated. "My father was once very explicit. No need to go into detail. There were other such machines at other camps."

Lewisohn had started to say something else but stopped in mid-sentence and looked directly at Dalham.

"I am quite impressed!" he said, his eyes sparkling with appreciation. "But then perhaps I shouldn't be. Your father must have been a wonderful resource of knowledge."

He paused, then continued: "But there were no other such machines as big as this one, I assure you. It could handle quite a workload."

He rubbed his eyes for a moment.

"The inmates who somehow survived, their health returning, were then shipped out to other camps, to serve the Nazi cause, and not incidentally, that of some of the German industrialists."

"I have heard about that connection from others."

"Particularly in light of what has been happening over the past few weeks, I suppose."

"That's right, Elliott."

He stood suddenly.

"Kent—I may call you that, I trust?"

"Absolutely."

"Good! Kent, would you walk outside with me? It's become very stuffy in here."

Dalham nodded without reluctance; he was feeling similarly.

The prison yard was empty then. In the distance, snow-capped mountain ranges formed an incongruously majestic backdrop.

"Cold air, Kent, clean and pure," Lewisohn observed.

"Not the same back at Chelmno, was it?" Dalham asked softly, knowing that the trauma would never completely leave those who underwent it.

"Oh, no, not the same at all! Awful odors then, Kent."

He was visibly shuddering.

"I was very ill, to be sure," Lewisohn continued. "But my mother and father were much worse. When it was apparent that they would *never* become labor slaves, the Nazis gassed them and put them on the conveyor belt leading into the *Knochenmuhle*. But..."

He stopped, turning his back on Dalham.

"Around the side, please," he asked, "where there are no windows."

Dalham followed the other man.

Lewisohn leaned back against the brick wall.

"I watched their bodies approaching the opening into which they would disappear. Kent, I...I saw my mother *move*! Ever so slightly, ever so..."

He was overcome again, unable just then to continue.

"Elliott, you don't have to finish," Dalham said as he rested a hand on the other's shoulder.

"Oh, but I do," said Lewisohn, "oh, but I do. You see, that memory keeps coming back periodically. I try to forget it but it returns, and it returns most often when least expected. And then I must find someone else who will listen because...because it helps me to talk out what happened, like cleansing a wound. And yet for me that wound never fully heals, and then I must sponge it out again through telling someone, through releasing that awful moment into the air. Maybe...maybe that's it, Kent; the good clean air taking away the awful poison yet again."

He shook himself as though disposing of some snow that had clung to him in the midst of a blizzard.

"My mother turned her head ever so slightly, opening her mouth. Could she have seen me then? I can never be sure. But I knew she still lived! My mother alive! I screamed, 'She's alive, she's alive! Stop it! Get her out of there!' The soldiers heard me, and one of them went up to my mother, examined her quickly, and then hit her with the butt of his rifle. Seconds later, she had disappeared into that...that..."

His face was white at the recollection.

"What happened next?" Dalham asked gently, after waiting a few moments for the other man to calm down.

"Few realize it but Himmler himself had never been fully aware of what was going on at Chelmno. Sooner or later, though, word leaked out. He had ordered that the Knochenmuhle be dismantled, but it remained in service until 1942. Himmler, angered when he found out, sent a special commando unit to Chelmno with orders to destroy the machine and get rid of the mass graves by fire and dynamite, graves that were little more than repositories for what was left of the bodies after that evil machine had its way with them."

"Himmler had a streak of conscience?"

"Who can say? Was it simply a reaction to an order disobeyed? Concern about the harm to the Nazi image? That's a wild one, isn't it? Chelmno wasn't a national camp as such but strictly a local 'enterprise' set up by *Reichstatthalter* Arthur Greiser in conjunction with the Polish police. Or had Himmler, upon learning of what was going on, been unusually sickened by the truth, as he was later when he visited the Auschwitz camps—and then retaliated by humiliating Greiser and others who were involved?"

"Were you shipped elsewhere?" Dalham asked.

"Yes, by special orders of Heinrich Himmler."

"*What?*"

"Apparently he got word of what had happened to my mother."

"Of course he would never *free* you altogether!"

"Of course! That would set a precedent. But he did make sure I was sent to Theresienstadt."

"The so-called humane camp."

"Yes. Jews often tried to bribe Gestapo agents to change their papers so they could go to Theresienstadt," Lewisohn said, grinning slightly at the other's display of knowledge. "In time, though, it changed, becoming nearly as bad as the others."

"And then?" Dalham asked.

"I managed to escape, and lived with Polish partisans until the war ended. I learned a great deal about explosives. I was small and light on my feet in those days, kept thin by the rigors of life on the run, and proved to be a big help to them. They all became my brothers, my sisters. Many of them had lost their own families, too."

The purging process seemed to be ending.

Elliott Lewisohn stood up straight, smiled sheepishly.

"Forgive me," he said, embarrassed. "They think me so tough here, these inmates do."

"You survived, Elliott. You survived conditions that I wonder whether I could ever have endured. Take the average inmate here. Consider how *he* would have fared."

"None too well," Lewisohn acknowledged.

They turned back toward the prison yard.

"Kent, my friend?" Lewisohn said as they walked.

"Yes?"

"In there is a 22-year-old with the name of Heinrich Himmler."

"I know. This cadre wanted a *total* link with the old regime. That was one of their devices. Each one took a different Nazi's name."

"Kent, it seems to go deeper than that."

They stopped walking.

"What do you mean?" Dalham asked, puzzled.

"He knows *everything* about Himmler. The one named Josef Mengele knows *everything* about the death doctor of Auschwitz. The others know *everything* about their namesakes."

"Careful research, Elliott. What's so special about that?"

"It's *more* than research. Trust me, please. It's far, far deeper than that."

In a few minutes they were back in the warden's office. Lewisohn reached into the center drawer of his desk and took out a single sheet of paper.

"May I read something to you, Kent?" he asked.

"Certainly."

The words came slowly but with underlying passion:

> *I am no child, afraid of darkness.*
> *God has led me through so many*
> *nights with a light of fire.*
> *Surely no darkness is too dark—*
> *   with Him.*
> *When I walk with Him, even the*
> *night shines as the day.*
> *The darkness is as the light...*
> *Egypt, Babylon, Greece, Rome...*
> *Crusade, Black-Death, Exile, Crema-*
> *   torium,*
> *Pharaoh, Haman, Nero, Hitler...*
> *I have lived too long,*
> *experienced too much,*
> *Known too many nights, not to see*
> *That they are, like the day,*
> *Only a moment of eternity.*
> *This night too shall pass,*
> *And in the morning light*
> *We shall behold Thy face, O Lord,*

in righteousness;
And in Thy light shall we see light.

"The Jews are a sad people, Kent," Lewisohn said. "We have our bursts of laughter. We have our parties, our fiddlers on the rooftops. But beneath it all is the sense of being doomed, of always wandering in the wilderness. That was why, at first, there was so little resistance to the Nazis. We seemed to be accepting yet another manifestation of our destiny."

He smiled as he started to put the quotation away.

"But then we invariably bounce back somehow," he said with a bit of wistfulness. "Millions may die yet millions more survive. But not my parents, Kent. It was not the Lord's will that they join me throughout any more years of my life. I have been without them for a long time. Sometimes I can scarcely remember what they looked like when they were well, when they were happy. But I *always* recall, in great detail, my mother's face as she lay on that conveyor belt, life fluttering her eyelids, the pain, the fear that must have consumed her."

He slammed his fist down on the desk.

"That's what happened to my beloved parents, Kent. And yet now instead of rushing out into that corridor with a rifle, and doing the same thing to those who honor human monsters by embracing their very names and following the same cause—if you can dishonor that word by calling it a cause—instead I must pray to God that it is enough for me now simply that the words of a single quotation cool my rage and sustain me in its absence through the long days ahead."

He held out the sheet.

"Would you like to take a copy?" he asked. "I have others. Perhaps those words will have special meaning for you one day."

Dalham thanked him.

"Are you ready to begin?" Elliott Lewisohn asked.

Dalham replied that he was. They left the office, and the warden personally escorted him to the isolated cellblock where the new prisoners were confined.

Dalham hesitated and then went inside that first cell.

The young man named Paul Joseph Goebbels turned and faced him.

36

ONE wing of the maximum security Federal prison had been designated for the new inmates. The men previously incarcerated in those particular quarters were shifted elsewhere, the bulk of them to other facilities altogether.

The attempt at secrecy was total. But criminals, after years on the street and in prison, often develop a special sense, a sense that allows them to pick up on what is going on around them—which is why such a large percentage manage to evade capture for so long. So hints and rumors spread throughout the prison, these of particular interest to the black and Jewish inmates.

"I think I know what's going on," one would say.

"Not that Fascist group," another would reply. "I lost some relatives in the Birkenau section of Auschwitz."

"Here?" a third man, black, would add. "They torched a friend of mine near Dalton, Georgia."

Finally, special guards were stationed in the corridor leading to that wing.

Four men with names borrowed from a brutal Nazi past:

Heinrich Himmler, Paul Joseph Goebbels, Josef Mengele and Reinhard Heydrich.

Most of the media coverage assumed, logically, that they had done nothing more than appropriate their new names out of some twisted desire to be as complete a recreation of the Third Reich as possible, down to the final details.

"It is chilling, this attempt to foster a mirror-image of such a monstrous time," commented the director of the Center for Study of Nazi War Crimes on national television. "They are so zealous in their dedication to it that they even appropriate the names of the original devils."

Media attention seemed to focus on that aspect of the organization's six-month campaign of violence and subversion.

"Here is another example," the director said during the prime-time interview, holding up an amateurishly drawn map, and pointing to one portion of it. "What we know as Poland has been renamed Warthegau by these beasts."

He put down the map and stared directly at the camera.

"That was the official name of western Poland after its annexation by the Third Reich!"

But he didn't stop there.

"Look at this," he added, unrolling some parchment-like paper and holding it in front of him for a close-up. "It is a scroll found at one of their camps. I shall read the words!"

> We are ENEMIES OF THE JEWS, because we are fighters for the freedom of the German people.
> THE JEW IS THE CAUSE AND THE BENEFICIARY OF OUR MISERY. THE JEW IS RESPONSIBLE FOR OUR MISERY AND HE LIVES ON IT.
> That is the reason why we, AS NATIONALISTS and AS SOCIALISTS, oppose the Jew. HE HAS CORRUPTED OUR RACE, FOULED OUR MORALS, UNDERMINED OUR CUSTOMS AND BROKEN OUR POWER. THE JEW IS THE PLASTIC DEMON OF THE DECLINE OF MANKIND. TO BE A CHRISTIAN MEANS: LOVE THY NEIGHBOR AS THYSELF! MY NEIGHBOR IS ONE WHO IS TIED TO ME BY HIS BLOOD. IF I LOVE HIM, THEN I MUST HATE HIS ENEMIES. HE WHO THINKS GERMAN MUST DESPISE THE JEWS.

By the time he was through, the director was weeping.

"Every word of that was written by Paul Joseph Goebbels fifty years ago," he said, his voice shaking. "It was to become a manifesto for the Holocaust. Yet this copy was found not in Berlin or any other German city, but freshly printed in a small town in Illinois!"

There were other exponents of the so-called "Fourth Reich" theory. The deeper Kent Dalham dug into the facts, the more sense that concept made to him when viewed within the twisted logic that obsessed the neo-Nazis and their skinhead surrogates. Yet he wondered about other questions: *Why now?* And most critically, *What gave them their power?*

At that one he shivered as a once-tenuous connection appeared increasingly strong in his mind.

Aparicion.

He never got very far from that word and its implications. In all the weeks of real death, real violence, real destruction and chaos, something as intangible as a young boy's apparent fantasy had nevertheless maintained his attention.

When you see an army of thugs attempt to turn a midwestern American town into a replica of a bomb-leveled German town, he thought, *that stark reality should make stories of phantoms and apparitions lose their potency and be filed away as delusions.*

And yet what else could explain, fifty years ago and now, the rare ferocity of what had happened?

Goebbels.

The young man facing him was short, thin-faced, quite pale.

He was not more than 20 years old. Dalham noticed that he walked with a limp.

"I have been put in charge of the investigation surrounding the events of the past six months," Dalham said.

"What is your name?" Goebbels asked.

"Detective Kent Dalham."

"English?"

Dalham nodded.

"At least they sent no Jew," the other replied, smiling. "At least they did that."

"Why do you call yourself Paul Joseph Goebbels?"

"Because I am...," he started to say, then stopped himself. After clearing his throat, he added, "Because Herr Goebbels was a great man."

"You call him *great?*"

"I do. He and Bormann were loyal to the end."

"But he committed suicide," Dalham interjected. "Before that, he ordered the deaths of his wife and six children. Is such a man great?"

"Acts of necessity."

"That's the same discredited defense other Nazis used at the Nuremberg Trial. It didn't hold water then nor does it now. Goebbels was considered perhaps the only true intellectual in the entire Nazi hierarchy. How *can* you offer the doctrine of necessity as a viable issue? That is supposed to cover it all? Whatever is necessary, is. Whatever isn't, isn't."

"Your last two sentences express it well, Kent Dalham."

A pause.

"You walk with a limp," Dalham observed.

Goebbels was silent, a haunted expression settling on his face, the dark circles somehow deeper in an instant.

Dalham studied him, thought back over the research of the past couple of weeks.

Paul Joseph Goebbels.

In the early 1920s, he despised the future Führer, at one point demanding that the "bourgeois Adolf Hitler be expelled from the National Socialist Party."

Later, almost inexplicably, he became a follower of Hitler, calling him "either Christ or Saint John."

"Why the change?" Dalham asked. "Why did your namesake switch gears so radically?"

"Because Hitler was the only one he *could* follow. He was the messiah of the German people."

"And of Herr Goebbels in particular?"

"Yes."

"Was Goebbels so insecure that he needed a crutch like Hitler to lean on?"

Goebbels winced at the word *crutch*. Prior to then, he had not been paying much attention to the questions, answering them only in a bored monotone, his shoulders slightly slumped. But this time he stood up straight, an intense expression on his face.

"I paid the price of my deformity, facing the ridicule of everyone around me."

"You also? As well as Goebbels?"

Dalham was becoming quite fascinated by the apparent switches in personal reference. Since he didn't believe in reincarnation, convinced that the doctrine was yet another delusion, he knew there were only two other alternatives: schizophrenia or demonic possession. For the moment, he was counting on the former.

Goebbels flushed briefly, aware that he was being played with by a man who just might be his intellectual equal.

"*Goebbels* was often ridiculed because of his crippled foot," the young skinhead said. "Do you know what they called him behind his back?"

"Many things," Dalham remarked. "To which expression do you refer?"

"The little mouse-doctor!"

The skinhead's eyes were wide, his nostrils flaring. Goebbels had been victimized by whispers behind his back virtually all his life. Even after he had joined the Nazi party, a special classification had had to be concocted to allow his entry since he wasn't of the tall, blonde Aryan appearance so preferred by Hitler and the others.

Nachgedunkelnter Schrimpfgermane.

Roughly translated, that meant "a dwarflike German who grew dark."

He was also known as "the malacious dwarf," "Wotan's Mickey Mouse" and "the he-goat of Babelsberg."

"Some even said you were born with a clubfoot," Dalham added, "and you were called a reincarnation of Lucifer himself."

"I could not *help* what became of me," he said, not entirely successful in his attempt to speak with total detachment. "I fell ill with osteomyelitis."

"Yes, inflammation of the bone lining."

"My parents were perusaded that I needed an operation," Goebbels went on."The result was that my left leg became four inches shorter than my right and was forever weak and scrawny. For a long time I had to wear special shoes and braces."

Dalham decided to play to the arrogant side of Goebbels' fractured ego.

"But to compensate," he said, "I have read that you, Herr Goebbels, developed into nearly as magnetic a public speaker as Hitler, with a powerful, booming voice and an electrifying manner. Wasn't that so?"

The other beamed with sudden pride, getting to his feet, pacing the small room, confident.

For a moment he went back and forth between *Goebbels* and *I* when he spoke, switching in an instant, but settled, briefly, into just the first person.

"...and I had to show them, show everyone, I was worthy! And I did!"

"By wooing the German people with the brilliance of your mind and, not incidentally, murdering the Jews."

Goebbels swung around on one heel.

"I didn't *always* hate them, you know. I studied with their kind at the university. Professor Friedrich Gundolf, a Jewish historian, taught me a great deal."

"So Hitler corrupted you then, is that what you are saying?"

"It is *not* what I am saying! I learned the *truth* from him, and the truth set me free. I wrote to him, 'God gave you the words to describe what is ailing in Germany. You began at the bottom like every great leader. And like every great leader you grew greater as your task became greater.'"

"You made that statement in 1926, didn't you?" Dalham asked, choosing the words deliberately.

The other broke out in raucous laughter, shaking his index finger at Dalham several times.

"Goebbels, you mean," he said after calming down. "Clever of you, Kent Dalham. Quite clever indeed."

"But you said that *you* wrote to Hitler. How could *you* have done so? Hitler has been dead for more than 40 years."

It was obvious that Dalham's attempt to confuse the young man was beginning to work.

"Yes, yes, that's right. I did say that, didn't I?"

"But why? It was Goebbels who penned those words, not you. Yet you said that you had done it."

The other walked to the single window in the room, which overlooked the prison yard.

"Goebbels...I...we...we're going to do it all over again, rebuild everything."

"We? You and..."

"And the rest of the Third Reich."

"The Third Reich is nothing more than a nightmarish memory now. Why do you continue to refer to it?"

As Goebbels spoke this time, his voice changed, becoming deeper, more powerful.

"What we *demand*, what we will *have*, Kent Dalham, is clear-cut and radical; therefore in the long run, revolutionary. The upheaval we seek is to be achieved first of all in the spirit of the people. We will teach them to fight against the withering poison of the international Jewish-spirit! There *must* be extirpation of the foul Semitic immorality, a death sentence imposed on each of them in punishment of their crimes and the stench of their awful deeds!"

"But what about *your* crimes? The destruction of an entire town a few weeks ago. The slaughter of millions decades earlier. You yourself should escape free of punishment?"

"We will be *rewarded*, not punished."

His back still to Dalham, he made a gutteral sound of contempt and added, "What about the atrocities committed in the Russian labor camps?"

It was not a surprise to Dalham that the skinhead mentioned this. As many as 80,000 Germans died in camps at

Schumachtenhagen and Neubrandenburg in what was to become East Germany. They were starved to death, they died of exposure to freezing temperatures or rampant disease, or else they were shot. To hide the evidence of what had happened, the Russians buried the victims in mass graves that many knew about but few had the courage to protest. Those that did were murdered by KGB agents.

"You conveniently omit mention of those," the skinhead was saying, "and your own government's treatment of the Japanese during World War II in those so-called 'relocation' camps. It seems that all this is somehow unimportant."

"What we did to Japanese Americans was wrong, I admit," Dalham replied. "My father did what he could to help. But they weren't stuffed into ovens, and they weren't gassed, and whole masses of them weren't shot and then—"

"But what about the Indians, your so-called native Americans," Goebbels interrupted. "Whole generations have been driven to alcoholism as a result of the corrupt treatment they've received. What about the slaughter at Wounded Knee?"

He turned around defiantly.

"I *thought* you would question me in the manner you have," Goebbels added. "And by your very manner, you presuppose me to be unequal to your tactics, a piece of cake, as the expression goes."

He whipped out a folded sheet of paper from the left pocket in his trousers.

"I must read something to you," he said.

"Go right ahead," Dalham told him, knowing that the other would do so anyway.

Goebbels glanced over the sheet once, and then:

> so i agreed to move
> i see me walking in sleep
> down streets down streets grey with
> cement

and glaring glass and oily wind
armed with a pint of wine
i cheated my children to buy
i am ashamed
i am tired
i am hungry
i speak words
i am lonely for hills
i am lonely for myself[4]

"Is *that* a soliloquy from a happy American who has been treated with the slightest decency?" he said after finishing.

"There is a *great* difference between—," Dalham started to say.

The one named Goebbels shook his head in angry dismissal, and then his whole manner changed. The feeble pretense at any separate identity vanished. The small, crippled body was as ramrod straight as could be managed. The right arm shot up.

"*Heil Hitler!*"

Dalham stood.

"Your Führer is dead!" he declared. "Your *messiah* is dead and buried. Unlike Christ, he never rose from the dead, never ascended into heaven. He went the other way, Paul Joseph Goebbels. He's in hell right now, with the rest of the vermin."

The young man's gaze, his eyes dark, locked in on Dalham's own.

"Do not be so sure," he said, smirking. "Do not be so sure at all."

37

i am ashamed
i am tired
i am hungry
i speak words
i am lonely for hills
i am lonely for myself

Dalham had hoped to have some effect on the Goebbels clone, but true to the special talent of the real Goebbels decades before, the reverse had happened.

Years earlier, he had had to spend time on an Indian reservation, investigating a murder case. He had never seen any tribe's living conditions previously, though everyone else at the Bureau had some personal story to tell.

It was a revelation he would never forget.

Open sewers, the smell of excrement in the air. Children in rags, their skin dirty.

Men stumbling about or sitting on the ground, hopelessness on their faces.

"Where did the majesty go?" someone named Sammy White Horse asked as the two of them walked together. "The wind against our cheeks as we rode grand horses? The pride that we had because we tamed the land beneath our feet and made it serve our needs?"

He stopped for a moment and looked at Dalham without blinking.

"We were here first, and your kind took it from us," he said simply.

Dalham never forgot those words, that afternoon, the stench that was everywhere...

He saw the reasoning adopted by Goebbels. It was ironically quite biblical in origin: the verse admonishing those who would condemn the actions of others first to clean out the filth in their own lives.

Yet the flaw in the *way* this was used seemed obvious. Christ meant it as a cleansing, peace-making command, but Goebbels was taking his stance only as justification for his infamy in the face of the infamy of others.

...if thine eye be evil, thy whole body shall be full of darkness. If therefore the light that is in thee be darkness, how great is that darkness!

Goebbels and indeed the whole subversive skinhead movement were convinced they had the light, the clear, shining light of justice on their side, reinforced in their minds by those periods in history when Germans were on the receiving end of barbaric behavior. Yet in fact it was not light at all, but darkness so intense that they had been swallowed up in it.

38

"HOW can we truly deal with sin in the lives of others until we have routed the sin that haunts our own past?" Dalham mused during dinner with Elliott Lewisohn at an Italian restaurant a few miles from the prison.

"There is some hypocrisy in all of us," the other man reminded him. "Do you and I allow our conception of God's will for our lives to guide *everything* we do? Isn't there some passage in your New Testament about those occasions when, knowing what is the right thing, the honorable course of action, we often choose the wrong, the sinful deed?"

"Yes, Paul wrote that," Dalham agreed. "It's part of that warfare within us, the flesh against the spirit, and the spirit against the flesh."

"A constant battle."

"It is."

It was a battle Arthur James Dalham had fought every day of his life; in his case it was a tendency toward materialism.

"I like good *things*, Kent," he admitted to his son. "I like leather upholstery on our furniture. I pick the best wood paneling for our home I can afford. I spend more money than I should on cars. I buy the best clothes. As you know, we've never had a problem getting any of that, son. But sometimes I wonder how much of the life we lead has money as the foundation, and how easily we'd adapt without it."

The younger Dalham had protested that it was better to have that sort of tendency than one anchored in perversion or violence or drugs.

"True, Kent, in a sense," his father had replied. "But when, really, is one sin *better* than another or even *less* sinful? Should we be proud because we only cheat *a little* on our income tax when somebody else has molested and then killed 35 teenage boys? God deals with both harshly, son. *None* of us have cause for pride, that kind of pride, anyway."

While spending time at the prison, Dalham had grown to feel morally quite superior to the skinheads.

Why shouldn't I, Lord?

I have killed no one except to prevent the murder of another, or in my own self-defense. I have never taken narcotics or anything of the sort. I was always faithful to Valerie.

And then he realized that, more than once, he had lied. More than once he had taken God's name in vain. More than once, as a teenager, he had had sex with a girl. There had been many sins in his life. He had broken a number of God's laws. He might as well have transgressed all of them!

"For me it's a battle to try to stop myself from rounding up those kids and—"

Lewisohn's voice broke into his thoughts.

"—doing to them what they did to the poor souls at that camp in Oregon. Who knows how long this thing will drag on? If somebody's got the money to finance all this, then hiring a smart lawyer won't be a problem. They probably have a petty cash account waiting to be spent!"

Dalham could understand how Lewisohn felt. Strangely he could also understand, increasingly so, why any skinhead felt as he did.

"You can't excuse them, Elliott, never that, of course," he said. "But do we write them off? Do we label them purely as monsters? The original Nazis, yes, but these kids? If we do, then we must also ignore conditions that are virtually the same for hundreds of thousands of runaways. How many of *them* will drift into neo-Nazism? Will we have a vicious cycle here, fighting some kind of revolution every few years?"

Lewisohn was growing impatient.

"I can't worry about sympathy for kids who think that Goebbels, Himmler, Mengele and Heydrich are admirable human beings!"

He looked sharply at Dalham.

There was a note of urgency in the warden's manner, and something else that Dalham couldn't ascertain but which made him feel uncomfortable.

39

THE Lord will cause you to be defeated before your ene-mies,'" read the 21-year-old who had taken on the name of Reinhard Heydrich. "'Your carcasses will be food for all the birds of the air and the kingdoms on earth, and there will be no one to frighten them away.

"'The Lord will afflict you with boils...and with tumors, fes-tering sores and the itch, from which you cannot be cured. The Lord will afflict you with madness, blindness and confusion of mind. At midday you will grope about like a blind man in the dark....Day after day you will be oppressed and robbed, with no one to help you.'"

He slammed the Bible shut, and still holding it got up from the edge of the bed on which he had been sitting.

"That, Mr. Kent Dalham, is a picture of life in one of our concentration camps!" he declared with unconcealed triumph.

"So you were an instrument of Almighty God, then?" Dal-ham asked.

"If I were to believe in Him, yes, I could say that."

"But you don't."

"I could *never* accept a deity who had designated the Jews as His chosen people. Such a god is too ignorant to be worthy of my worship."

He opened the Bible again.

"Here is further denunciation of the Jews in yet another portion of the Old Testament: "'You will eat the flesh of your sons and the flesh of your daughters. I will destroy your high places, cut down your incense altars and pile your dead bodies on the lifeless forms of your idols, and I will abhor you. I will turn your cities into ruins and lay waste your sanctuaries. I will scatter you among the nations and will draw out my sword and pursue you.'"

He paused, for emphasis, and then added, "'You will not be able to stand before your enemies. You will perish among the nations; the land of your enemies will devour you.'"

And then he threw the Bible on the floor.

"That land is our fatherland, Mr. FBI Agent, the *Deutschland* that we love and serve," he said proudly. "That enemy is all Aryans. And we *are* devouring the Jews, limb by limb, organ by organ."

"Past tense," Dalham reminded him. "You are lost in insane dreams of half a century ago."

"Dreams can be reborn," Heydrich said in a manner that suggested he knew something the other did not. "Dreams can resuscitate an empire!"

Dalham smiled.

"You are a parrot," he said sarcastically. "You mouth threatening words that mother an infamy concocted by others."

Heydrich stiffened.

"You are what Hitler always considered you, the ultimate yes man," Dalham continued. "You were the ideal front man, young, charismatic, while Himmler was colorless and dull. Your obsequity, so constant, so *obvious*, must have made Hitler, Himmler, the others laugh at you behind your back. But you were useful."

"I followed *orders*!" Heydrich screamed.

He realized then what he had said.

"*Yes!*" he declared, relishing the thought. "It was *I*—then and now. Indeed! I did so well that, at one time, it was thought I would succeed Hitler as Führer."

"True, you were mentioned as a successor. But you built your reputation on brutality, on death and maiming, on pain and destruction. You gloated before the agony of your victims!"

"And I got the ultimate revenge," Heydrich cackled, no longer able to control himself. "Because of me, the Czech resistance suffered devastating blows. The village of Lidice! Yes! It was obliterated, its citizens executed."

"Why, Reinhard Heydrich?" Dalham asked, standing this time. "Why did that happen?"

He stood before the thin-faced young man.

"What *caused* the destruction, Reinhold Heydrich? Tell me!"

"It happened because—"

He stopped, raising his left hand to his mouth. His face went through a twitching, trembling series of contortions.

He slid off the bed and sank to his knees.

"A bomb!" he exclaimed.

"Yes, a bomb. *Remember the rest of it?*"

The 21-year-old was struggling.

"The car—they threw it under the car!"

"That *is* what happened. And then what? Go on!"

"I...don't...know..."

He looked up at Dalham, his voice much softer this time.

"I always hated myself, you know. They kept saying that my father, Bruno Heydrich, was a *kike!* No one could prove it. But the whispers, the whispers kept on, and on, and—"

"And then one night, drunk, you saw yourself in a mirror, and in rage mixed with self-pity, you pulled out your pistol and fired two shots at that image, shattering it in a thousand fragments."

"Yes! How did you know *that?*"

"I have files on you, on your superior Himmler, on—"

"He was *never* my superior. He seduced the Führer into thinking that I was an intellectual pigmy compared to his surpassing brilliance. But without *me*, the Final Solution would have been an international joke!"

"What does genocide, the most fundamentally barbaric of acts, have to do with the intellect?" Dalham demanded.

The youth's face took on a disdainful expression.

What a fool! He thinks it is easy to construct camps like Treblinka and Dachau and the others. We had to be mathematically correct, figuring out the number of Jews that could be disposed of in a given period of time.

"If you only knew the planning, the very careful planning, if you—."

He cut himself off again. His body jerked once, twice.

The car!

Outside Prague.

"Two Czech partisans were parachuted in," Dalham said, sensing what was happening. "One of them, Jan Kubis, who became a hero to the resistance movement as a result, threw the bomb and—"

It exploded right under the car!

When my men discovered what had happened, they rushed me to a hospital.

"You were given extraordinary care," Dalham persisted, "but you had been critically wounded. *You died a week later!*"

The young man whose real name was unknown began crying.

This man is dangerous. He is trying to make me believe some lies.

I could not have died in that Czech hospital. I could not!

(Long pause.)

He's right. For the love of—.

I did!

I died there, the resistance jubilant...

Still on his knees, he leaned forward, the sobs tearing through his body, his manner bordering on hysteria.

"What...happened to me?" he said, his voice breaking. "I have fresh blood on...*my own hands now!*"

Dalham got down on the floor with him.

"I don't know just yet," he said softly. "The same thing has occurred with the others as well."

The young man's manner had completely altered. He seemed neither Nazi nor skinhead and not at all someone who had entered his 20s, but rather younger, more frail, and very frightened.

"I...I'll try to remember. I'll try to help...before...before they execute me! But...but..."

He fell to the floor.

"...I don't even know my *own* name anymore!"

He looked up at Dalham, a terrified expression on his face.

"Why don't I know who I am?" he pleaded.

Dalham had seen that reaction before. Kids were roped into cults, seduced by the leaders in every psychological and physical sense. And then when confronted with the stark truth, they often collapsed, literally unable to look at themselves in the mirror, partly out of disgust, partly because they no longer knew who it was that was reflected back at them.

And now, Dalham told himself, *it's one of the leaders themselves.*

"What caused all of this?" he asked as sympathetically as possible.

The other pushed away from him.

"Please," he begged, "please, don't make me think...don't make me think about *that.*"

"But you can never be free until you confront it," Dalham said.

"And when I do, will that mean I am free from the punishment the law has in store for me?"

"If it has anything to do with—"

"Insanity? That's what you're going to say, isn't it?"

"Yes. We just might save you and the others that way."

The one who had called himself Heydrich so confidently earlier was shaking with fear as he backed away from Dalham and seemed surprised when the wall stopped him from moving any further.

"Insanity?" he spoke the word musingly at first, then repeated it again, much louder this time, laughing hysterically until the cell started to waver in his vision, and he lost consciousness seconds later.

40

IN his motel room, Kent Dalham was leafing through the files he had been given about Aryans Underground.

Thousands of victims, he thought to himself, *put to death almost casually.*

He was sitting on the floor, the files on either side of him, several others on his lap, and leaned back against the bed, rubbing his eyes briefly.

Years before, as a teenager, he had had to put a dog named Rusty to sleep. It was a decision not made by his parents but rather himself. Rusty was his pet, more than that actually, a cherished companion, and he needed to face the matter directly, without passing the responsibility along to someone else.

He remembered taking her to the vet, watching while there was a final examination, hearing the results, the hopeless prognosis, and then having to decide on the spot, nodding his assent. Rusty was in continual pain from a variety of ailments, including kidney stones, leukemia and just plain old age, and there was no possibility of recovery.

Since I was three years old, dear friend, he had thought when the vet and an assistant picked up the old Irish setter, *and now no longer.*

Rusty turned for only a moment and looked back at him, her eyes bleary with the medicine she had been given for months in a failed attempt to help her.

He asked the vet to wait. Then he walked up to Rusty and kissed her on the forehead, and she licked his cheek with that long pink tongue of hers.

Good-bye, he had told her with his eyes because the words could not be actually spoken just then, and she seemed to be saying the same thing with hers, moisture collecting on her lower lid, and dripping over the end and down her snout.

Two weeks later, a parcel service delivered a small package about nine inches long by five inches wide. He opened it slowly. Inside the cardboard was a metallic container. After taking the top off, he saw the white and gray grains of powder and tiny pieces of bone, and he couldn't go back into the house for awhile but walked down the street to the little township park where he had taken Rusty every day on her "rounds."

He sat there on a tree stump for perhaps an hour or longer, looking up as other dogs came with their masters.

...their masters.

He thought how inappropriate that was, a dog not *mastered* at all if there were a right relationship between it and a human being, a dog instead part of a family of equals, treated with care when sick, held and loved and talked to in the midst of whatever happened to be afflicting it.

That was twenty years ago.

A long time to be without Rusty, a dog that had once saved his life. He had come near a rattler without noticing it, though Rusty did, and the dog jumped in front of him, killing the snake with one bite of her powerful jaws, yet not before she had suffered its own fangs in her flesh. He rushed her to the vet and she survived. But she was not the same, not nearly the same as before, more tired, suddenly older than even her advanced years. He realized, when the sorrow after her death had dissipated a bit and clarity returned to his mind, that in addition to saying farewell in that glance of hers, she also seemed to be thanking him for at last taking away the pain.

Years later, as he pondered those files, as he stood before that extermination camp outside of Portland, as he looked inside the crematorium, he remembered his own reaction to ordering the death of "just a dog," and he wondered how millions of human beings could ever have been burned to ashes by other human beings.

He had hesitated briefly, reaching in and picking up the bony tip of a tiny, tiny finger.

A child, he had told himself, *perhaps not dead, pushed into the oven with a flicker of life remaining, screaming at the awful heat. Indeed that was probable if these neo-Nazis were truly emulating their maniacal predecessors.*

Men outside, laughing, watching as the conveyor belt transported others into the crematorium, not caring at all. It didn't matter; garbage was garbage.

He flung the files on his lap across the room, disgusted.

Some time later, his emotions quieted down, he put the contents of those folders back together and continued reading.

Tomorrow, he told himself, *it will be one who calls himself Mengele...Josef Mengele, the butcher of Auschwitz.*

41

W HY would he want dolls, sir?"
The guard was genuinely puzzled.

Dalham had no answer.

"I can't imagine," he replied. "The Angel of Death playing with dolls!"

"But he's only a kid, sir. How could he call himself such a name?"

Dalham shook his head.

When he was taken to Mengele's cell, he passed by the others. Since this was the solitary confinement section of the prison, each cell was a separate room with no contact between them. What was spoken in one could not be heard in any of the others.

He stopped for a moment at Heydrich's cell. The youth who had adopted that name saw him through the single small window in the heavy metal door.

"What are you doing, Mr. Federal Agent?" the young man asked, trying to appear as tough as before but his very manner defeating him as his face mirrored his confusion and uncertainty.

"Continuing the investigation," he said.

"Do you know what will become of us?"

"I can't say as yet."

"Mengele may be the worst, you know. I must warn you that he—"

He stopped, struggling with himself.

"Not the worst," he added. "Hey, I take that back. I gotta tell you something."

"What's that?" Dalham asked.

"There's another."

"Another?"

"He's still loose."

Despite himself, Dalham's mouth dropped open.

"You didn't know that?" the 21-year-old asked.

"No, I didn't."

"Stop in after you finish with Mengele."

Dalham nodded, started to walk away, then turned back.

"What does the word *aparicion* mean to you? Anything?"

At that the other's manner changed, his cheeks twitching noticeably, color draining from his face.

"Later."

"Fine," Dalham agreed reluctantly.

As he walked down the corridor to visit Mengele, he found himself almost anxious to be done with this "interview" so he could return to the other's cell and get to the bottom of what had been only hinted at.

He's still loose.

Kent Dalham hadn't the foggiest idea who that was.

Josef Mengele was sitting on the single chair in his cell. On his lap was a rag doll. Gripped between both hands was another, this one looking very much like a Barbie doll.

"You seem surprised," the 25-year-old observed. "How could a monster regress to playing with dolls?"

"The thought *did* enter my mind," Dalham admitted.

"How can you be so sure I deserve the appellation?"

Dalham had anticipated that sort of question and had brought a thick file with him.

"In 1939, you joined the Waffen-SS and—"

"Brilliant research," Mengele interrupted sarcastically. "That hardly makes me a sadist."

"You began as an *Untersturmführer*," Dalham considered, "and you served as a medical doctor in France and Russia. Four years later, Heinrich Himmler appointed you chief doctor at Auschwitz."

The look on this youth's face was nearly ecstatic, as though reliving in his mind earlier joyous moments.

"Now we come to the interesting part," Mengele said. "Do you know about what I tried to do with those two boys at the camp, what I tried to create?"

Dalham nodded slowly.

"They proved that you hated the Gypsies as much as the Jews."

"No, *no*!" Mengele said, becoming agitated. "I hated them, yes, as did Himmler, but that wasn't what I meant."

"What *did* you mean?"

"Does your fine pile of research reveal to you the nature of my experiment?"

Dalham noticed that Mengele had begun twisting one of the doll's arms.

"You tried to create a pair of—"

Dalham cut himself off, finding it difficult to recall the details, the file complete indeed, complete in every detail, with even a picture of the children just before death claimed them.

"I failed because infection set in. What a shame I couldn't prove—."

"They died *in agony*!" Dalham interrupted, his voice rising more than he intended.

"The pursuit of scientific objectives *often* can be painful. You know that as well as I do, Mr. Kent Dal—"

Mengele's eyes widened.

"Arthur James Dalham was *your father*!"

"Congratulations. You're the only one thus far who has made the connection."

Mengele's earlier agitation was increasing. He had twisted that one arm off the doll by now and was working on the other.

"None of *them* were haunted by this man!" he said. "Very few ever went to trial. Your father joined with Wiesenthal. They hounded me—"

"—from Rome to Buenos Aires to Paraguay, and then on to Brazil."

"To a grave at Embu, a grave they deluded themselves into thinking was mine."

"They checked the dental work. The false teeth were yours, the remaining real teeth were also."

"Of course!"

Dalham examined the expression on his face, the way he held his head, the fingers that had pulled apart the second arm on that doll and were now working on its midsection.

"Do you not know of dental surgery?" Mengele went on. "It can be very painful, but the price I paid was worth it!"

Dalham was becoming fed up with such fantasies. He stood abruptly, glowering at the young man.

"Cut out the charade, Mengele or whatever your name is!" he said.

"That is my name," the other protested.

Dalham was pacing the cell.

"Nonsense. Mengele would be in his mid-seventies if he were alive today. You're far younger than that."

The doll was totally in pieces by now. Mengele looked at it, surprised, and tossed the fragments on the floor. As he was reaching for another, Dalham strode forward, grabbed the remaining dolls and threw them to one side.

"Your namesake did *that* to helpless human beings!" he said. "He tore them to pieces in the name of some kind of perverted science."

"But I *am* Josef—" the other started to repeat.

They were interrupted by another voice.

"*Special Agent Dalham!*"

A prison guard was standing in the door, distraught.

"What is it?" Dalham snapped.

"Sir, I need to tell you something."

"Go ahead."

"Not here."

Dalham reluctantly went out into the corridor. Behind him, the young man was starting to gibber, "That *is* my name! It is! The Führer gave it to me!"

Dalham stopped short and started to tell the guard he'd have to wait.

"No, sir, it *can't wait*! Heydrich or whoever he is...he's *dead*!"

Dalham hurried to that cell. The door was open.

Heydrich was on the floor in the far corner.

Part of his head was caved in.

"He must...have banged...himself against...the wall," the guard said, confused. "I should have been more alert. I...I'm going to catch..."

Dalham entered the cell, saw something out of the corner of his eye.

On the wall—written in red:

LORD LUCIFER

TRIUMPHANT

The guard beside him asked the obvious: "Sir, how could he have written that *after* he bloodied himself? Those injuries were fatal!"

42

OTHER agents were brought in within 24 hours to investi
gate the death of the skinhead who insisted upon the
name of Reinhard Heydrich. Evidence was scant.

"It happened quickly," said Nathan Barker, a robust man in
his early 60s, who had been with the FBI since the 1940s.
"Whoever did it went in, got the job done quickly, and was
gone."

"He didn't commit suicide then?" Dalham asked.

"No, Kent. He was *thrown* against the wall. It was one quick
motion. No man could do that to himself, at least without trying again and again, but even then the chances are slight."

"The prison's highly structured, guards everywhere, especially in this wing, especially with *these* prisoners."

"I don't know exactly how whoever did it managed to get
past that kind of security."

Barker was about to leave the prison with the others after
questioning inmates and guards alike throughout most of that
day, when he drew Dalham aside.

"Kent, there was one instance when a man..." he started to
say, then shook his head, as though to clear it.

"What's wrong, Nathan?"

"It's so silly," the other man said as they stood to the left of
the prison's main gate, the remaining agents waiting outside.

"Tell me. I won't laugh."

"It was in the 1960s. Some guy had gotten loaded up on
drugs and taken a machine gun and killed half a dozen people
at a shopping mall. I happened to be there at the time. And I
had him in my sights, Kent. Suddenly he dropped the gun, and
I thought he was going to surrender. He didn't. Instead he
bashed his head against a concrete wall with such force that,
well, there was very little left of the skull."

"He must have been on PCP," Dalham speculated.

"Yeah, I suppose so."

"You don't sound very convinced."

"I've thought all along that there was more to it."

"What do you mean?"

"Kent, that guy was also a practicing Satanist."

43

"WE are immunized by our infamy," the thinnish 20-year-old of average height was saying as he sat upright in a high-backed chair, "and by the fact that we are here in the United States, not at Nuremberg in an atmosphere of collective vengeance."

"Explain that," Dalham asked.

"Take Noriega," the other said. "All that talk about a fair trial."

"The cornerstone of the American judicial system."

"Your Achilles heel. A fair trial is a long process, every bit of it paid for by the tax dollars of the Americans who are suppose to loathe what we stand for."

He smiled arrogantly.

"Every home in this nation will know of us, every American speaking our names for a long time to come. The media will ensure that. The longer the trial takes, the more coverage we will get!"

Dalham was silent.

"How long was it before the Night Stalker in California was *convicted?" the youth continued. "Appeals could delay his* execution for years."

"That's hardly a guarantee of immunization from punishment for your crimes."

"The longer we live—"

"—the greater the likelihood your followers can somehow free you, I gather. Yet no one has made a move to spring loose Noriega or Ramirez. How come?"

"Noriega's followers clung to him on the basis of greed, fear. Ramirez inspired no one. Yet the principle is the same. They survive, yes?"

"And Aryans Underground encourages loyalty, which sets you apart from those two, is that it?"

"Precisely. We offer a belief system."

Dalham knew that this young man, with the owlish-looking face, the almost feminine hands, was unfortunately quite correct.

"Our captivity will not discourage those who look up to us."

"And execution would make you martyrs. Either way you can't lose."

"Oh, yes. Look at what crucifixion did for the followers of Christ, turning them from a ragged band of wanderers in a small country to many millions the world over."

"You omit one key detail: Christ arose from the dead," Dalham reminded him.

"As *we* will, should we die, through those who keep the dream alive."

"You're saying then that those who commit the most grievous acts are guaranteed special treatment," Dalham interpolated.

"Of course! As I said, the United States prides itself on the dictum of a fair trial. How is that *possible* now? Tabloid newspapers proclaim our guilt. The evening TV news rehashes detail after detail. How *can* we be treated with impartiality? Answer that!"

"Even in the hysteria of the postwar months, the Nuremberg Tribunal tried hard to be objective," Dalham pointed out, "and justice was swift."

Looking at him through wire-rimmed glasses, the skinhead named Heinrich Himmler had the manner of a man who was suffering a few moments with someone only slightly more intelligent than a retarded chimpanzee.

"Everyone there *hated* us!" he declared. "They could hardly wait to hang us! Surely even you can realize that. Our guilt was assumed from the beginning."

Trying to maintain control of himself, he shifted to a seemingly dispassionate recitation about the Nuremberg trial.

"One of your leading historians wrote: 'It is, of course, recognized that a particular crime may cause such emotional reaction that it is difficult, if not impossible, for the one charged with its commission to receive a fair and impartial trial. To some extent that may have been true at Nuremberg.'"

He paused for effect, then continued: "If one expects to conduct a trial and to administer justice, one should take a different approach from that of the famous judge Roy Bean, who used to apprise an accused that he would give him a 'fa'r and squ'ar' trial, and then hang him. Punishment should not be considered until guilt is established. And one approaching such a matter while embroiled in passion is scarcely apt to give an accused a fair trial. Or, if he actually does do so, few will believe it. The cry then seems to be for vengeance rather than punishment. Punishment should be conceived as a vastly different thing from vengeance."

Himmler sat back, crossing his arms in defiant self-satisfaction.

"There!" he barked. "There you have it! Infallible reasoning. We cannot expect justice, not at all—but we *can* expect liberation as everything drags on and on for the sake of a veneer of impartiality. Your legal system since Nuremberg has become mired in the manueverings of attorneys and appeals and stays of execution. None of that existed for my kind fifty years ago! Which is why your courts have become so clogged. But it serves us well. May the clogging become even worse!"

"But you fail to take into—" Dalham started to say.

"Do *not* interrupt me," Himmler said with utter coldness. "When our followers rise up again, which they will in time, do you expect the Europeans to come to *your* rescue? Or will they simply say, 'It's an internal problem. We can't get involved'"?

Dalham looked at the one named Himmler intently.

"But then the Allies had no corner on hypocrisy," the agent said. "Hitler initially postured as a man of peace, God's man for the rebirth of his nation. He dropped that pretense soon enough."

Again in rebuttal, with the same icy intonation, Himmler went on to recite the humiliation faced by the Germans after World War I.

"He had the *obligation* to achieve triumph for the German people in any manner necessary. Look at the nation in those days! By January 1923 the mark had gone from 8.9 per dollar to 17,972. And that wasn't the end of its deterioration," he said. "On November 15th that year, the valuation was 4.2 billion marks to the dollar! Germans were living out of garbage cans and gutters. We had to leave our cities and eat food fed to cows and pigs. We became a nation of beggars."

"And Hitler turned you from beggars into murderers!" Dalham cut in.

"The warden of this prison must surely feel differently," Himmler said knowingly.

"You are *aware* of that?" Dalham said, reacting with more surprise than he intended.

"Of course. The one who ordered his salvation should know about it, wouldn't you say?"

Dalham hesitated, certain that Lewisohn would have said nothing to the youth. Yet since this was not a paragraph in any history book, how could he know?

"You seem at a rather sudden loss for words," Himmler observed.

"I was wondering, actually, how someone as intelligent as you could be so specious in your reasoning in so many areas," Dalham told him, hoping to bait him out of that unflinching demeanor and into an outburst of some intensity. "You come off sounding like a second-rate Alfred Rosenberg who could hardly be called a superior intellect himself. He was, you must surely agree, a pompous, overpraised hack—hardly the fount of eternal wisdom that he called himself more than once. Yet you swallowed his teachings lock, stock, and barrel, and now you regurgitate them syllable by syllable."

"I *took* those teachings and added to them my *own* insights!" Himmler said, his face flushing slightly.

Dalham knew he had hit a nerve, though perhaps a minor one.

"But you were a poultry farmer near Munich," he added. "You raised *chickens*! That hardly requires any soaring intelligence."

"You try to bait me by your insults," Himmler replied. "You think me so stupid that I will reveal something to you out of anger."

"You claim to be a man of loyalty, fidelity. You were raised in a devout Roman Catholic family. Yet you fathered several illegitimate children. I call that hypocrisy!"

Dalham was sitting in a chair across from the youth, studying him. Himmler had been of average height, with the look of a mild-mannered schoolteacher; so it was with this skinhead. And there was a physical similiarity between the others and their Nazi counterparts as well.

"You seem quite well today," Dalham said, switching tact abruptly and, he hoped, disconcertingly. "No stomach spasms just now?"

Himmler shook his head.

"Any headaches?"

"None, thank you."

"That's a bit unusual, isn't it?"

Himmler said nothing.

"How long will that last though?" Dalham persisted. "You always tried to help yourself through homeopathy, mesmerism and herbalism. But nothing did the job for very long. You had to take more and more drugs, go into longer sessions with your hypnotist, consume a greater number of exotic herbs. *All of it producing no lasting help!*"

Himmler remained silent.

Dalham was becoming exasperated though he dared not show it.

"And it all got worse when you visited Auschwitz!" he spit out the words.

Himmler was still silent but a single tear had begun a slow trip down his left cheek.

"You were called *gnadelos* by others," Dalham continued. "They thought you merciless. You understood that. You said once, 'I know that there are people in Germany who feel sick when they see this black tunic.'"

"Please shut up," Himmler said.

"Have I hit something at last? After that truncated time at Auschwitz, did you find yourself overcome with depression more severe than any of those previous bouts?"

"I left early that day for *other* reasons!"

"You're lying, and you know it. You fainted on the spot because you had no stomach for seeing the results of your orders. You oversaw camps being *built*, yes, but how convenient it was that you were never around when they were filled to capacity with the subjects of your pseudointellectual theories."

"I must ask that, as my jailer, you extend to me—"

"How could it be otherwise?" Dalham interrupted. "Though your Roman Catholicism gave you a sense of conscience, you were successful in burying it so long as you could generate the Final Solution by remote control."

"I *wanted* them dead!" Himmler said as he stood.

"But when you saw *how* they died, when you smelled the rotting piles of meat that had once been human beings, men, women and children alike, when you heard their dying moans courtesy of an SS colonel who let you witness their fate in a gas chamber as Zyklon-B was pumped inside, when you—"

"Yes, yes, *yes!*" the skinhead named Heinrich Himmler shouted. "I...he...he had to get away. He *had* to!"

"Because you knew you couldn't go to confession *ever again!* How could you tell *anyone* how you felt? The truth about the monstrous evils that you perpetrated? How could you express yourself to another human being without losing your mind in the process? So you concocted greater and greater crimes, trying to bury your guilt in the midst of the maniacal passions that had been driving you, driving you, driving you from the very beginning."

Himmler raised a fist in Dalham's direction, his face beet-red.

I saw their faces, twisted in agony. Even the children, still clutching a parent's hand!

And this fool smiling at me, proud that he had carried out MY orders!

That memory from Auschwitz had never faded, had remained as vivid as it was a day afterwards, a month, a year.

I had difficulty eating beef during the time to follow. I could not look at a roast without seeing a human body in an oven. I could not cut into a rare piece of steak, the blood dripping onto my plate, without...

Suddenly he collapsed on the floor. He seemed torn by some convulsion, some awful struggle inside himself. German words escaped his lips in a torrent, in the midst of blasphemies spoken in English, the two languages colliding and being interspersed in a chaotic jumble.

Dalham, never having confronted a case of authentic demonic possession before, couldn't tell whether this was one such instance. But from all he had heard, from what other agents had told him, the skinhead's behavior seemed dangerously close, and he knew he had to let the Holy Spirit lead him.

Dalham bent down beside the convulsing body.

"Claim the name of Jesus Christ!" he told this Himmler clone. "You haven't forgotten that name."

"I don't know, God, God, God, I—"

"It's just been pushed deeper and deeper into your subconscious," Dalham persisted. "But it's still *there*."

The youth was torn with wracking sobs.

"God help me!" he cried. "God help me—you don't know how terrible it's been, first pretending that I was Himmler, then *believing* it."

"You *aren't* Himmler," Dalham said softly.

"But I saw this—this thing. It smiled at me. It spoke with a thick accent. It wanted my soul and...and..."

"Listen to me! I can't explain everything that's happened. I *can* say this."

The young man tried to turn away but Dalham grabbed him and forced him to pay attention as they looked at one another.

"You were *never* Himmler. It was a satanic counterfeit. Its domination needn't continue any longer. Claim Jesus as your Savior. Let His Spirit come into your body!"

"Jesus, Jesus, Jesus," the other started repeating over and over, "Jesus, forgive me, forgive me, Jesus, Jesus—"

Just then a wrenching scream tore past his lips. He fell limply forward, and Dalham caught him.

A few moments passed.

The young man sighed once, opened his eyes, looking ashamed and uneasy at the same time.

Dalham smiled reassuringly.

"What *is* your name, son?" he asked.

The other looked up at him.

"Jerome, I...I...yes, Jerome," he said. "I think my name is Jerome."

His expression was fearful, begging.

"I don't know what to do now. Tell me what to do?"

He held out his hands.

"I can't get them clean," he said. "I just can't get them *clean!*"

44

DALHAM had total access to the prison, to the guards as well as the inmates. He spent time with men who had been incarcerated for a staggering variety of crimes—rape, murder, armed robbery, drug pushing, income tax evasion.

One he found fascinating was a mafioso chieftain named Francesco Giancetti.

"People keep asking me how a religious man could do what I'm accused of doing," Giancetti mused after Dalham and he had finished eating lunch at the mess hall and were heading back to the inmate's cell.

"The thought occurred to me," Dalham acknowledged. "You've spoken about the Lord more than once, and not in vain."

"Have I used even a single profanity?"

Dalham shook his head.

"But the streets are supposed to run red with blood when I give the order?"

"That's part of it."

After they had reached the cell, and the guard accompanying them had slid the door shut, Giancetti sat down on a plain little chair. Dalham sat as well.

"I knew Christ before I knew the gun," he said simply.

"Then why did you ever take up the gun?" Dalham asked.

"Because I knew my mother and father before I knew Christ. And they knew their mother and father *before* that. And my grandfather and my grandmother used to fill my mind with stories about *their* parents."

"Guns have been a family heritage, is that you're saying?"

"For a long, long time. We grow up with violence. We often die with it."

"But Christ does not want you living as you do. It is not a way that pleases Him, surely you know that?"

Giancetti was silent for a moment or two, then: "Each day I come to Him for forgiveness."

"And each day He gives it to you, but—"

"Someday, somewhere His patience may run out, and then..." Giancetti finished the sentence for him.

He shuddered visibly, the color draining instantly from his face.

"Are you all right?" Dalham asked.

Giancetti nodded, then leaned forward conspiratorially.

"You are a nice young man," he said.

"Not so young."

"Twenty years my junior! Listen, Kent Dalham, this prison is going to *explode*!

Dalham pulled back.

"Because of the skinheads?" he asked while assuming he knew the answer.

"That's the spark, yes," the other man said. "But there's more to it than that."

"I don't know what you're getting at, Giancetti."

"Evil, my friend."

"More so here than in any prison?"

"Yes, yes! There are Satanists here."

"That doesn't surprise me."

At prisons as well as Army bases. Men doing the things of darkness in allegiance to Lucifer. No, Mr. Mafia Boss, it doesn't surprise me.

Giancetti was becoming exasperated.

"Don't you see what I'm trying to tell you? The skinheads are here. The Satanists are here. And a large percentage of the inmates happen to be Jewish. Not every gangster, as you call us, is Italian after all!"

Four skinheads.

Each was holding a knife in one hand.

In the background was a large photo of Adolf Hitler.

Dalham told him about what had been discovered.

"It's going on *here* too," Giancetti assured him, "and in other prisons across the country."

"Satan worship?"

"What better conditions, I ask? Evil men imprisoned for their sins—all under one roof. And now four more!"

"Then those kids, if I can any longer call them that, are at least safe, since they are with others like them."

"*No!*" Giancetti blurted out, then lowered his voice. "The three remaining skinheads are liabilities now. They've been discovered. They have to be replaced. It may not be overnight. It may take awhile. But there will be others. The cancer is only in remission, my friend."

"You're saying they're in danger? Here?"

Giancetti nodded, a look of utter conviction on his face.

Dalham was annoyed. He had had to listen to an old criminal's ravings. He was ready to ignore these as such.

"I'm sure Warden Lewisohn will take care of everything," he said, shaking the other's hand and then asking the guard to let him out.

The skinheads are here. The Satanists are here. And a large percentage of the inmates happen to be Jewish.

As he started to walk down the corridor, those words still in his mind, he heard Francesco Giancetti break out in sudden, harsh laughter.

45

DALHAM was about to leave the prison, anxious to return to his motel room, stretch out and try somehow to relax.

It was near dusk. A few inmates were still out in the prison yard though they soon would be heading back inside for mess call.

Dalham noticed a young man standing to one side, rubbing something between his hands. Ordinarily he would have paid little attention except that another, older inmate was walking past, only to stop suddenly and confront the younger one. A fight ensued, the older man grabbing whatever the other had been holding and throwing it on the ground, then stomping his foot on it several times.

Dalham rushed toward the two. The older inmate looked at him, uttered an expletive, then swung a fist toward his face. Dalham avoided contact and karate-chopped the man, who crumpled to the ground instantly.

"What was that all about?" he asked the younger inmate.

"He don't want me to have nothin' that's the Lord's," the other replied.

Dalham bent down, picked up the object.

A crucifix.

"This really isn't a good luck charm, you know," he said as he handed it back to the inmate. "But you were rubbing it like that's what it was."

"Yeah, I know that for sure. I'm proud of Jesus. I want people to know He's my Savior. But I ain't perfect. I do things that ain't right. Maybe I *was* hoping for a little luck."

"What's his problem?" Dalham asked, indicating the older inmate who was still on the ground, nearly unconscious.

"Look at his pocket. The left one. See that leather strap."

"I see it."

"Pull it out. Look at what's at the other end."

Dalham did just that.

A pentagram.

Symbol of satanic worship.

"It's all over this place, and not just here."

"What do you mean?"

"Other prisons, too. The devil's own underground."

Dalham had the older man sent to the infirmary to be checked for injuries. He talked with the young inmate for a couple of moments longer, then left, intending to spend more time with him that following morning.

46

*T*HE riot was well-organized. Inmates had prepared every detail carefully. In less than half an hour they had achieved their goal: The three skinheads were captured and taken out of their cells.

"Why is it so easy?" one inmate mused. "I don't understand why."

Communications in and out of the prison were cut.

Soon this would be discovered by those on the outside. There was little time to satisfy the revenge that had driven them to this point.

Himmler, Goebbels and Mengele were cursed, kicked.

"Monsters!" the cries arose.

After a rope had been put around the neck of each, the inmates laughed.

"At last!" one shouted. "You can't escape this time."

Something happened then.

Each skinhead started jerking spasmodically, then shrieking horribly.

"What evil?" an inmate said, shuddering.

A terrifying sight, with the bodies looking like poorly manipulated puppets.

"They must be insane," said a guard who had been subdued by the inmates, his hands tied behind him, and forced to watch along with other guards and the warden himself.

"That's not it," Lewisohn told him.

"How can you say that? Look at them!"

Lewisohn said nothing further.

The three skinheads quieted down moments later. There was now nothing but fear on their faces.

"Hang them, hang them!" an insistent chorus began.

And so they were.

47

*T*HE *riot seemed to have begun as a kind of collective roar by the inmates, an emotional reaction to their neo-Nazi fellow prisoners. None of those involved tried to escape. After the three skinheads were hanged, the inmate leaders—over the protests of some of the more defiant prisoners—simply opened the gates of the prison and allowed the Feds to come in. All guards were released; none were hurt. But there was one fatality besides the skinheads themselves, a young inmate found with his throat cut and a crucifix clutched tightly in his left hand.*

One by one, the other inmates were questioned.

"We don't know what came over us," one old-timer said, "some kind of madness."

He paused, then added, "Maybe we're not so different from the ones that were hanged."

Dalham entered the prison yard after the inmates had returned to their cell blocks.

The bodies of the three young men were still hanging from the makeshift gallows.

He stood in front of each one. Now they seemed not at all the monsters they had pretended to be, but three kids, fear frozen on their faces as they died.

"I wish I had put everything in a neat file, thoroughly researched, all the answers properly assembled," Dalham said. "But I have only pieces, Elliott. And now these kids, the ones who could fill in the rest of the puzzle, are gone."

Lewisohn was standing next to him.

"It was out of your hands, Kent," he said, a strange edge to his voice. "This would have happened sooner or later, even if they had been split up as a group and sent to different prisons. If not a hanging in each case, then someone would have knifed one; another might have been beaten to death; the third might have been poisoned. It's almost impossible to safeguard kids like these. From those who hated them on the outside, yes, but not from men inside who were determined to seek revenge for the recent crimes and for those fifty years ago."

"But they weren't even *alive* then!" Dalham protested.

"True, but it's a grave they dug for themselves when they set on pedestals the idols they worshipped."

"What if they couldn't help themselves? What if it was demonic possession?"

Lewisohn looked at Dalham in amazement.

"Is that an official speculation?" he asked.

"Of course not."

"Then you can't *personally* believe that stuff, can you?"

It was Dalham's turn to be amazed.

"Do human beings *typically* engage in what the Nazis did, what these skinheads *wanted* to do? Humanity has a sin nature, yes, and it's *capable*, obviously, but I wonder whether it doesn't take some awfully intense oppression by Satan or outright possession for people actually to go beyond mere capability and engage in the kind of carnage we're talking about. I don't know whether that's sound from any psychological or scriptural perspective, but it makes you wonder, anyway."

"What about pure insanity?" Lewisohn asked.

"Sure, insanity is a possibility. But then you have to ask another question."

"What's that?"

"Exactly what was the cause of their insanity?" Dalham posed. "What drove them over the edge?"

"Abusive parents. Drugs. The causes aren't exactly obscure. You know them as well as I do, Kent."

Dalham's expression betrayed his mindset.

"But you're convinced that there's more to it this time, aren't you?" Lewisohn said.

Dalham nodded.

The warden sighed as he shrugged his shoulders.

"We'll never know, will we?"

"If you assume that it ends here," Dalham told him.

"You don't?"

"I'm not a prophet, but I just can't believe that the skinhead movement is finished."

"Because hatred is still here, in some form or another? Is that what you're hinting at?"

"It is. History suggests that bigotry remains long after the original bigots have been stopped."

"Every Jew knows the truth of that, I've got to admit, Kent. It's been nearly half a century since World War II ended. We're yet fighting for our survival. Jewish blood still flows in the alleys and the gutters and the dusty streets of Israel itself."

They talked a bit longer and then Dalham left, but not before giving instructions about the bodies, which would have to be autopsied. He would come back later and question the inmates.

He returned to his apartment, sank down on the bed and fell asleep in an instant, every bone in his body hurting.

And then, in the middle of the night, he awoke with a start.

I wish I had put everything in a neat file, thoroughly researched, all the answers properly assembled. But I have only pieces, Elliott. And now these kids, the ones who could fill in the rest of the puzzle, are gone.

He was drenched with perspiration as he recalled those words.

...the ones who could fill in the rest of the puzzle.

After taking a moment to calm down, he reached for the phone next to his bed and called an emergency line at headquarters.

Elliott Lewisohn was sitting at the desk in his office when Dalham entered.

"This is a surprise!" he said cheerfully. "Did my secretary fall asleep? She didn't tell me you were here."

Dalham sat down on a chair in front of the desk.

"Tell me why, Elliott," he said.

"Why? I don't understand. Why what?"

"Why you cooperated with the prisoners in the riot?"

"Cooperated with—!" Lewisohn started to say, then cut himself off, and bowed his head.

When he looked up again in a few seconds, his eyes were wet.

"How did you find out?" he asked.

"It seemed too neat, too easy, the supposed top leaders of the skinhead revolution all gone in an afternoon. This is supposed to be a maximum security prison. And you are known to be one of the best wardens in the entire Federal prison system."

"And you couldn't believe I would be so sloppy, is that it, Kent?"

"That's *part* of it. I also turned up something else."

Lewisohn looked at him with a touch of fear.

"And what would that be?"

"I checked your background, Elliott. I learned a great deal."

The warden sighed wearily.

"You know about Stier, don't you?"

Dalham nodded.

"I do. I got the bright idea of looking at the earlier years, just after World War II."

"What did you find out?"

"That you worked briefly for one of the elder Stier's companies soon after the war ended. I wondered why this wasn't discovered earlier. But then Stier had his tentacles in many companies in those days. It's only been since his son has been under suspicion that further investigation has been done. But it's a long leap from that to ever realizing the connection with you."

"Is that all you have, Kent?" he asked.

"It is. And it was a long time ago."

"You made me think you'd uncovered everything!" Lewisohn exclaimed, realizing that he had been tricked.

"But you caved in more easily than I thought you would. Does conscience have anything to do with that, Elliott?"

A shudder tore through the massive bulk of the man.

"God knows you're right," he said. "God knows I considered the irony of cooperating with the devil so that the demons I hated could be exorcised from this place. I who condemned inmates selling out to the Nazis at *every* camp during the war!"

"But their survival was at stake then. While we can't condone their treachery, we can understand the appalling conditions that drove them to it. You had none of that *today*. It all was decades in the past. What *could* this man have promised you that was so compelling you couldn't turn him down? What did he promise you, Elliott?"

Lewisohn reached out and picked up a photograph of his mother that had been on his desk, looking at it with longing.

"You don't suspect, Kent? You have no idea of what went on here? You think I talk about demons strictly as a metaphor?"

He slowly put the photo back where it had been. Then, in an action too swift for even a veteran FBI agent to intercept, Lewisohn swiftly took out a revolver and fired it at his temple. He toppled off the chair, hit the floor with a thud.

Dalham rushed to the warden's side.

"My...mother...he...he...promised to..."

Blood spurted out of his mouth and over the front of Dalham's suit. A spasm tore through his body.

"He said I...I could...could..."

Lewisohn reached up, feebly grabbed Dalham's lapel.

"I must warn you: Stier's...not the the the...top. It's...it's..."

Less than a second later he was dead.

48

DALHAM continued his assignment at the prison by trying to find out as much as possible about exactly what went on.

Francesco Giancetti was the only one willing to help him.

"You know," Dalham said as the two of them sat in a private room adjacent to the warden's office, "I get the impression that it's not so much that they are unwilling to cooperate but that they—"

"—are *unable* to do so, is that what you were going to say?" Giancetti interrupted.

"Yes, that's right."

"As though they had no will of their own?"

"Exactly!"

Giancetti stood and paced the small bare room.

"When I told you I knew Christ before I knew the gun, I was quite serious, my friend."

Dalham rebelled at the images in his mind then, of men killed gangland style, of a vast network of pornography and drugs and prostitution, the profits of which flowed into the bank accounts of scum like Giancetti. Such a man talking about knowing Christ!

"You continue to have a great deal of trouble with that, don't you?" Giancetti said. "I can tell by the expression on your face."

Dalham cleared his throat.

"I do," he admitted. "As I said before, you have as much blood on your hands as any of the skinheads."

"Does becoming a follower of Christ guarantee perfection?"

"No, but it should be at least an *attempt* to please Him."

"I am making that attempt, Kent Dalham."

"I don't know what you're getting at."

"Let me tell you what happened here."

Francesco Giancetti's story was an astonishing one, but Dalham tried to interrupt as little as possible because it was told with complete conviction, and he had no impression that the mob chieftain was trying to bamboozle him.

After their previous meeting, Giancetti had become restless.

"I think your reaction to my claim of faith in Christ got to me," he said. "I couldn't sleep. I got up and paced my cell. It was awful."

That was when he saw movement in the corridor directly outside.

"A man, quite tall," he recalled. "I didn't recognize him."

"An inmate?" Dalham inquired.

"No, he was dressed in a business suit."

The man turned and looked at him for an instant.

"My blood ran cold," Giancetti said. "His eyes seemed to be entirely dark, his expression..."

His hands were trembling.

"Please believe that seldom happens with me," he said, embarrassed. "He seemed, ah, totally evil."

"Couldn't that be imagination?"

Giancetti sat down in front of Dalham again.

"No, my friend," he continued. "I have seen *evil* more than once in my life. I have served it to my enemies again and again. Evil and I have been companions for a long time."

The eyes were empty of life. They were cold, dead orbs.

Looking into them was like a descent into an abyss, at the very bottom of which was hell itself.

"Some guards were with him," Giancetti went on. "I could hear only snatches of what they were saying."

...it has to be tonight...they cannot be allowed to stay alive...we're losing them...but that will mean starting over again...oh, yes, I know...somewhere else...we lose a lot of time...it is but a battle in a longer war...ultimately Satan has promised...

"Less than an hour later, it happened," Giancetti told him. "This place went crazy."

He had heard shrieking sounds.

"Awful sounds," he said, recoiling at the memory, "as evil as the eyes of that stranger."

The Himmler skinhead ran past his cell.

"Who was chasing him?" Dalham asked.

Giancetti looked at him, an ironic grin curling up the edges of his mouth.

"Not who," he said, "not who at all. He was being chased by *something*."

Dalham wished he could label all this as the deluded nightmare of an aging gangster with guilt so heavy it had finally affected his sanity.

"I *saw* something and yet I saw *nothing*."

"You're making little sense."

"I saw some *shapes*, Special Agent Dalham. They were..."

He lapsed into silence.

After a few moments Giancetti started speaking again.

"One of those shapes turned and faced me," he said. "For a split second we had intimate contact."

"Intimate? Explain, Francesco. That sounds pretty strange."

"Oh, it *was* strange. It seemed to delve into my very soul. And I could see beyond it, as though it were standing in front of a doorway."

"A doorway?"

"To a place of flames and torment."

Giancetti broke into tears then.

"I could imagine myself among those flames. I could imagine myself crying out but no one helping me. I could see the souls of all my victims over the years. Some were not there but most were. I gave the orders to murder them. How many would have escaped the flames if they had lived longer, if they had had more time to accept Christ as their Savior and repent of their sins?"

Then had come the laughter.

Laughter echoed throughout the prison.

"It was the sort of laughter that chilled every bone in this aging body of mine."

"And then the hangings?" Dalham probed.

"I could see it all from the window in my cell."

He wanted to cry out for them to stop but knew that would be of no avail.

"I sank to my knees," he said. "I begged God to forgive me. I begged Him to sweep away the hypocrisy that had been a part of my life through all the killings."

Giancetti had bowed his head then, those words coming almost as a prayer.

Dalham got up from his chair and walked over to the man.

"Can we pray together?" he asked.

"Oh, God, yes," Giancetti said softly.

As they were getting down on their knees, Dalham felt a curious draft of cold air and heard a sound like that of a cat's claws on tile. But then both passed, and he assumed it was nothing more than his imagination, yes, that was what he assumed.

49

VIOLENCE by skinheads virtually ended after their leaders died in prison. The movement seemed to have deflated.

The towns that had been affected began to rebuild.

And in Europe...

Dalham sighed, near-exhaustion nibbling at him.

"Will there now be peace in the world? No more Federal judges killed by bombs? No more blacks doused with gasoline and burned alive? No more wealthy Jewish businessmen knifed to death?"

Dalham looked at his friend Doug Buchanan. "Of course, I meant that, shall we say, sarcastically," Dalham admitted. "But in all seriousness, what do *you* think, Doug? After all, some high-level leaders died in that prison."

Fellow agent Buchanan became perceptibly more cautious. "It does *seem* that way with what happened there. Well, let's put it this way: That crowd certainly has lost some important battles."

Dalham knew that his friend was a child of the FBI, often reacting in a bureaucratic fashion, verbalizing his thoughts with diplomatic caution, a bit of conditioning that Dalham himself tried to shed periodically.

"But the war, Doug?" he asked, grunting. "Have they lost the war?"

"If what Lewisohn told you is true, then we dare not think *they* think that is the case," Buchanan pointed out.

"But what did he say, actually? He alluded to someone above Stier. But who could that be?"

"We may never find out."

"So let's cherish this moment before it's over, is that what you're saying, Doug?"

The other man sighed, then stood and walked over to a bookcase that extended from floor to ceiling.

"I told you a long time ago that I was a history buff. Here's some evidence of that. But this is only part of my collection, Kent. I've done the attic over as my personal library. These are just the books I refer to most. Want to see upstairs?"

"Sure would," Dalham told him.

After climbing up a pull-down stairway, what Dalham saw were hundreds of books, ranging from the classical period to the so-called Dark Ages to the Renaissance, Reformation and Victorian eras, on through to the present.

"Incredible!" Dalham reacted, surprised.

He glanced over some of the titles.

"*The Nazi Youth Corps*," he repeated. "That one's pretty revealing, I'm sure."

"It is, Kent. Take it home with you, if you like."

"A little late, though, to do any kind of good. You know, after the horses have left the barn, that kind of thing."

"I'm not so sure," Buchanan mused.

Dalham, noticing more titles, admired the scope of the other man's collection.

"I had no idea you were into it like this."

"Few people know. It's a private thing—sort of my sanctuary. I travel throughout time when I read these, Kent."

"And what have you learned?"

"That significant displays of human sin, of our corruption, may ebb and flow, may appear dormant for long periods of time. But it's like cancer, cancer that goes into remission and then flares up again later, unexpectedly. Yes, we *can* capture some skinhead leaders, and they *can* die in prison, murdered by their fellow inmates; yes, all of *that* can happen, and it has."

"But the cancer will come out of hiding, and continue its rampage," Dalham added.

"Yes, Kent, I daresay, worse than ever!"

Dalham half-grinned.

"Listen to the media," he said, "and you would think we've entered a new era, one that gives every promise of lasting for a long time."

"Listen to the media, old buddy," Buchanan observed, "and you'll be led right up to the gates of hell itself without ever knowing you're there."

It was getting late. Dalham had another assignment.

"Gotta go, friend," he said finally.

"Take *The Nazi Youth Corps* with you. You might find some of it quite fascinating."

Dalham accepted the book and was about to leave when Buchanan grabbed his arm, held it briefly.

"Kent, there is anti-Semitism all over Europe, not just in Germany, you know. It's growing throughout Eastern Europe. As one commentator remarked, 'The collapse of Communism has allowed old hatreds to resurface throughout those countries, including the Soviet Union.' The *Pamyat* is especially dangerous. I worry that we've gotten rid of a symptom in recent months but the disease itself is growing, not just here but in a dozen other countries."

Dalham and Buchanan were silent for several moments, surrounded by the profound nature of what had just been said.

"It *could* happen again," Dalham said finally. "Entire nations committed to infamy!"

Buchanan nodded sadly.

They embraced then as the longtime friends they were, and then Dalham went outside. The sun was directly overhead. Even the pain in his leg seemed muted.

He paused for a moment, glancing through the pages of the book his friend had just given him, remembering something he'd read earlier.

"At the very core [of their focused hatred] was an emphasis upon paramilitary training, *which they could always rely upon when necessary.*"

His mind provided the italicized emphasis. He skipped a few paragraphs.

"Some succeed in exorcising the 'demons' [that haunt them], liberated at last; others continue to be possessed by them. It is not a question of whether there will be a next time but rather *when* that next time *shall* occur."

Dalham heard voices.

He looked up from the pages of that book.

People were out in large numbers, walking, laughing.

"A beautiful day," he whispered aloud, though with a certain lack of conviction.

He passed by a newsstand, only vaguely noticing the front page of one of the papers, which read:

European Governments Scramble
to Plan for a New Age

Dalham smiled ironically at the latter choice of words, then glanced at the news dealer who looked bored. After all, nobody was reading newspapers or magazines. The weather was too nice.

And the world was at peace.

50

SOLOMON Hillel Schechter died a few months after Michael Fredrickson got out of the hospital. They were fishing beside a stream near the old Jew's cabin in Colorado, which he had bought years before.

It was a warm day, the sky clear, the hint of a breeze in the air.

They had become close friends in a brief time.

"For me, you are like God must be," Fredrickson told him as they sat on two flat stones.

"I don't know what you mean, Michael," Schechter told him.

"Forgiving. Isn't that what He's all about?"

"Yes. I didn't always see that, couldn't accept it for most of my life. I am a Jew, after all. My God has often been one of vengeance, an eye for an eye, that sort of thing."

"But Christ changed all that."

"He did, Michael."

"Do you feel less of a Jew now, Sollie?"

The old man looked at him, eyes twinkling.

"No! A thousand times no! I am *more* of a Jew now, not less. I am a happy Jew, a satisfied Jew, a Jew who no longer has to wait in despair but who realizes the Messiah has already been here, that in accepting Him today, I turn my back on the hypocrisy and the blindness that nailed Him to the cross in the first place."

Fredrickson's shoulders slumped.

"What's wrong, son?" Schechter asked.

"I have no right to be here with you as I am. You have no sense for letting me remain at your side."

...for letting me remain at your side.

Schechter thought over those words for a moment, smiling to himself.

If you only realized what joy I feel now. In an instant I have turned over to the Lord all my bitterness, all my anger, all my loneliness, and taken into my very being His beloved Son. I now have the Son of God and another son in the flesh by my side.

Schechter had spoken those words aloud though he hadn't intended it, as private, as deeply emotional as they were.

"I am your son, Sollie?" Fredrickson asked.

Schechter looked at him, embarrassed.

"Yes," he finally said. "Yes, that is the way I feel."

Michael Fredrickson put his fishing pole to one side, reached out and embraced this man whom he once tried to hate, and now whom he loved as a father.

Then he stood and started off toward the surrounding trees.

"Michael, are you all right?" Schechter asked, concerned.

"Yes, Sollie," the teenager said, "I just wanted to talk to God alone."

The Jew nodded with understanding.

Several minutes passed. Schechter caught a fish, a small bass. As he was pulling it in, he grew sad, watching the creature squirming on the end of the hook it had swallowed partway down its throat.

I cannot, he thought. *I do not need you to survive, little one.*

He took out the hook as gently as he could and put the bass back in the stream, and it swam away quickly.

He laid the pole down next to the boy's.

Birds.

How beautiful their song.

He looked around at the forest.

No more death camps, no more ditches filled with my friends, my loved ones. No more sooty clouds of smoke from—.

He thought he heard a sound, and turned.

His eyes lit up.

Not Michael.

Not that son.

Michael Fredrickson finished his time of communion, wiped his eyes of the tears that had formed, and walked back to the stream.

Sollie!

Lying half in the water, half on land.

Father!

He walked slowly forward, at first his legs almost paralyzed, then faster, rushing to the old Jew's side. He bent down and lifted the upper part of that fragile, fragile body, already the warmth gone, already the warmth gone.

He thought he heard a sound, and turned.

The flapping of wings, just barely audible, but enough so that he could find them.

Good-bye, Sollie...

A small, pure white bird took flight toward the clear, clear sky.

51

KENT Dalham paused before getting out of the car, the noon sun making him squint.

I don't know if I can face him, he told himself. *I don't know if I can say what I want to say. I've spent years trying to isolate myself from anything that would remind me of...*

Brett Fincher and his daughters Laurie and Susan.

They're hurting. It's only been a few weeks. What could I possibly do to help?

He had gotten out of the car by then, and was walking up the pathway to the front door.

I won't make it. I'm no expert on how to survive a tragedy. I didn't do very well in the midst of my own.

He was turning away when a tall, broad man in his mid-30s came to the door and opened it, smiling at him.

"Mr. Dalham?" he asked.

"Yes, are you Brett?"

"I am, sir," he replied. "It's nice of you to drive out here. Maggie told me some nice things about you."

"She did?"

"That final day, she called from Oregon and promised that she'd be home soon."

"I told my wife the same thing," Dalham admitted. "When I got there, it was too late."

"She said you seemed always a little sad."

"There is some sorrow that can never be resolved."

Fincher sighed a bit wearily.

"Yes, I know."

They spent the rest of the day together, the two men getting along well.

"The kids are at camp," Fincher told him. "Here's a photo."

It was a shot of the four members of a family now reduced to three.

"How do you just let go?" he asked. "How do you deal with the fact that you've been sleeping alone for nearly two months?"

They were sitting in the backyard on two wicker chairs.

"I used to reach out by reflex and try to put my arms around Valerie," Dalham recalled. "I'd pretend that she'd gotten up to get some ice water, especially on a hot summer evening. And I'd wait and wait and wait. When she didn't come back, my little fantasy died, and I fell back, and sometimes I cried for a long, long time."

Fincher threw his head back and looked up at the sky, clear of even the smallest cloud.

"There are times when I wish Maggie and I had never met," he said. "Then I wouldn't have known her and wouldn't be missing her so much."

...missing her so much.

Dalham thought over how often he had said those very words to himself and to others right after the tragedy. He seemed compelled to spill his feelings to anyone who would listen. Then later, he retreated instead, refusing to talk about the car exploding, about the blood that seemed to be everywhere, about having to identify what was left of their bodies in the local morgue.

I had come to a point where it was nearly as though they had never existed, that they were just figures in a wonderful dream from which I awoke one day to a harsh and cold reality.

I could never even kiss them for the last time. The coffins were sealed tight...

Dalham turned and put his hand on the other's shoulder.

"There's one thing you can't *allow* yourself to do," he remarked.

"What's that?" Fincher said, his voice cracking a bit.

"You can't fall into the trap of thinking that not knowing her and not loving her would have been better than having your insides torn apart."

"Can you blame me?"

"No, I can't, Brett. I've been there. Remember, I lost the kids, too. I was left with no one at all."

Fincher's shoulders slumped.

"Forgive me. It's just so awful, smelling her perfume still in the house, seeing her picture, remembering the special dinners she used to prepare. But the worst is thinking of when we used to make love, and now there's just an empty spot. In the summer, when it was so humid and Maggie and I were covered with sweat, and I could see her body glistening with beads of it in the moonlight..."

He cut the thought off as though it were a television program he couldn't bear to watch, switching abruptly to another channel. He whispered something not quite intelligible, then looked directly at Dalham.

"It's funny in a way but, you know, the girls seem to be adjusting better than I am."

That did appear to be the case. They took over the cooking, the housework, so much else, as though eager to prove how well their mother had taught them such duties.

"I think that's deceptive, Brett," Dalham pointed out reluctantly. "They may just be trying to act strong for your sake."

You're more fortunate, Brett, than I am, Dalham thought. I return to an empty apartment, with only a few snapshots, some clothes I kept, a few toys, other odds and ends. But you have living products of your marriage.

"They may just be trying to act strong for your sake," Fincher repeated these words, then paused, thinking this over, before adding, "I'm just afraid that I'm not doing very well at it myself."

In the midst of what they were saying to each other, Dalham felt that he didn't have to ask the other man about his Christianity. He had seen clues about the house: some Bibles and plaques with Bible verses—not that these were proof of Fincher's faith, but they gave some hint at least.

"The best moments and the worst are all wrapped up in the same little dream I have every so often," Fincher said wistfully.

"What sort of dream, Brett?"

"I imagine that I see Maggie walking along a street of gold, with angels at her side, right after the Lord had called her home."

Valerie, the kids! Just like that—one night, when the pain seemed to be tearing him apart. And then he awoke, covered with sweat.

The shared recollection hit Dalham hard. Until that moment he would have said that he had already gone through that valley and would never have to walk it again.

Wrong.

Oh, Lord, I just want to hold them again, just once, Lord.

Dalham suddenly burst into sobs.

"It's like that with me," he managed to say in ragged little bursts. "For Valerie's sake, I'm glad that she and the kids are with the Lord. But here, now, in my flesh, I..."

He couldn't go on for a moment.

Both men were silent then, allowing their tears to dry, images retreating back into some deep region of their minds after being abruptly, jarringly resurrected.

Dalham recalled a strange little moment, after Valerie and he had finished making love, and he was holding her in his arms, when she seemed to sense, in some way, that they wouldn't live to be old together."

"It would be wonderful," she said, "but I just don't know."

"It's not a premonition, is it?" he asked, concerned.

"No, but it may be something the Lord is trying to tell me," she went on, "that still small voice from the Holy Spirit whispering, whispering, whispering."

"In words? You hear them, Valerie?"

"Oh, no. Not in words. Actually I'm not really sure what I'm trying to say."

"*Could it be, my love, that you are simply saying we should never take one another for granted?*"

"*Yes, that's probably what I mean,*" she said, and kissed him passionately.

A couple of years passed after that moment, and they both forgot it, wrapped up in lives that were much more real than some unexplained feeling about the future.

Until that morning, that morning of awful violence, after he found out what happened, when Valerie's words came back to him with jarring force...

Finally Dalham spoke, coughing a couple of times before he did so, his throat having gone dry in the interim.

"How many parents out there are going through so much worse?" he said.

"The ones whose kids have become skinheads?" Fincher queried.

"That's right. I know what happened to mine. Many of *them* will never find out. Did they join Aryans Underground? Or die from a drug overdose. Maybe AIDS is eating away at them. Yet their mothers, their fathers can't even hold their son, their daughter for the last time."

"That must be worse than anything—raising a child and then losing that child in such an awful way," Fincher agreed.

Fincher bit his lower lip for a moment, then asked: "Kent, how do you face all this stuff day in and day out?"

"For a while, I was filled with disgust at what I saw, the kinds of people who would rob, or rape, or murder, or hook countless teenagers on drugs. I wanted to go out there and destroy each one of them."

He stopped briefly, trying to get his thoughts together with some degree of coherence.

"But, Brett," Dalham continued, "that's actually not the worst problem I've had to face. There's another that's the real bummer."

"Not caring at all, I'll bet. That's what you're going to say, isn't it?"

Dalham was stunned.

"How could you have known?" he asked.

"It's only been a little time without Maggie, and yet even so soon I find myself trying to harden up, to deny my emotions, thinking that's the only way I'll be able to survive."

"Try imaging what it's like after a couple of decades. You face scum like terrorists, the mafia, others. You see the results of their vendettas, maimed and dying people, their blood flowing in the gutters like so much rain water!"

He was shaking as he spoke.

"And then it's not just in your job. Some crazies do it to your family and wipe them off the face of the earth!"

"I understand, Kent. You don't have to say it all again."

"But I do, Brett, I really do. It's like a poison that builds up. Only when you lance the wound is there any relief. Trouble is, the wound keeps getting infected."

His eyes widened as he remembered what Lewisohn had told him about the warden's own hatred. He mentioned this to Fincher.

"We all have that poison in us, in one form or another," the other man said, nodding. "For some, it's against the Germans. It's a great irony that today Germany is one of our staunchest allies, and they seem to be doing whatever they can to make sure that no German government, present or future, is ever again responsible for anything like the Holocaust. Responsible Germans seem as terrified by the neo-Nazi phenomenon as Americans are.

"But any anti-German phobia is only part of the picture. For others, it's hatred against blacks or Hispanics or someone else. I guess it's part of the price we pay for having a sin nature. It wouldn't surprise me if some other movement were to spring up a few years from now that was directed against another group. People seem to need other people to hate."

"And so we try to overcompensate by draining *all* emotion away, by pretending that we just don't *care* anymore," Fincher interpolated. "Eventually that works. Eventually we have such a thick skin that we could witness almost anything and it wouldn't get to us."

"A hardened heart is essentially what you're talking about," Dalham added. "I know what that's all about, Brett. A hardened heart may work for a while but we *are* human, and some cracks are bound to surface. That's when the *real* pain starts, I mean, being forced to look at it all, forced to reexamine yourself and see what you allowed yourself to become. Then we have only one avenue: getting down on our knees and asking the Lord for cleansing. I talk from experience, Brett, as I guess you can tell."

Dalham stood, stretching his legs.

"In moments like that, God's love really comes through," he said. "At least that's the way it was with me. He promises, not to give us all the desires of our heart, but to fulfill all the genuine *needs* we might have. Mine was for that cleansing I just mentioned. I saw it happen as well between Michael Fredrickson, a hate-filled skinhead, and Solomon Hillel Schechter, an embittered old Jew. They should have loathed one another. Michael had suffered and Sollie had suffered. Each hated what the other represented. For Michael, it was an older, uncaring, even abusive generation; for Sollie, it was the spectre of Nazism rising from the ashes.

"What they experienced within themselves and between themselves had enormous impact on me, Brett. It was another example of God's love, an example so profound that I could do nothing but submit to what He wanted in my own life."

Dalham cleared his throat, which was suddenly quite choked up.

"But to achieve any of this means a bruising struggle deep down in your gut. It's not a situation that can be wished away. Years of pain, memories that won't let you be at peace—none of that can be submerged in a sea of pleasant smiles. Certain preachers are mistaken when they say that all we have to do is think positively, to somehow will ourselves into being happy and cheerful all the time. They claim that such introspection, such direct confrontation with our pain, is altogether pointless because we don't *have* to go back into the jungle of our emotions to know that the jungle exists. Ignore what causes our unhappiness, they say, and it will somehow go away in time, covered by the shed blood of Jesus Christ.

"The appeal of this kind of mush is undeniable. It's all part of that easy grace heresy. But if it were really so simple, no Christian would ever have to face despair for very long. It's like layering on dollops of New Age stuff over biblical truth. What a deadly pollyanna view of life! I keep thinking of what the Bible says about those in the last days who will have a form of godliness but will be nothing more than satanic counterfeits!"

"They're disgusting," Fincher added. "They're disgusting because they try to make people almost doubt their salvation if even a single negative thought enters their mind. That's of the devil, they'll say!"

"And I say to them, look who's talking!" Dalham said, virtually spitting the words out.

Dalham started pacing.

"There's something else, though," he said.

"What's that?" Fincher asked.

"It's something just as deep as the rest, but I'm not sure I've been able to handle it successfully."

Fincher waited patiently, realizing that such deep emotions, once buried, couldn't be rushed out into the open without causing the severest trauma.

"I've dealt with my bitterness and my anger, yes, but that's been mostly related to *me*, to *my* personal tragedy. What terrifies me is that I haven't felt *more* outrage over what the skinheads did in Oregon, over what they planned to do all across the country. I mean, I should have been beside myself with righteous anger. But I was too busy with my own grief to worry much about anyone else!"

He stood still, abruptly, as though coming up against an impenetrable solid object.

"I looked at the bodies in that camp, and I thought of *my* wife, *my* children. I saw what had happened in a town set ablaze by the skinheads, and I once again flashed back to the puddles of blood on the asphalt in front of *our* house. But hundred of families were going through at least an equal nightmare!"

He sat down again, as though he had been a balloon and suddenly all the air had gone out of him.

"I was horrified, Brett; of course I was. I vomited up my disgust more than once. But that was when I was *at* the camp. Later, away from it, in a motel room, or in a car or wherever, it was...it was..."

He stopped briefly, hating the truth that had surfaced in his mind.

"Business as usual," he finally said. "After this case, there would be another, then another after that. Names in a file; electronic images on a computer screen."

"Part of the job," Fincher offered.

"But where does the job *end*, and where do *I* begin?"

Toward evening, Dalham decided he had to leave.

"Why not stay?" Fincher asked. "We could grab some chow at a restaurant near here."

Dalham was tempted. But he did have a new case to go over. He couldn't afford the time.

"I just can't," he said reluctantly. "The Bureau makes so many demands on us."

Fincher nodded.

As they stood and walked toward the front of the house, Fincher asked again, "You won't reconsider, will you?"

Dalham gently told him about the pile of folders back at his apartment.

Finally the two men shook hands, and Dalham got into his car and drove off.

Valerie, he thought after getting only a few blocks away, *the man needs me.*

He laughed.

After all this time, I need him!

He turned the car around and started back to Fincher's house. Nearly there, he suddenly braked the car as two sentences from a very old letter came back to him.

I am putting up a portion of my estate to benefit him financially when he retires. As you know, I have substantial sums available to me.

Dalham started laughing.

Amazing, Lord, he thought. *Amazing indeed.*

The honking of a car behind him stirred him from that temporary reverie.

He drove the remaining two blocks, his body's adrenalin pumping furiously.

To his surprise he saw Fincher standing on the front steps, waiting for him.

"How did you know?" Dalham asked after he had gotten out of the car.

"I heard some brakes screeching," he said. "Was that you?"

"It was."

"Besides," Fincher said, "I would have come back myself."

"Kent, it's not difficult to see that we're alike. At least we know the same kind of pain."

Dalham could hardly wait to tell the other man the part that he could.

"Brett," Dalham said. "I think I know what's supposed to happen between us."

"I don't understand."

"Kids, Brett. Helping them."

Fincher was silent a moment.

"Maggie would have appreciated the irony."

"And the forgiveness, Brett, the cleansing in both our souls."

"Yeah, great idea. But doing it right, the building, the equipment, the rest, wow, Kent, all that could be expensive!"

Kent Dalham was smiling broadly.

"Do you know something I don't?" Fincher asked.

"I think you could say that," Dalham replied as the memories of a meeting many years before came back to him, the gaze from a coarse old face holding his own in a kind of visual lock, the smell of ancient wood in the air.

"A man so many people hated..." he thought aloud, though barely above a whisper.

"Kent, are you okay?"

"I was just thinking of someone I met only once."

"He must have been special, Kent. I can see that on your face."

"Oh, he was, my brother, he was."

A short while later, Kent Dalham retired from the FBI. At about the same time, Brett Fincher sold his computer business.

They formed an organization called Children of the Furor.

Fully funded.

Epilogue

HE'D had to leave that building quickly, that penthouse office, those six computers, and seek a different place.

The setback made him tremble with anger that seemed to rumble up from deep within him. But he knew, after numerous moments in the past when victory was close but in the end snatched from him, that there would be yet another opportunity.

"It's only momentary," he told an aide as they hurried into the awaiting car.

"I realize that, sir," the aide replied. "There's still a war in progress. This has been only a battle."

He admired this young man, tall, blonde, good-looking, a perfect Aryan, with the indispensable trait of unquestioning loyalty.

"From all that I have discovered about you, I think it is safe to say you would be a good replacement," he said. "In fact I know it."

The aide blushed.

"I'm honored, sir. But I'll need additional training, a great deal of it."

"You will have it."

"By the way, will I do the killing, sir?"

"Oh, yes, that would be fine. That would be fine indeed. I'm delighted you brought up the matter. Such things can be a little awkward, you know."

"Thank you, sir. I try to be alert to everything that's going on."

The car was driven out of the city to a remote airstrip. After issuing last-minute instructions, he got on-board, then turned and waved to the aide, shouted a farewell, knowing that it would be only a short while before the young man was flown to the new headquarters as soon as his mission was accomplished.

The plane took off, leaving the aide standing there for a moment on the isolated runway.

He smiled, sighing with satisfaction. He knew exactly what to do, knew where to find the man he was to assassinate, knew how to kill him without being noticed.

Now, it's my turn, he thought. *Rudolf failed, and I will replace him!*

He looked toward the plane that was rapidly disappearing from sight.

"I won't let you down, master," he said aloud. "I never have. I owe you everything, *mein Führer!*"

He turned, and in that moment, gun firmly holstered near his armpit, his mind filled with an image of Rudolf Stier's body jerking eerily in a kind of death dance as the bullets pounded him, the illusion of his youth was suddenly gone, gone, gone, replaced by something altogether different.

Notes

1. *The Nazis and the Occult* by D. Sklar, Marboro Books Corporation, copyright 1977 by Dusty Sklar, All rights reserved.

2. *THE HITLER YOUTH; Origins and Development 1922-1945* by H. W. Koch, Marboro Books Corporation, copyright 1975 by H. W. Koch. All rights reserved.

3. *Less than Slaves* by Benjamin B. Ferencz, published by Harvard Univerity Press, copyright 1979 by Benjamin B. Ferencz. All rights reserved.

4. "Relocation," a poem by Simon J. Ortez, Acoma Pueblo poet, reprinted from *Keeper of Concentration Camps*, University of California Press.